SOUL MAGE

LISA BLACKWOOD

SOUL MAGE

HUNTRESS VS HUNTSMAN:
SOUL MAGE SAGA / BOOK 1

Lisa Blackwood

ABOUT THE BOOK

A stoic warrior-maiden and a villainous priest-king make the most unlikely alliance in the history of the five kingdoms.

When a rescue attempt to save a clutch of dragon eggs from the soul mages goes terribly wrong, Warrior-Priestess Verdria of High Rock finds herself on the wrong side of a portal, deep in enemy territory.

She soon learns she's in the heart of the soul mage's empire and when Honryn, the future priest-king of the mages, takes a liking to Verdria and saves her life, she's pretty sure she's facing down a 'fate worse than death' scenario.

Just when she thinks things can't get any worse, Priest-King Honryn introduces her to the Royal Court of the Soul Mages, the most morally corrupt and blood-thirsty court in existence.

Life is cheap.

Souls are currency.

And Verdria has caught the fancy of the young priest-king, and while he doesn't want to steal her soul, he's set on winning her heart.

And she's equally set on having his heart, after she's carved it out of his chest.

But when she discovers Honryn's most monstrous secret, a secret he's even hiding from his fellow soul mages, she's moved to pity and offers to aid him.

SOUL MAGE

CHAPTER 1

Honryn

"May you trip and bite off your cocks," Honryn muttered as he gazed up into the jeweled eyes of the winged serpent god. Light from the burning cauldron at the base of the statue reflected in the large, faceted jewels, giving the eyes an almost lifelike sparkle. Blessedly, that was just an illusion. The serpent god did not inhabit the mortal domain. Not yet anyway. Never, if Honryn had a say in his future.

Staring into the snake's face with its open mouth and its arm-length fangs was always preferable to being at eye level with the statue's large, double phallus. And looking up into its face helped him resist the temptation to snap off the statue's pair of engorged members and shove them into its gaping maw.

Not that he could ever indulge in such juvenile behavior, no matter how much he might wish. More than his own life was at risk.

Which was why he was always careful and kept his words soft enough the other priests and priestesses sharing the great temple's inner sanctum wouldn't hear him over the drone of their own chanting. With another glower at the statue of the winged serpent god, its stone wings—not to mention other body parts—on full, rampant display, Honryn schooled his scowl into something more benign and continued with his 'prayer' chant.

"May your venom sacs rupture and your fangs rot from your head." As he whispered the words, he reached down and cut another of the iridescent blue scales from his wrist and tossed his God's blessing into the fire like so much trash.

Of course, he made certain the other clerics in the sanctum with him thought he was making a blood sacrifice in honor of their great Serpent God during these sessions each morning.

He flashed his own teeth at the statue and tossed two more scales into the flames of the cauldron. As the blessed scales burned to ash, he continued the next part of his daily chant, taking great pleasure at desecrating the most holy of temples within the entire empire.

With a savage grin aimed up at the statue, he continued. "I give you back your blessings. I deny you my magic. I deny you my body. And I most certainly deny you my soul. You can take those scales and shove them right up your ass for all I care."

Having repeated a similar chant for the last twelve years of his life, since the scales had first come in, Honryn had concluded long ago that if the god heard and was livid, the deity either lacked the power or the ability to punish his own future priest-king.

That suited Honryn just fine.

"One day I shall see your great temple crumble to dust, the most corrupt of your people perish, and your empire fail and vanish into the sands of time." Honryn spat out the words with more vigor than was perhaps wise. "Let this empire suffer as its victims have and become another civilization lost and forgotten by history."

The sound of pounding feet approaching interrupted Honryn's next words. He used his right hand to cover the wrist of the left, as if to staunch the flow of blood, though there was very little. But it wouldn't do to have anyone see the bounty of blue scales lining his wrists that he needed to rid himself of each day.

If anyone ever figured out that he possessed such a 'great' blessing and was carving them out of his flesh in the greatest of blasphemies, the ensuing carnage wouldn't be pretty.

He faced the room calmly and readied himself for a potential attack. It wasn't like his older brothers hadn't tried to assassinate him a time or twenty before. Though assassins were never so loud.

The other clerics had fallen silent, their faces turned toward the back of the temple and the source of the approaching footsteps. His fellow priests and priestesses all radiated emotions ranging from disbelief to outrage.

Honryn only smiled coldly. Perhaps he'd get to kill a few more of his fellow soul mages this day. Death was always on the table as a punishment for anyone interrupting the holy morning rituals.

By the heavy tread of boots and the jangle of metal bits and buckles clanking together, a company of guards was about to breach the sanctity of the temple.

A first in Honryn's experience.

Hmm…

It looked like today was going to be an interesting day.

How delightful.

Honryn sheathed his knife and retrieved his leather bracer from where he'd tucked it into his voluptuous black robes. He was still lacing up the bracer when a group of ten guards halted just outside the threshold of the temple's inner sanctum.

Ah, so whatever brought them here wasn't something they really wanted to die for. How very regrettable. Also, none of them were members of his own Elite personal guards. IIis guards were too intelligent to come barging into the temple. They would have sent a member of the priesthood to carry a message to him.

Not looking up at the newcomers, he continued to tie the laces. But he didn't need to look upon them to learn more about each soldier. His magic expanded out and tasted all the souls in the room, their desires, fears, and intentions. It was the usual mix of duty and fear and awe at being in his presence.

Which didn't tell him anything particularly useful.

As a precaution, he wrapped his unseen power around their souls, all the souls in the immediate area—both the soldiers and the clerics. If his father or uncle had discovered his secret and these guards were here to capture him—which was unlikely, they would have come in much greater numbers—he preferred to be prepared to deliver swift deaths so none within or without could warn the rest of the emperor's elite royal guards.

While Honryn had made plans for every contingency, those plans would take time to instigate.

Dividing his consciousness, he sent half of it to hunt out the locations of his mother, twin sister, and the rest of his people while simultaneously directing a question at the now bowing guards.

"I assume you're carrying some dire news?" he drawled. "Though I cannot fathom what would be a compelling enough reason to warrant such an action as to disturb me during the morning rites. Tell me, what is so important that I might spare your lives for this disturbance in the heart of our Father's most holy temple?"

Reading his mood, his fellow priests and priestesses summoned their own magic, readying to act on a moment's notice should he order them to kill the guards for this very grave insult.

The guards' leader, a tall, lithe man with the supple musculature of a sword master, bowed deeper before answering. "Your Holiness, forgive the intrusion, but the emperor has sent word that he requires your aid in a task of utmost urgency. He would have come himself, but he cannot return in time, so commanded me to carry the message."

His curiosity piqued, Honryn wondered what his sire might need him to perform that was of great enough importance to send his guards into the temple. A sacred area that Honryn was well within his rights to defend with lethal force from any perceived slight to the Lord of Serpents.

The guard swallowed audibly, telling Honryn that the male knew his fate was being decided.

"The matter is time sensitive."

"I assumed as much." Honryn let a touch of ice grace his words.

"Of course, your Holiness."

He hated that term, but Honryn pushed his irritation aside for another time. He'd already scared a few years off the guard's life. That would have to do for now. And since Honryn *did* want to know what had brought the guards here, it was likely time to switch back to benevolent spiritual leader for a bit. "Come, tell me what you know of this errand while we walk."

The guard heaved a sigh of relief so strong it was almost comical as he straightened, but he didn't hesitate and immediately jumped into the subject that had brought him to the temple.

"The mages on the scout ship sent to the distant western continent have been reporting in regularly. They had successfully loaded the stolen dragon eggs some hours ago, but in their latest report, they said dragons have found the ship. They are attempting to outrun the beasts…"

Good luck to them, Honryn thought, and had to fight back a grin of amusement. He would shed no tears at the thought of that ship burning to ash. Unlike its two companion ships that had been lost to a storm, the remaining ship had none of his people onboard. He'd always thought it a great injustice that the two ships with actual good souls onboard had gone down and the surviving ship was the one stacked with his father's loyal subjects.

Those two lost ships had taken with them Honryn's plans for a peaceful future away from all this.

"The emperor requires your aid in building a portal strong enough to cross that distance and extract the dragon eggs and our men," the guard continued, unaware of the direction of Honryn's thoughts.

"I shall come at once and send for six of my most powerful brethren."

It was advantageous that the weaving of great spells was forbidden in the temple. And that he'd said he'd come didn't mean he'd hurry. After all, it would hardly be dignified for the Priest-King Elect of the Soul Mages to be seen running.

And should the dragons reclaim their stolen eggs in the meantime?

All the better.

As for the brethren he would call to aid him?

He would indeed call upon the most powerful mage-priests and mage-priestesses. Currently, those individuals were scattered across the island at the other temples overseeing morning rites. He wouldn't mention to the guards that he was now fully capable of creating a portal over that distance by himself.

Honryn was careful not to let any of his thoughts show, merely smiling benignly and nodding for the company of guards to lead the way, his own entourage of temple clerics following close on his heels.

CHAPTER 2

Verdria

"The unholy bastards are making a run for the open ocean!" Verdria shouted to her dragon mount, trying to be heard above the wind and the raging seas below them. The task would have been easier if she'd shared Rhavana's gift for dragon mind-speech. But so far, her fellow warrior-priestess was unique among their sisterhood in her gift to speak with her dragon mount Kolaith.

Perhaps it was because Rhavana and Kolaith *actually* liked each other?

Verdria's mount wasn't nearly as pleasant as Kolaith and hadn't even judged her worthy of knowing his name. Yet while the great ornery, black-scaled beast couldn't hear her thoughts, her comment about the soul mages' ship making for the open ocean must have reached him, for he roared out an ear-shattering agreement and put on another burst of speed, closing the distance between them and the ship.

New to riding dragon-back, Verdria let out an involuntary whoop as her assigned dragon mount arrowed down from the sky, streaking toward the ship and its cargo of stolen dragon eggs.

The sky was dark with wings all around her as more of the flight darted toward the boat. Below, Verdria noted the mages were scrambling around on the deck. She might not be that familiar with sailing, but that movement didn't seem random or what was required for controlling that great behemoth of a ship with its three masts and multiple sails.

The mages had to be taking up defensive positions. As if confirming her theory, her battle magic tingled along her skin, warning her of a gathering foreign power in the air. Moments later, a bolt of shimmering black energy jumped from the ship, leaping high into the sky, targeting the lead dragons closing in on the boat.

Chaos erupted across the sky. Dragons banked sharply in all directions, attempting to avoid the lethal black bolts while their riders shouted in bravado or fear even as they counterattacked with their own magic.

Verdria held back, knowing her magic was much more lethal at a closer range.

More of the black lightning-like power arched up from the ship, whipping in multiple directions. Unfortunately, the vast expanse of the dragons' wings also created large targets for the mages' bolts.

Several lethal tendrils of power found their targets. Verdria could only watch in helpless rage as dragons and their riders fell from the sky to crash into the waves below. But some of the tension in her shoulders eased when other dragons peeled off from the primary flight to assist their fallen brethren.

The burning in her lungs warned Verdria she'd been holding her breath. She released it and dragged in another when she saw all the dragons in the water were still alive and swimming. They were too far away for her to see how their riders fared, but her fellow priestesses and the centaurs in human form had been harnessed in and situated high on the dragons' shoulders. They were likely safe from drowning, even if they were unconscious. Then, mentally nodding to herself, she focused back on the danger of the soul mages.

Soon, she promised herself, her one hand tightening on her saddle harness while the other closed around the staff of her great axe. *I'll have the chance to avenge all my sisters dead at the hands of the monstrous soul mages.*

She just had to get to the deck of that ship, and then her axes would sing the most pleasing of sounds.

Unfortunately, many more of her sisters and their new centaur and dragon allies might die before they ever touched boots to the ship's timbers.

Verdria cursed the situation that forced the dragons to hold back their lethal fire. Instead of this melee, the dragons could simply have swooped in and vaporized the ship with their fire, and then circled to watch the soul-stealing mages drown or burn. She'd have been more than happy to watch either outcome.

But with the dragon eggs aboard, they couldn't set the ship ablaze until after the warrior-priestesses and their centaur allies boarded the boat and located the eggs. If the dragons were indiscriminate with their elemental fire, they risked the eggs going down with the ship. And with so few remaining female dragons, losing even a single egg would be devastating.

Verdria thumped her dragon mount's shoulder to get his attention, since she didn't know the big, over-grown goose's name. All she'd learned from Rhavana was that this elder had lost his mate and offspring to the mages centuries ago, but time had not dimmed his great need for vengeance. And now that the enemy had returned, the ancient dragon once again hungered to deliver death and destruction upon the mages.

After the fourth thump on his shoulder, he rolled a giant eye in her direction. She grinned at the black-scaled dragon.

"Try not to die," she shouted over the wind.

"You either," he barked out in the first bit of mirth she'd seen him exhibit in the few hours they'd been partnered up.

The call of the horns rang out, signaling the riders nearest to the ship had detected the mages had exhausted their prepared spells. The mages would now have to create every spell from here on out during the heat of battle, a tactical disadvantage.

It was what they'd been waiting for.

Verdria unclipped from her harness and used it to climb down the beast's shoulder and then slid down his foreleg, trusting that the scaly bastard would at least catch her if she slipped, since she was risking her life to save dragon eggs.

She didn't relax until after his fingers curled into a cage around her body. Then, with a roar, he folded his wings tighter to his side and arrowed toward the ship at greater speed. All around them, other dragons executed the same maneuver.

Wind whistled in Verdria's ears. Ignoring the quivering, nauseous feeling in her stomach, she focused on the approaching ship's deck and the soul mages running for cover. Over the distance, she started picking out her first targets.

It was better than listening to the roars and cries of the dying as many of their allies were destroyed on approach.

The mages weren't out of the fight yet, their strikes

coming faster and landing much more accurately, taking several more dragons and their riders out of the battle.

But then her dragon mount was through the wall of deadly bolts of black magic and slicing through the air directly beside the ship. With only a sharp bark of warning, he tossed her toward the deck.

Verdria's training kicked in, and she tucked and rolled as if needing to bail off a horse galloping full out.

The deck rushed toward her. She hit it a moment later, the impact jarring a grunt from her. The ship's decking proved a lot less forgiving than a grassy meadow. With gritted teeth, she ignored the scream of abused flesh and forced herself up into a defensive stance.

A few feet away, a dark-haired centaur in human form landed on the deck just as roughly. He paid his landing no more mind than she had and was already shifting to his four-legged form.

Verdria saluted him with her axe, and he grinned wolfishly back at her before turning to seek the nearest enemy.

Other priestesses and centaurs dropped down all around the ship, their sudden arrival causing chaos on deck for a moment. But soon the soul mages rallied, switching from attacking the dragons in the sky to fighting the priestesses and centaurs now aboard the ship.

She only had a moment to glance up and see her dragon mount sail clear of the ship and out of immediate danger before the first soul mage was upon her.

Her throwing axe made quick work of him, the embedded battle magic in the blade cutting through whatever nasty spell he'd been about to toss at her before lodging in his chest. Before he collapsed forward onto the deck, her great axe took his head. After retrieving her throwing axe, she stepped over his body, already on the hunt for her next target.

Verdria narrowed her eyes and tracked the nearest soul mage. Another male. He leaped up a set of stairs from below deck, a long, curved blade fisted in his tattooed hand. More tattoos swept up his wrists and arms, but his clothing hid any others he might have. As for his hair, it was short and dark like the other mages she'd seen, his cheeks fuzzy with the beginnings of a beard. Dark lashes stood out against his pale skin. His sparse facial hair made him look like a youth, but she wouldn't hazard to guess a mage's age.

Instead, she welcomed him to dance with her and her axes. They circled each other. The dull clack of metal on metal, the wet sounds of tearing flesh, and the screams of the dying bombarded her senses from all around her as others engaged in battle. But those sounds hardly registered. For the first time in days, she had a physical enemy directly in front of her and could at last vent all her grief and helpless rage upon him. But he looked so young.

He seemed to sense her hesitation and sneered at her, spitting words in the tongue of the soul mages. She might not know what he said, but from his tone and expression, it was an insult.

At that moment, she was glad for his foolish emotional outburst. It would let her kill him without hesitation. Killing men. A foreign concept to a warrior-priestess. Her people bore so few boys; all males were protected and cherished.

Baring her teeth, she mentally reminded herself that the youthful looking male in front of her was a soul mage, an evil creature that might look like a man, but he couldn't be considered human.

He came at her suddenly, ropes of black twisting magic leaping up from his outstretched hands. While his magic might be potent, hers was stronger, her blades sharper than his spells.

She swiftly took this fellow's head.

"For my fallen sisters," she growled at the headless corpse as it slumped to the ground with a heavy thump. Then she spun away, already hunting for the next soul mage in need of killing.

Her battle magic and the drive to avenge her sisters lent her strength as she clashed with one soul mage after another. It was a swift, bloody business. There was no time for fancy footwork or elegance. No more hesitation after the first youthful looking male. The only requirement was butchering the mages before they launched one of their bolts of black magic that would incinerate everything it touched.

But as she fought more of these unnatural opponents, she soon discovered that fearsome power wasn't even their most terrifying magic.

She witnessed more of their dreadful magic in the form of one deadly little nightmare of a spell that, while far more subtle than bolts of black lightning, was even more insidious. Only feet away, a centaur was hit by one of those spells. It coiled around the helpless male for a moment before sinking below his skin. He jerked to a halt, all motion ceasing. A heartbeat slid by and then he collapsed to the ground in the boneless manner of the unconscious or the dead.

She wasn't given the chance to check if he still lived for another enemy attacked her. She leaped over the unmoving male and dived behind a crate to avoid the same fate that had befallen the centaur.

Momentarily safe from soul mage attacks, she took a beat to catch her breath and assess the situation. But even as she poked her head around the edge of the crate to take in her surroundings, she didn't miss when a small, crystalline object emerged from the centaur's body. The small crystal globe hovered above his chest, the soul trapped within the crystal glowing with fiery light as if the soul inside were still putting up a fight.

But she knew from the reports that there was no escape for the soul unless an outside force destroyed its crystal prison.

As she watched, a soul mage stepped forward, scooped up the soul crystal, and called on another spell. This time she could feel how much stronger he was, harvesting power from the trapped soul to fuel his spells.

Baring her teeth, Verdria lunged from her hiding place and re-entered the fray.

Her battle magic rose within her, fed by righteousness and rage. And when the mage launched an attack at her, she merely braced herself and channeled her battle magic into her crossed axes. Then, with a mental push, she directed that power at the mage's spell rushing toward her.

With a deep hissing and crackling of power, the two opposing magics battled. But, unlike the mage, Verdria didn't hold her ground, not dependent solely on her magic. Instead, she forged ahead, muscles straining against the force of his magic, and charged her opponent.

The maneuver caught the mage off guard, and she broke through his defenses. Grinning at his surprised expression, she plunged her axe through his forehead and down into his chest before pushing the body off the blade. Breathing hard, heart pounding, adrenaline rushing through her veins, she barely noticed the hot wash of blood and gore.

In a fleeting break in the battle, Verdria glanced around and took in the scene. Too many of her people and their new centaur allies were dead or dying. But almost as many dead mages littered the deck. She noted the surviving soul mages were now fighting shoulder to shoulder, perhaps having learned that it was better to fight as a team.

She briefly wondered why they hadn't figured that out sooner. Clearly, it wasn't part of their training. But then again, from the mages she'd crossed, it seemed they relied heavily upon their magic for offense and defense. So perhaps their magic didn't play well with another's power?

But they weren't unintelligent and were now adapting their fighting style.

Verdria narrowed her eyes, seeing movement behind the mages standing shoulder to shoulder. At first, she thought it was another line preparing to surge forward, but she changed her mind a moment later when she witnessed three of them disappearing below deck.

Whatever they were up to, it couldn't be good.

The dragon eggs!

If the mages knew they couldn't escape with the eggs, would they attempt to destroy them before Verdria and her people could rescue them?

Likely.

With new dread fueling her, she glanced around at her people and then spotted Rhavana halfway across the deck on the port side of the ship. Yelling, she waved to the other warrior-priestess. Rhavana spotted her and bolted across the deck, dodging blasts of the mages' magic.

"Verdria, what is it?" she asked between pants.

Pointing where the mages had disappeared, Verdria shouted above the sounds of battle. "A group of mages disappeared below deck. Down those stairs. It can't be for any purpose beneficial to us or the dragons."

Rhavana's gaze followed where Verdria pointed. "They're going for the eggs!"

"That was my thought as well."

"We need to get down there," Rhavana said, echoing Verdria's thoughts.

Verdria didn't need any convincing, and together they charged the enemy line, the other warrior-priestesses and centaurs thundering behind them.

CHAPTER 3

Verdria

Verdria's hunch proved correct. After they'd broken through the line and the enemy scattered, she and Rhavana took advantage of the chaos to slip below deck. When they followed a few mages below, they found the men were heading to a richly appointed chamber. Two arrows from Rhavana's bow and a well-aimed toss of Verdria's throwing axe ended the mages' lives swiftly and relatively silently.

With sweat rolling down her back and dripping from her temples, Verdria ignored her muscles' complaints and went to retrieve her smaller axe while Rhavana scouted around the chamber. Once she'd recovered her axe, Verdria joined the other priestess studying the room.

She noted it was likely the captain's quarters or some other important dignitary judging by the lavish furnishings.

The only out-of-place items were five straw-lined crates strapped to the floor. It had to be the dragon eggs. Walking closer, she spotted a pearlescent shimmer within, not even the straw able to hide the glow of the magic clinging to the large eggs.

Now that they'd found them, they just needed to get them off the ship. Verdria turned away from the eggs and studied the room once more, paying particular attention to the walls and windows where symbols had been burned into the wood by magic.

She narrowed her eyes, taking in the symbols glowing malevolently with power.

Yeah, that couldn't be a good sign.

"We just have to figure out how to get them off the ship," Rhavana said, as if reading her mind.

"That might be easier said than done," Verdria pointed toward the walls and windows she was study-ing. "See these markings?"

They were pulsing with what Verdria could only call an evil light. And it seemed to grow stronger the longer she watched them. "I think someone doesn't want us to remove the eggs from this room."

"Likely," Rhavana agreed. "But let's try the windows

first. The crates are too big for us to carry, but if we can push them to the windows, a dragon can snatch them up one at a time and carry them away from the battle."

"Good plan." Verdria nodded, glad to have at least some form of a plan even if they still had to figure out parts of it, like breaking through those evil-looking spells. "Windows first."

Not seeing the point in hesitating, Verdria launched herself at the nearest window and swung her great axe at the glass. The spell snapped awake as soon as the axe was a finger's width from touching the glass, repelling the blow with a bone-jarring counterforce.

Verdria stumbled back with a curse as the axe bounced off the glass as if she'd struck stone. After catching her balance, she rubbed her shoulder and glared at the symbols.

"Nope on the windows," Verdria muttered angrily, but she was already looking for other ways out.

Rhavana called out to her. "Help me check the rest of the symbols. They may have been done in a hurry after they arrived with the eggs. One might be flawed, weaker than the rest."

One could only hope, Verdria thought to herself. Out loud, she added, "Good point."

Together, they began searching the exterior walls. The first three Verdria approached all seemed as powerful as the one she'd already attacked and nearly shattered her axe upon.

But after a moment, Rhavana made an excited sound, drawing Verdria's attention. "Think I've got something here!"

Verdria rushed over and stood at Rhavana's shoulder, leaning over the shorter woman for a better look. "Light seems weaker. Let me try. Might want to stand well back."

Rhavana nodded and turned away to point her arrow at the door. It was wise. The sound of Verdria's axe was likely to draw any able-bodied mages to their location. But that was for Rhavana to worry about.

Verdria had her own task—getting out of this moons' cursed room with the dragon eggs.

Leaning closer and tilting her head to the side, she noticed something she'd missed before. Behind the glow of power, the spells were painted upon the wood with ink or blood. Verdria's lips twisted in distaste. Knowing what she did of this particular enemy, she'd bet her favorite axe the dark substance staining the wood was blood.

Yet knowing the spell was painted upon the wood gave her an idea. Once again, she used her beloved battle-axe like it was designed for chopping wood. But this time she went at the ship's timbers instead of directly at the symbols.

Her first strike didn't sink into the wood as she'd hoped, but nor did it bounce her axe back at her. The spell here had more the consistency of maple sap thickened over a fire far too long. She renewed her strikes. When the first wood splinters pelted her, she grinned and continued to chop with a more aggressive rhythm. Wood continued to fly at each of her strikes, and once she had a goodly sized hole, she grabbed at the rough edges of the timbers and pulled sharply, her muscles flexing and battle magic bolstering her physical strength.

With renewed energy, she fought past the ship's resistance, tearing away one chunk of wood after another. As pieces of the soul mages' spells fell away, the ring of symbols shivered and began to destabilize.

Rhavana joined her by the small but ever-widening opening, momentarily taking her eyes away from the door to view Verdria's work. "I think that's sufficient for a dragon to break through now. Let's push the crates over to the opening. I'll contact Kolaith and relay our plan to him. He'll alert the other dragons."

Verdria nodded sharply in agreement at her fellow priestess's plan, and together they began cutting loose the crates.

Rhavana paused after a moment. "Wait. Found something!"

She carefully lifted out a small wooden chest. When she cracked open the lid, a soft blue glow seeped out. Opening the cover the rest of the way, she breathed out a sigh of relief.

"I think I just found the soul crystals of Kolaith's sister and her mate."

"More good news," Verdria muttered. "Now let's get them out of here."

Cutting the last of the crates free and then putting their backs into it, the two women shoved the containers toward the opening one at a time.

While Verdria was working on shifting over the fourth crate, Rhavana used her link to her dragon mate to tell Kolaith they were ready for him.

"I'm here," Kolaith said as his fist punched through the hole, enlarging it enough to snatch the first crate. He was gone in the next moment, and another dragon, this one a green, reached for the second crate. Next, a bright blue dragon snatched the third crate.

"Three down. Two more to go," Verdria called loudly to the other woman. "Better get our backs into it before more soul-mages show up."

Rhavana rushed to her side, and together they shoved the second to last crate within reach of the dragon waiting outside the ship. He wasted no time in grabbing it.

They were shoving the fifth one across the floor when the door, windows, and walls all seemed to shiver and roll strangely to Verdria's eyes. Power flared brightly from the remaining symbols.

"Now what?" Verdria asked as she put more effort into pushing the last crate.

Knowing her luck, it wouldn't be anything good, she reflected.

Rhavana huffed beside her, helping to shove the last crate over to the hole in the ship. "I don't have the slightest idea, but I doubt it's a good sign."

They weren't left wondering long. Magic bled from the symbols, the dark power rushing down the walls and across the floor, where it formed a pool. Then, two heartbeats later, an intense white light burst out of the velvety darkness, blinding her for a few precious moments.

Spots danced in her vision, and she blinked rapidly until they slowly retreated. Once she could see again, she froze in alarm.

A door shimmered in the air where there hadn't been one before.

"Moons," Verdria cursed when her brain made sense of what her eyes were trying to tell her. "That's a first."

Only fuzzy, grey shapes could be seen moving beyond the door, as if she were looking through thick fog. But those shapes were human-sized and could only be more soul mages.

Reinforcements? Probably. But that wasn't her greatest concern currently. The door was and what its existence meant.

She'd never seen such a power. But this must be how the soul-mages had slipped out of their camp and made it to their ship without leaving a trail. That a soul-mage controlled a power able to open doors between distant locations was terrifying.

How could her people fight an enemy capable of creating such portals? An enemy possessing an advantage which allowed them to move spies and troops in and out of anywhere at a moment's notice was terrifying.

"This is bad," Verdria whispered. "We need to warn the others."

"Already done," Rhavana said. "Kolaith is ordering the other dragons to swoop in and snatch the rest of our people from topside."

While Rhavana might have warned her big dragon lover in time to save their other allies on board, this new power wielded by an unseen soul mage seemed to have other plans for Verdria and her friend.

Verdria watched the magic race along the windows and walls until even the door was swiftly covered in shifting shadows that promised death to anyone foolish enough to venture too near.

And just like that, the situation had shifted from certain victory to sudden doom. For them, at least.

Well, Verdria mused as she swung her two axes with deadly grace, limbering up her muscular arms and shoulders once more. *If I'm going to die, I'll make sure to take as many of them with me as possible.*

The foggy shroud concealing the other side of the portal receded, showing her in sharp detail just what was waiting beyond the shimmering door. A man stood with his arms spread wide and his head tilted back as sinuous waves of a dark, velvety magic flowed from his body.

The male was a prime specimen, tall and broad-shouldered. Handsome in the face, too—not that she'd ever seen many males up close to use as a comparison. But his dark eyes, with their thick lashes, were pretty. And his broad cheekbones and sharp nose complemented his strong jawline in an equally pleasing way.

Smirking, Verdria made a mental note to mess up that pretty face of his before he died.

A black robe with silver embroidery had fallen from his wide shoulders to hang from his lower arms, leaving his chest bare. An expanse of pale, hairless skin met her gaze as it swept down a muscular chest and farther to his defined abdomen. His lower half was equally impressive, though it was encased in a snug pair of black pants that looked like someone had sewn them on to him.

All that exposed skin called to her, the perfect target for her axes to sink deep.

But it was what he lacked that was the most interesting. He bore no tattoos upon his body, and his skin didn't have the signature pallor that most mages possessed. Nor did he have that deeply sunken look to his eyes, like their dark power fed upon the mage as much as the souls they trapped in crystal.

In short, he looked like no soul-mage she'd ever set eyes upon.

With a small part of her consciousness, she wondered why his skin was unmarked by the tattoos that all soul-mages adorned themselves in. It was strange that he didn't use the tattoos to store up additional power like other mages. At least, that's what the ancient texts had mentioned were the purpose of the mages' tattoos. They weren't just harmless body art.

Lack of tattoos notwithstanding, he was undeniably a soul mage, that velvety black magic declaring what he was as clear as if he'd shouted the truth in her ear. And that handsome bastard had to be the most powerful one in existence to do what he was doing without needing the additional aid of a bunch of tattoos.

Moons above! She didn't even see any soul crystals on his person. And with what he was wearing, it wasn't like he had loads of places to hide them. Well, she supposed some could be hidden in the voluptuous robe that was currently falling off him.

Standing behind him were several other soul mages with the usual tattoos and soul crystals on display. Even though she couldn't see any magic coming off those men and women, perhaps their leader was drawing power from them in some way unseen to her eyes or other senses?

The man she'd instinctively labeled as the leader reached out and waved one elegant hand toward the room. The symbols all around the chamber grew brighter, saturated with even more power. Soon they began vibrating with their newfound energy.

Did he not have a limit to how much power he could summon?

"Bloody moons!" Verdria hissed, tearing her gaze from him to study whatever he was doing in more detail. What she saw wasn't reassuring in the least. But she didn't let that distract her from hunting down any sign of weakness in his spell work. And she saw one potential weakness she might be able to exploit.

"We've almost got this last crate close enough to the hole for a dragon to snatch," Verdria said as she used her great axe in a sweeping motion to gesture at the distance. "The opening isn't completely closed over by whatever magic shield that soul mage is weaving. I think our battle magic should be able to break through if the dragon can't manage it on his own. We can escape with the crate when the next dragon—"

"Priestesses," called an impossibly beautiful voice that shattered Verdria's concentration and froze her next words in her mouth. She glanced back at the too-pretty male.

His hypnotic voice continued, seemingly to wrap itself around her soul. "If you wish to live, come to me. The ship is doomed, as is everyone on it or near it. But you need not die. I'm sure I can find a use for two such..." His gaze flicked from Rhavana to land on

Verdria before widening slightly as he took all of her in, "...two such very large and powerful warrior-priestesses."

Verdria laughed as she shifted her great axe from one hand to the other, and then drew her second, smaller axe. "I always wanted to try my hand at capturing a centaur in a one-on-one fight but never had the chance. Maybe I'll see how a soul mage of your power sizes up in battle, Pretty One."

The other soul-mages cursed and spat out angry words in their own language at her insult, clearly understanding her words even if she didn't understand theirs. When she looked at them, she noted their enraged expressions. Rage made fools of people, and fools were easier to kill in battle. A grin spread across her lips. There would be much killing. So very much killing.

But the brief exchange had revealed something else. The soul mage leader had spoken in her native tongue. Clear, with hardly any accent. She preferred not to dwell on the how and where he'd learned to speak her language so well. Besides, she had other concerns just now.

Three of the soul mages had swept around their leader and were now advancing upon the portal with murder in their eyes. Their powerful reactions to her 'Pretty One' insult told her that the lead mage was someone they held in great esteem.

Verdria grinned at the male she'd labeled as the 'Pretty One.' This male was surely a high-ranking member of their society, a noble or commander of some sort. Perhaps he was even their king?

What a prize his head would make!

Then she remembered she'd likely still be overwhelmed by the sheer number of enemies she'd face on the other side of that portal. But cutting down a military leader or even their king? What a worthy last act that would be.

But what if she could spur him into crossing over to her side?

"You're such a pretty male. Once I defeat you, you'll make a fine decoration in my bed." Not that Verdria would ever take a mage to her bed. She'd die first, but she wasn't above lying to a mage to stoke his anger enough that he'd make a fatal mistake.

Before she could really formulate her plan, the male surprised everyone by laughing at Verdria's comment. Then he called back his people before allowing his eyes to run down her body, pausing at her chest for several moments before returning to her face. "I look forward to such a fight, my Fierce One. Cross the portal and we shall see how you fare in a battle against me. Loser ends up in the winner's bed?"

Verdria laughed, the sound deep and joyous. "I shall cross your portal when I'm ready, Pretty One."

"Why not come now?" he asked, a smile gracing his lips.

His smile was the most seductive thing she'd ever seen, she mused.

Their brief exchange had stalled the other soul-mages, but Verdria didn't fool herself. If she and Rhavana didn't escape, death awaited them.

"You're running out of time. Come," the mage leader said, his melodic voice urged them again as he gestured at the spells painted on the walls. As she'd originally guessed, they'd been designed to destroy the ship and everyone on it.

Outside, a dragon roared, announcing his presence.

Verdria grabbed Rhavana by the arm and shoved her at the crate. "Push, damn it! And tell your dragon lover to be ready to grab this."

Behind them, she heard the leader of the soul mages issue orders in his own language. She assumed it was an order to capture them and retrieve the dragon's egg.

Her assumption was proven correct as a dozen mages swarmed through the portal. Unfortunately, there were too many to pick off with a few of Rhavana's arrows or Verdria's axes.

But if she held off the onslaught for a few moments, the distraction she might offer could be enough to give the dragon a chance to scoop up Rhavana and the crate and get out of range of the ship before it blew.

With a savage grin, Verdria turned to Rhavana in the

moments before they were overrun and jerked her chin at the last crate.

Together, they put their shoulders into it and pushed the crate out through the large hole in the wall. A dragon swooped down and snatched it before the container and its precious cargo hit the waves.

"Time for you to go," Verdria said to her fellow warrior-priestess, grabbing Rhavana by the shoulder and belt and tossing her out through the hole.

"Hey!" Rhavana shouted in rage even as she caught a handhold and stopped herself from falling into the ocean. "What do you think you're doing!"

"Saving you." Verdria glanced down at the other priestess, where she hung from the side of the ship like the stubborn woman she was. "We don't both have to die."

Rhavana scrambled for footholds, but the ship's planks were too smooth. She seemed to realize it as well and pleaded with Verdria. "Jump with me. No one has to die."

"That's not true. You heard the pretty soul mage. He wants us. If I don't stay and fight and give him a chance to capture me, he'll just blow the ship and we'll all be dead. If I fight them off long enough for everyone else to get away, then my death will have had a purpose."

"I'll stay and fight with you."

"No, you won't," Verdria said, allowing her gaze to track Kolaith swooping alongside the boat. A moment later, he curled a claw around Rhavana and plucked her from the side of the ship.

Sensing she was out of time, Verdria spun around to see a mage just as he was reaching for her with some kind of spell glowing between his fingers.

"I don't think so," she told him, a savage grin drawing her lips up as she buried her throwing axe in his skull.

The first of this new group of mages fell to her power. He wouldn't be the last.

And she'd make sure their leader fell to her battle magic or die trying.

CHAPTER 4

Verdria

Many bodies slumped lifelessly around the chamber. Drops of blood dripped from her two axes, the liquid hitting the floor with soft little plopping sounds. Only her harsh breathing disturbed the otherwise now silent chamber.

Death was still coming for her. Verdria didn't fool herself about that. Many more soul mages waited on the other side of the portal. As a Warrior-Priestess of the Moon Goddess, Verdria didn't fear death. After all, far worse fates could await a soul than a glorious end in battle. That didn't mean she would go easily.

"Priestess, come to me if you wish to live."

The darkly seductive note in the voice had Verdria adjusting her grip on her great axe as she eyed the speaker.

But she wasn't fooled by his pretty face, outwardly calm expression, or his offer of aid spoken in that beautiful voice.

She knew what he was and what he really wanted—her soul.

And every moment she stalled this soul mage from his goal of blowing up the ship was a moment longer for her fellow warrior-priestesses and their allies to escape to a safe distance.

Once again, Verdria briefly eyed the evilly glowing symbols now burning themselves into the sides of the ship. They pulsed so swiftly, the illumination was almost a continuous glow. She had little time left before the spells unleashed their destructive power, but one thing was sure—she was still breathing.

That meant there was still time enough to kill a few more of the monstrous soul mages.

Her gaze snapped back to the leader of this group, where he still stood safely on the other side of the portal. She glowered at him through the threshold, debating how best to entice him to dance with her in battle.

Her eyes narrowed further as she noted something else. The velvety, black power holding open the window to that other location spun slower, the outer edges of the spell slowly blurring.

Fading, she realized.

The portal spell was gradually closing.

Either the strain of holding the portal open for this long weakened the soul mage, and the spell was beginning to close, or he was intentionally allowing it to shrink.

"Come, priestess," he called once more in that deep voice of his.

His words drew her gaze back to his.

Grinning, he held her gaze boldly. "I can see you are too proud to surrender easily to anything, even death. Cross the portal and live to keep on fighting for a little longer." He paused, and then one elegant, long-fingered hand gestured down the length of his body in a sensual motion, as if offering her a delectable feast. "Perhaps you'll even take me into death with you? I sense you would like that very much."

She arched a brow and allowed her gaze to slide down his body once more. For all that the soul-devouring mages were rotted spiritually by their particular form of corrupt and twisted magic, this fellow had certainly maintained a pretty enough body on the outside.

Then the velvety black magic rising from his bare skin expanded suddenly, billowing outward, and she realized he'd used his own body as a distraction. She cursed herself for being a fool, even as three more thick tendrils formed from the magic twisting around the mage.

The sinister energy crawled through the air, each tendril slithering toward the powerful portal spell where they latched on, feeding more power into the magical gateway.

"Priestess, I may be powerful, but even I have my limits. This is your last chance at life." His rich tones were like black velvet magic against her senses, easily the most seductive thing she'd ever heard. He could probably read off the items on a ledger and still make every woman in his vicinity take note of him, mesmerizing them with his voice until they were thinking about stripping him bare.

Focus, she mentally barked at herself. Once again, she wondered if there was some magic in his voice.

If there were, best she swiftly slit his throat to safeguard her soul when she died. There was no way she planned to let them get her soul. She'd fall on one of her axes first.

"Life, you say?" She smirked at him as she slowly spun her favorite weapon.

"There isn't much time left," he said with what almost sounded like the barest hint of a pleading tone. "If you wish to live, you must come to me. You have my word that I will not kill you."

"Hmm. Trust the word of a soul mage? Really?"

Verdria laughed. "How naïve do you think I am, Pretty One?"

"Naïve? No, Priestess, I would not call you that." He cocked his head as his gaze roved over her. "Determined. Focused. Lethal. I imagine any or all those terms apply to such a fierce one as you."

"Flattered. Truly. But I don't think I'd like your kingdom's hospitality very much."

He smirked at her words. "Priestess, I didn't say you would enjoy my company, only that I wouldn't kill you."

"That doesn't sound fun at all, Pretty One."

Slowly his merriment shifted to what, impossibly, looked like concern.

"You are nearly out of time. Come to me now if you wish to live. The ship is already lost. Even if you jump, you won't be able to escape my spell's destructive power."

"I already know I'm going to die. But you were right earlier. I'm just trying to figure out a way to take you with me, Pretty One."

His smirk returned, and he released that rich laughter of his again. The other soul mages still looked equal parts confused and angry.

Their leader's rich laughter halted whatever the other mages had planned, and several of them glanced back over their shoulders at the commander as if seeking some instruction or even a hint of what he wanted.

Verdria could relate. His laughter wasn't the reaction she'd hoped to cause. Anger would have been much more helpful. Oh well, just because she couldn't provoke the leader into a mindless rage didn't mean she couldn't change targets.

She shifted her grip on her throwing axe. Then, with a skillful toss, the axe sliced through the air, crossed the portal's threshold, and planted itself in the back of the closest soul mage's head.

Her target collapsed in a heap. The sudden thud had several mages turning back to her, their gazes showing surprise for a moment before rage overcame their shock. These remaining men and women were no warriors, she concluded. The first batch of mages to cross the portal had been much more of a challenge. Trained warriors, she'd assumed. They certainly hadn't been foolish enough to show their backs to her.

She shrugged and then grinned savagely at them. "Well? What did you expect? The idiot gave a warrior-priestess his back."

Only the leader seemed unsurprised, having never taken his eyes off her.

She returned his intense gaze, accompanied it with another shrug, and then took a two-handed hold on her great axe. She nodded toward the dead man. "He was too stupid to live. You didn't want him serving under you, anyway."

"You're correct, of course," he said, his tone giving nothing away.

But if she wasn't mistaken, there was a mischievous light glinting in his eyes. She was entertaining him.

Not exactly my plan, she mused to herself.

"Come, Priestess. Step through the portal and show me how good you are with that axe of yours."

"Now you're just flirting."

"Perhaps I am."

She mulled his admission over. While she didn't know if this would qualify as flirting, more than one of her mentors had hinted that men often thought with the rod between their legs instead of their heads. Perhaps this mage had a weakness for any nice pair of tits? Verdria would use that to her advantage if possible.

Her smile stretching, she gestured him forward. "Why don't you come here? I'll show you what I can do with my axe."

"I think not, my Fierce One," he said, a laugh of delight following swiftly behind the unwelcome endearment. "However, you're far too intriguing for me to allow you to die pointlessly."

With a flick of his wrist, tendrils of velvety blackness broke away from the portal, lashing out in her direction.

She danced backward, her goddess blessed battle-axe slicing through each of the tendrils as they reached for her. Only swift footwork and her skills with her axe kept the tendrils from surrounding her. But there was another problem. A greater mass of sprawling dark magic blocked all other routes of escape. Even the hole in the back wall was now covered with a latticework of shifting, malevolent darkness.

Had he been toying with them all along? Had he let the dragon escape with Rhavana and the egg? That…

She frowned. That made little sense.

But now she was effectively trapped. The portal was the only avenue of escape. Not that she wanted to go that way. But as the mass of lashing and twisting tendrils continued to contract around her, forcing her closer to the portal, she knew she would not have a choice soon. Perhaps he planned to interrogate her. He'd only need one priestess for that, she supposed.

She hated a mystery, but this was one she didn't plan to live long enough to solve.

"You want to see what I can do with my axe, Mage?" She taunted him as she summoned her battle magic, the full force she could summon at once. Then she took a running leap and launched herself through the portal.

Landing on the other side, she grinned at the startled mages surrounding her. They regrouped quickly.

Using her hefty axe, she knocked away the first sword in her path.

At her mental command, a dozen spears of her battle magic coalesced out of the air in a semicircle in front of her. She tightened her will around them all, invisible fingers of power closing around each spear. Then, in the next moment, she flung them outward, guided by her will.

Using so much of her power in such a way burned through her reserves at an alarming rate. But she only had one chance at killing her ultimate target.

With a loud battle cry, she launched herself into the large hole she'd made in the mages' ranks, her long strides carrying her toward the leader of the soul mages.

The few mages still standing ran into her path, attempting to block her from reaching their leader. With her fierce grin never faltering, she cut them down with her axe and equally deadly battle magic, never taking her attention off their too-pretty commander. Though her battle magic did warn her as more guards came rushing into the room in a desperate attempt to get between her and the male she wanted. She ignored them, knowing they were too far away to prevent her from reaching her goal.

But their very desperation to reach Pretty One *was* confirmation he was someone of importance. Slaying him would be a worthy last kill before she fell on her axe, her own magic slaying her before the mages could capture her.

A swift death by her goddess-blessed blade was the only insurance she had to prevent the soul mages from harvesting her soul. And it needed to be a quick death—no prolonged lingering.

"As you can see, my arm is strong. And my axe is sharp, Pretty One!" she shouted at him when only two mages remained standing between them. He hadn't run and she mentally willed him to hold his ground. The other soldiers were almost upon them. If he ran now, he could escape her.

The last two mages fell before her blades, and finally only a handful of strides stretched between her and her primary target.

"Impressive," he said with appreciation clear in his tone.

Not running was a mistake on his part.

She aimed a wolfish smile at the mage as she closed the last of the distance between them and swung her axe. "Are you ready to face the gods, Pretty One?"

"Perhaps another day?" he said, joy still sparkling in his gaze. Then, in a swift move, he raised one hand. His fingers opened before she could reach him, revealing a bright glimmer of magic. It swiftly expanded outward, leaping between them.

His power struck her shields as her axe was in the apex of its swing. Her battle magic crumbled before this strange new onslaught. Within moments, her magical defenses were in ruins, and his energy was sinking below her skin. In those moments, she realized he'd been toying with her all along. He could have captured her at any time. She also noted he commanded another power, and this second magic wasn't the dark, oily energy of a soul mage. Worse, her magic hadn't reacted as it would to a hostile power.

But she didn't have time to reason out what type of power it was at this exact moment. The only thing she *did* have time for was one loud curse, and then her limbs grew heavy, her feet suddenly rooting themselves to the ground.

No. No, no, no! Now she battled panic as well.

"You dishonorable coward! What did you do to me?" she shouted at him as numbness crawled down all her limbs. Her fingers went completely numb, her great battle-axe slipping from her grasp to crash to the floor beside them.

He stepped forward before his guards could stop him. "I would hardly call saving your life a cowardly act, Fierce One."

"Go fornicate with a mountain goat, Mage."

She slumped forward, her unresponsive body losing the battle with gravity.

He caught her in his arms but staggered back a couple of steps under her substantial weight, likely not expecting her to outweigh him. If it had been within her power, she would have grinned at his surprise as she rammed a blade between his ribs and into his little black heart.

But all that was beyond her ability at present, and her head dropped forward to rest on his shoulder.

"Now that I have saved you, what should I do with you?" he asked in that darkly beautiful voice of his.

"Put a blade in my heart to put me out of my misery?" she muttered against the warm skin of his shoulder.

"I think not."

"You'd be doing yourself a favor. I'll do everything in my power to make you miserable, you soul-stealing bastard."

"I enjoy challenges, my Fierce One. It's foreplay for me."

His delighted laughter echoed in her ears even as all her other senses continued to go as dull and useless as her body.

She wasn't sure what was more humiliating, being caught so easily or being held in his arms. Only his strength kept her from crashing to the floor. She'd rather land on her face than be held in a soul mage's arms.

Not that he cared what she thought. He called out orders to his surviving people, completely ignoring her, a difficult feat with him holding her up. But he seemed to manage it just fine.

CHAPTER 5

Honryn

The priestess was a substantial—though not unwelcome—weight in his arms. Now, while his spell temporarily held her immobile, and she wasn't trying to take his head, Honryn could study her. He hoisted her higher, wrapping his arms around her waist to hold her up.

Of course, her head flopped back down on his shoulder. From this angle, all he could see was her curly red hair barely contained in two braids as big around as his wrists.

Red was a color not seen in the hair of the empire's people. Certainly not that bright shade of hers. She'd likely never know it, but she had her flame-colored hair to thank for her life. It was that bit of brightness in the ship's dark interior that had caught his attention.

But it was something else entirely that held his attention now.

Something deeper.

Something below the skin.

She was brave, her spirit fierce as she'd faced him down. He'd admired that about her. And it had been refreshing to have someone challenge him. He'd long since cowed, destroyed, or bent most of his enemies to his will.

But this new warrior-priestess had challenged him. And, oh, how he'd liked it. He'd also noted that her fighting styles were excellent as she'd cut down all his brethren in her path.

He wouldn't mind crossing blades with her to test himself against her training. The warrior-priestesses of the Moon Goddess were renowned warriors, as he knew firsthand.

A bit of mirth flowed through his soul. Of course, he and his Fierce One would have to have a very long talk first. Otherwise, she'd try to take his head with the first swing in the practice ring.

As much as her battle skills had caught and held his attention, now that he held her in his arms, something else ensnared him.

Her scent.

Blessedly clean and untainted by the stench that accompanied the magic of the soul mages.

It was a battle to stop himself from burying his nose against her neck and stand there for the next hour, inhaling her fresh scent. Even the tang of sweat and blood wasn't enough to hide her otherwise pure fragrance.

Goddess. As soon as he was alone with her, he was going to bury his face in her hair and forget about everything for a short time.

Just the thought of being alone with her had him itching to be away from everyone else, to hurry back to his chambers. It wasn't her beauty that compelled him, for she had little—too big and mannish and crude by the standards of the empire. But perversely, he liked her all the more because she wasn't dainty and the ideal of beauty as far as the nobility was concerned. And since she was the type of female his people would automatically dismiss or even snicker at behind fans and veils and masks, that made him like her even more.

And it was more than just that, he realized. He liked her size, the feel of her muscular body in his arms. He already knew she'd be an equal for him in the practice ring.

Another part of his mind noted she'd likely be an equal partner in another type of physical endeavor as well.

He gave himself a mental shake and told a particular body part to behave.

I'm well aware it has been a very, very long time since I've bedded a woman, he thought a touch bitterly. *You don't need to keep reminding me.*

But even that wasn't the reason he wanted to get this priestess alone.

It was his power's dual nature.

Both halves of his magic wanted to explore her, learn her battle magic. Discover her strengths and weaknesses.

But unfortunately, that would have to wait until later. To reveal the two sides of his magic's nature would be a death sentence here in the empire's heart.

And he also had another pressing matter to attend to if he didn't want to find himself on the receiving end of his uncle's displeasure. As the Priest-King Elect, only the current Priest-King outranked him, as his uncle would remind Honryn if he stepped too far out of line. While his uncle allowed Honryn to run roughshod over just about everyone else, including the emperor, he wouldn't take kindly to what he'd perceive as a slight to the Serpent God, such as if Honryn didn't get back to the temple and finish the morning rites.

His uncle's benevolence only stretched so far, and Honryn had already been testing it extensively of late. There had been growing contention between them about Honryn's continual rejections of all his uncle's candidates for a potential consort for his heir.

The problem was that Honryn literally couldn't get intimate with any woman without betraying one of his closely guarded secrets, even if he actually found a woman he could stomach, which posed a rather large problem since he needed a mate before he could take up his uncle's mantle at the Festival of the Wine Moon.

Glancing down at the woman in his arms, he narrowed his eyes in thought.

Hmmm. Perhaps Fate had delivered a solution to his situation that had seemed untenable until the moment he'd looked through his portal spell and first spotted the red-haired priestess on the other side. He already knew both sides of his magical nature liked her by how his power had responded to her. And if he could gain her trust, she might be willing to keep his secrets, unlike a mage woman.

His choice would undoubtedly upset the court and his father and his brothers. Maybe even his uncle.

Honryn grinned suddenly. He did so love to ruffle feathers.

What a delightful day it had turned out to be.

Glancing around, he realized his elite temple guards and the members of the city garrison were silently awaiting his orders while he'd been inspecting the newest member of the court. The city garrison guards were too far below his rank to address him directly, while the temple guards were too respectful of his station, and his Elite personal guards were too well trained to question him out loud, but he could see the silent questions building behind all the shuttered expressions.

It was on the tip of his tongue to order the city guards to transport her to the temple, where he could monitor her while he finished up morning rites, but it would also take time to locate a cart to transport her across half the length of the upper city. The guest quarters of the royal palace were closer. He could have his warrior-priestess installed in one of those rooms and have the servants clean her up while he returned to the temple and completed morning rites. The sooner that was done, the sooner he could return to his warrior-priestess, and they could have a long talk.

He turned to the captain of his Elites, where she stood looking on in respectful silence. While her expression gave nothing of her inner thoughts away, she was no doubt annoyed at him. He'd used a portal to travel from the temple complex to the palace, leaving his personal guard behind where they'd waited outside the temple's sanctum. Clearly, they'd discovered their charge was gone and rushed across half the city to rejoin him.

But whatever she might be feeling inside, Elite Captain Sanjah let nothing of her emotions show on her face as she observed him while silently awaiting his orders. He'd always liked her because while she *was* a competent swordswoman, she was also efficient at overseeing whatever else needed to get done promptly. He could trust her to make sure the servants settled in the new warrior-priestess. And there was the bonus of the captain being a closed-mouthed woman. She wouldn't spread rumors about Honryn's latest rescue.

He directed his next words to her.

"Take a unit of the city garrison and have the priestess carried to the guest wing, then summon a few of my personal servants to clean her up and see to any injuries she's suffered. I'll return when I'm able and do a proper healing on her."

"Yes, Your Holiness. I'll see that your warrior-priestess is safe and settled in."

He didn't miss how his captain had stressed the words 'your warrior-priestess' when she'd spoken. Clearly, he'd allowed his expression to reveal more than was safe.

Then he nearly rolled his eyes at his thought.

Anyone with even one good eye could see what his Fierce One was, thus know her importance. As one of the Priestesses of the Mountains, women of her blood-line were immune to the plague. That meant she was fertile as well as being a warrior strong in body, mind, and magic. Any children she birthed would be powerful hybrids, strong in magic. And his brethren valued magical strength above all else.

Even the regular city garrison guards were smart enough to deduce what Honryn's apparent interest in this outlander woman might mean.

His captain took the priestess from Honryn without another word, but he noted when she grunted softly at the warrior-priestess's weight. Two of the city garrison guards stepped forward to aid her.

"My spell will keep her immobile for hours yet," Honryn said, needing to say something to the soldiers. "The most she'll be able to do is speak once she wakes. Make sure there is someone to translate for her. At present, I don't have time to perform the language spell upon her."

"Of course, Your Holiness."

Honryn turned and started away and then paused and glanced back at the guards struggling to lift the warrior-priestess. "Make sure everyone knows she is to suffer no abuse. The warrior-priestess is my... personal guest. I shall return to attend her as soon as I'm able."

His captain bowed her head. "She shall want for nothing."

Nodding, Honryn strode off, reluctantly attending to his duties when he'd much rather spend his time learning about the mountain woman.

CHAPTER 6

Verdria

Her hearing was the only sense which hadn't completely abandoned her when the mage leader's spell had hit her. Verdria had heard him speak to his people—not that she could understand his native tongue. But she was aware he'd issued a few instructions to the guards, and then she'd been handed off to another pair of arms. The new person holding her up was smaller than the commander and more slightly built. A woman, perhaps?

Verdria's guess was confirmed when the person attempting to hold her upright muttered a soft, barely heard curse in a feminine voice. At least, she assumed it was a curse going by the tone and how softly it had been uttered.

Then again, the guard could have been commenting on the weather for all Verdria understood of the foreign words.

Still, she would have smirked at the woman's grunt of exertion as she tried to hoist Verdria's limp form higher, but like the rest of her body, her lips were numb and unresponsive from the commander's powerful spell, so no smirking. But anything that she could do to make a soul mage's life more difficult was a small victory worth celebrating. And she would not fool herself. With a heavy feeling of despair in her middle, she knew her victories were likely to be few now that they had captured her.

The sound of two more guards approaching reached Verdria's ears, and soon there was a person at each arm and one at her feet. Then, with a sharp word from the female guard, the three of them hoisted Verdria into the air and carried her down a long corridor, one which branched many times. She knew that bit about her surroundings only because she could feel as they slowed for each turn or fork in the tunnel.

They walked farther into the building until the scent of exotic flowers and incense faded to be replaced by the more familiar scents of beeswax candles and burning torches. The change suggested they were going deeper into the palace, where neither breezes nor natural light reached. After too many twists and turns for her to track, her guards halted once more.

There was a scraping of a key being inserted into a lock and then the sound of a door being pushed open. By the slight grunt accompanying the sound, the door was large and heavy enough to require a little muscle power to open it, or the door hadn't been opened in a while.

She dismissed that last thought in the next moment.

The room smelled of fresh linens and soap and more of the beeswax candles.

And the best part—her eyelids finally obeyed her silent command and opened.

Well, a tiny crack, at least. She'd take that as a sign of improvement.

The guards carried her through a large, lavishly appointed outer chamber and then into an equally large bedchamber where they deposited her on one side of the bed. She noticed the dark-haired woman seemed in command of the two men. However, Verdria couldn't determine any rank difference between the three strangers. The woman and two men were all dressed similarly, with metal-decorated leather vests over shirts of billowing fabric. Long, loose pants made of the same material covered them to their sandaled feet. Every bit of their attire was dyed the same light-swallowing tone of black.

With a few words to each other, the three guards

turned and left the room. Verdria tracked them by the sound of their footfalls. Not an easy feat on the carpeted floors. Their sandals made less noise than boots did, but she could still tell the two men only went as far as the outer chamber's entrance, where they stood guard. From their position, they could probably see into the bedchamber and monitor her. The woman's even softer footfalls vanished out into the hall, as she either left to return to her superior or to run some errand.

Verdria would never know until she had time to learn the language.

If she lived long enough to learn it.

She'd been prepared to die back on the boat or in the battle on this side of the portal, but now that she'd been captured and the time of her death was out of her hands, she didn't want to die. Not like this. Not as a slave, or worse. A strange shivery feeling took up residence in her middle. It took some moments to process it was fear.

As she stared up at the room's strangely smooth, cream-colored ceiling, waiting for whatever came next, she fought to stay calm.

Calm would better her chances of gaining her freedom later, or if that was impossible, at least aid her in getting her hands on a weapon and dying in battle like she'd planned back on the ship.

Though a not-so-small part of her knew she might

better serve her people if she could live long enough to learn something of tactical value about this kingdom and escape back to her own with the knowledge.

After all, the five kingdoms were working on renewing the old alliances. If she could get whatever she learned here back to her lands, then her people and their allies might be able to use that information to destroy the soul mages once and for all.

Verdria had often thought her ancestors had made a mistake centuries ago when they stopped short of hunting down the homeland of the defeated soul mages to ensure they would never again be a threat to the five kingdoms.

She could link her present predicament directly back to her ancestors' past mistakes.

Now fate had given their descendants a chance to correct that oversight. And Verdria feared that failing to destroy the enemy this time might doom all five kingdoms. The mages had clearly been building up their numbers once more.

A commotion out in the hallway caught her attention, and she instinctively tried to force her body up and off the bed, but all she managed to do was turn her head a little.

Small wins, she reminded herself.

That slight turn of her head allowed her to look out the bedchamber door and witness as a group of richly dressed men and women pushed passed the two guards on the outer door and forced their way inside. The tall man in the lead was wearing a uniform similar to the guards. Though the newcomer's uniform had more ornate touches, definitely more silver gems stitched into the vest. It wasn't until he was closer that she realized those decorations weren't gems; they were soul crystals. A dozen souls adorned his vest, and more hung from around his neck, his pierced ears, and at his wrists. Soul crystals even studded his weapons belt.

Horror curled in her stomach at the thought of souls being treated as objects of wealth or rank or… or fashion. The fingers of her right hand slowly curled into a fist. Realizing what she'd just done, she flexed her fingers, trying to work more strength and feeling back into her numb body.

To judge by his fancy attire and the number of soul crystals he wore, she'd guess him to be of a much higher rank than the guards who had carried her here. And his similar uniform suggested they were part of the same military force, which could only mean he was a senior officer, and was likely why the two guards had allowed him within.

Verdria didn't need to understand his words to know he was attempting to order the two guards to leave.

And it was clear from the guards' body language they didn't know how to handle the situation. Though at least they'd put themselves between the newcomers and the door to the inner chamber, protecting Verdria. For now.

They were outnumbered but seemed to be speaking in soothing tones.

The man in the lead of this new group wasn't appeased and snarled out more orders, nearly spitting in the face of the two guards.

Verdria still couldn't understand a word of what he shouted, but it was clear he was enraged and wanted to get into the inner chamber. And since she was the only thing new inside, she could only assume he wanted to reach her for some purpose she wasn't likely to enjoy.

The guards were shaking their heads, talking swiftly. Still trying to reason with him?

'Let them keep him distracted,' she prayed to her goddess. *'Keep them all occupied for as long as you can.'*

With another act of concentration, she willed her legs to move. Her sluggish limbs obeyed, moving a very slight distance, but it was enough to renew her hope and spark a rebellion in her warrior's soul.

A moment later, the higher-ranked man shouted out something that sounded like a threat. Or perhaps it was merely an order from a superior to a lower-ranking guardsman?

Whatever the meaning of the words, the two guards shifted out of the way reluctantly.

Farther back, off to one side of the mob of twenty-some angry nobles, a young servant girl stood looking on in shock. Verdria was surprised to see a child. They were so rare in the mountains.

She hadn't even seen or heard the girl when the three guards had first carried Verdria in. But the girl must have heard the yelling and come to investigate. And by the way she bolted out the door as Verdria watched, she assumed the girl went to get help.

Wise child, Verdria thought. *You don't want to be anywhere near the bloodshed that's about to unfold.*

She flexed her fingers slowly, working the feeling back into them as the icy chill of the mage spell reluctantly eased more of its hold.

Verdria knew little about this kingdom, but the too-handsome man who had captured her was clearly a power to be reckoned with, but so too was this older man, judging by how the others deferred to him. Though if Verdria was the type to place wagers, she'd bet the mage responsible for her capture was the more powerful of the two men, in magic if not in rank. Whatever brought the older man here, it must be a conviction strong enough to make him willing to face the mage leader's displeasure.

Verdria's gaze slid back over the newcomers. The group wasn't quite an angry mob, she realized. These men and women were still too controlled for that. She could feel their anger, though. For the moment, their fear or respect for the nameless leader seemed to hold them back.

That knowledge didn't ease Verdria's concerns, for they seemed willing enough to sit back and watch whatever the older man had planned for her.

She willed her battle magic to wake, but it remained beyond her reach even though her body was coming back under her control.

Quickly assessing the situation, she frowned. Even if the servant girl had run straight to a superior, any help the girl could raise would likely come too late to save Verdria's life. If she wanted to survive the next few moments, Verdria knew she'd have to fight.

The older mage was now standing at the side of the bed, looking down at Verdria, his skin pale and tight around his eyes, his aged face drawn in lines of more than rage, she realized. There was grief there, too.

"Warrior-priestess, do you know what you have done?" he asked in her language, his words clear, though accented.

'No,' she thought to herself, *'but I'm sure you're going to tell me, anyway.'*

He narrowed his eyes at her silence, his mouth tightening with some powerful emotion. "I had two sons. Sons any father would have been proud to call his own." He drew a long dagger from his belt. "Now I have none because of you."

Well, she mused, he certainly was one for getting to the meat of the conversation. Verdria usually liked bluntness, but she also liked to be in full command of her body.

The two guards assigned to Verdria rushed forward, once again speaking swiftly and urgently. The man froze, looking somewhat astonished, and then he loosed a bitter-sounding laugh.

He looked down at her, his molten gaze still promising her a bad time in her immediate future.

"These two tell me His Holiness has said that if anyone attempts to kill you, he will destroy that man's entire House." He paused and then glanced down the length of her, a puzzled expression on his face, as if he was trying to determine what about her warranted such an action. "To destroy an entire House over the fate of one warrior-priestess is a touch bloodthirsty even for him."

The two guards took turns speaking to the older man once again. He frowned at them and motioned them to silence, turning his attention back to her.

"They think he plans to make you his consort." The male continued to look down at her, his gaze just as cold and harsh as before. "In case you don't know our Priest-King Elect, he is fully capable of carrying out horrors far greater than any soul mage before him. He'd lose no sleep over killing another man's entire House. He'd kill others of his own bloodline if he considered them a genuine threat. He has in the past."

"Thanks for the history lesson, but if your sons were

some of the men I killed, that's regrettable. But your kind shouldn't have returned to the five kingdoms. Kill me. Don't kill me. It won't change anything. Everyone dies eventually."

"Yes, they do," the man agreed in a calm and icy voice. Though that cold killing rage still gleamed in his gaze, but his voice was calm when he continued, "Which is why I'm only going to mark you, so you never forget my sons or me. But you will live—live to mate with our great and terrible future priest-king. After all, that is surely a fate worse than death. I will watch you each day, rejoicing as he sucks out more and more of your spirit, reshaping you into his consort, into his tool."

He smiled as he pressed the cold tip of his dagger against the skin of her cheek, below her right eye. "A consort doesn't need to see to spawn his offspring."

She fisted the fingers of one hand and glowered up at the older man. Maybe she could take down this soul mage where she'd failed with the commander?

Unleashing an echoing battle cry, she knocked his blade aside and then lunged up at the mage's throat, enjoying the moment his eyes widened in shock.

CHAPTER 7

Verdria

*E*ven without full command over her magic and still being partly immobilized by the commander's spell, Verdria had no plans to go down without a fight. Unfortunately, that was easier to boast about than to accomplish. Her lunge came up short and the older man escape before she could capture him and snap his neck. Now the mob was upon her, shoving and kicking and punching as they sought to bring her down.

She fought them. Several going down under her more powerful blows, but someone swept her legs out from under her, and the others were upon her before she could regain her feet. Rolling onto her side, she attempted to escape the boot toe aimed for her ribs. She was partially successful, but only partially, still catching the blow on her side. Her ribs bitched about the impact. She hadn't heard a snap, and the ache was more of a dull throb than the white-hot lance of agony that heralded a broken bone.

She scissored her legs, taking down two of her opponents. They in turn conveniently took down three more mages, giving her the chance to regain her footing. Pain throbbed along her side in what was likely a few cracked ribs, but she wasn't out of the fight.

Not yet.

The soul mages came at her again, landing far more blows on her than she was on them. In the back of her mind, she wondered why they hadn't just used magic on her. Maybe they knew they didn't need magic to end her. It would only take a few more hits before she went down for good.

When she went down again, she wouldn't be getting back up.

As she fought, she kept telling herself it was better to die this way, better than becoming a consort to the priest-king of the soul mages. She would embrace death. But even as those thoughts crossed her mind, she fought to live, kicking out, punching, screaming, and head-butting her opponents.

Surrendering to death early was a type of defeat.

Verdria of High Rock had never been defeated in battle, not until she'd crossed paths with the soul mage priest-king—and that cheating bastard didn't fight fair. She wanted a second chance to beat that too-pretty man into the ground.

She'd be damned if she fell to this mob.

Kicking out, she crippled her next target. The youth, a soul mage dressed in rich fabrics and decorated with many jewels and soul crystals, dropped to the floor with a scream. He grabbed his knee and howled in pain. She cast a sneer at the male and then selected her next opponent.

But the mob's leader, the older man with more training than many other members of the mob, came at her again with a roar, tackling her to the ground.

Stunned, the breath knocked from her lungs, her body screaming in pain, it took her a moment to rally her brutalized body. That short time was all he needed. His hands were suddenly around her throat.

"I've changed my mind. I'm going to kill you after all." He snarled the words in her face, spittle splattering her on the cheek.

Her vision was fading when she squeaked out a single word. "Name?"

The man's brows rose. "What was that?"

He eased up on her throat a fraction, as she'd hoped.

"Name of my killer," she wheezed out. "Worthy opponent."

He gave a bitter laugh. "I am Lord Nuran of House Blythrun, and I will take your soul when you die and put so many spells upon it that when it is at last freed to return to the spirit world, you will then be enslaved as a whore to the two sons you've already sent there."

Verdria bit back a retort about how she'd kick their asses in the spirit world, too. Instead, she concentrated on pretending to be faint and dying and defeated.

"What?" she asked on a soft hiss of breath, allowing her head to lull to the side as her eyes drifted closed.

The fingers around her throat eased up a little more.

She waited, and as expected, he lowered his head until his lips were against her ear.

"Lord Nuran of House Blythrun will be the one to send you into the afterlife, Warrior-Priestess."

She twisted in his hold, clamping her teeth onto his neck, right over where his pulse beat the strongest. Channeling the last of her battle magic into added strength, she ground her teeth into his flesh as he roared in pain. She held on as he tried to pull away, to beat her off, landing blows to her head and stomach. Hot blood gushed across her face. She didn't relent even then, tearing his flesh more. The male on top of her howled again, fighting harder, but she brought her arms up and locked them around his neck in a depraved imitation of a lover's embrace.

Another soul mage reached down and tried to drag Nuran away, but she kept her arms locked around him, and her teeth clamped hard, her battle magic lending her the needed strength for this last kill. The amount of blood pumping across her face told her she'd succeeded.

Booted feet renewed their bombardment of her ribs, their owners not knowing it was too late to save their leader. This time she heard ribs snap; the expected white-hot pain lashed her side and stole her ability to breathe.

The other soul mages tore her opponent out of her embrace. She blinked blood out of her eyes in time to see them dragging away a dead body.

As they looked down at her in shock, she snarled up at them.

Yes. I am a mad beast. Come at me if you dare, she told them with her rage maddened eyes.

As if in answer to her silent challenge, several of the surrounding soul mages called upon their power and advanced.

Exhausted, her body bruised and battered, her battle magic depleted, Verdria watched as death came for her.

Sunlight from an east-facing window illuminated her enemies, and Verdria wished she'd been able to see the glory of the moons in the sky once more. But that wasn't to be.

She forced her eyes to remain open anyway, unwilling to cower away from anything, not even the inky jagged black swirls leaping through the air toward her, the spells promising a fate worse than death.

But the spells never reached her.

They should have. She had no defenses left.

Her eyes widened as she raised her head. She should have been dead. Yet, she wasn't. Something held the lances of power frozen, suspended in the air. However, there was nothing she could see preventing them from reaching her.

A moment later, she refocused beyond the suspended spells to gaze upon one of the soul mages. The man stood slack-jawed, the light dying in his eyes.

Dead.

He was dead, and his body hadn't quite realized it yet.

A moment later, his knees folded, his body collapsing to the ground with a heavy thud she felt in the marrow of her bones. Several other soul mages hit the ground seconds later. An invisible wave was rolling outward from her position, ravaging the startled soul mages before they knew what had hit them. She was still processing this sudden change of events when the commander she'd insultingly called 'Pretty One' strode into the room, his deadly magic whipping around him, not unlike a fan of scorpion tails hunting out and stabbing the last of her attackers.

The only surviving soul mages were the few who had hung back, unwilling to sully themselves in a battle, or perhaps too afraid of the man now walking among them to take part in an attack against a priestess he supposedly planned to claim as his consort.

A sudden shimmering over the bodies of her attackers momentarily drew her gaze from the too-handsome commander—no, she corrected herself—they'd called him the Priest-King Elect. Still, even though he was currently the deadliest thing in the room, she looked away from his person to see what his magic was doing.

Soul crystals were emerging from the dead mages' chests. Verdria's shock-slowed mind could hardly believe what she was seeing. He'd killed over two dozen of his own people in the blink of an eye.

The Priest-King Elect came to stand beside her. But he didn't so much as look down, his attention on the remaining men and women frozen in fear.

"By rights, I should kill the lot of you," he said. "However, our numbers are already depleted enough. I am being very merciful by letting you leave here today, but you've gained my attention now. If any of my rivals were still around for you to ask, they would say that my attention isn't good for one's long-term survival. If I should see any of you again, I cannot say if my benevolence would last."

All the surviving men and women, finely dressed nobles and guards alike, dropped to their knees and then prostrated themselves on the floor.

It was only when Verdria looked back at the leader that she realized he was looking down at her now, his expression unreadable.

He held out his hand to her. "Stand and come with me. No more harm will befall you. I promise you that, and I shall stay to see that my word isn't broken a second time."

Verdria slowly and painfully leveraged herself into a sitting position. She just stared at his outstretched hand, not moving to take it.

"Come with me if you wish to live, My Fierce One," he said in a gentler tone.

CHAPTER 8

Verdria

As she stared up at the mage's hand, offered in an invitation, Verdria knew this was one of those life moments, a culmination of events that led to a pinnacle. Accepting his aid might save her life, but it could also lead to her soul's ruin.

This future priest-king wasn't offering friendship. She knew that. He wanted something else from her. And she very much doubted it was for her to become his consort and squeeze out a child, as the other soul mage had crudely suggested. If she was wrong and he wanted a child, she'd disappoint him in that regard. Still, she didn't think that was what he was truly after.

But she would dig until she found out what he really wanted and then use that against him.

But first, she needed to live, and without aid, she wasn't at all confident she'd live to see the next sunrise. Every time one of her muscles shook or twitched, her chest and abdomen burned with agony.

Even through the agony, she forced her mind to focus. She needed to live for the potential knowledge she could bring back to her people. Fate was offering her a chance unlike any other warrior-priestess before her—the rarest of opportunities to discover the enemy's greatest weaknesses. This might even be the work of the moon goddess.

If that was the case, Verdria didn't want to be the one to fail her goddess and destroy her people's best hope.

Now she just needed to humble herself enough to ask a mage for aid.

As she half-sprawled broken on the floor, looking up at his hand with its long, elegant fingers, it dawned on her that he might lose face if she ignored his offer. Which made ignoring it even more tempting, but this might be her only chance to pretend to befriend this powerful man.

But her best chance to accomplish all her goals had just closed his fingers and let his hand drop back to his side without a word. He turned his back on her and walked away, calling out to someone in his foreign language as he did so.

She'd hesitated too long. He was leaving.

"Wait." The single word came out hoarse and broken sounding.

He halted and glanced over his shoulder. His intense gaze seemed to will her to find the power to stand, and she was somehow sure he couldn't offer his aid a second time without diminishing his position among his people. She could understand that. Mages were undeniably a particularly blood-thirsty breed. And if this was the heart of their kingdom, their court, it was most likely filled with the most cutthroat of their kind. To offer her aid a second time after she'd spurned him already might open him up for a potential attack.

Or he might just be nursing bruised pride that she hadn't taken his hand.

Verdria gritted her teeth and held back a scream as she painfully rolled to her hands and knees. It took three tries to reach her feet, and she was sweating and nauseous by the time she was upright. Her steps were awkward. She swayed badly. The throb of one fractured arm and multiple cracked ribs didn't help, but she made her way to him with a hobbling step. With each footfall, agony throbbed through her body, and her vision threatened to grey out. Every breath hurt. Every step hurt. But still she fought to hide her pain, unwilling to show more weakness to them than was absolutely necessary.

When she reached his side, he nodded and started from the room. Outside, she swore the corridor was spinning to confuse her. She couldn't even use her uninjured arm to steady herself against a wall, because the corridor she found herself in was too wide. She was certain she was about to pass out when warm fingers closed around her uninjured arm. They slowly slid down her arm until they could enfold her blood-coated fingers.

The strangest thing happened then. A trickle of familiar magic flowed into her.

It was impossible.

A trick.

Whatever caused the sensation couldn't be real.

The energy flowing into her felt like her people's magic, felt like the Moon Goddess's great power.

But the trickle was only very slight and then gone again, almost as fast as it had come. But she felt steadier for it.

When she glanced down, his hand was gone, leaving only a tingle behind in the tips of her fingers.

As impossible as it seemed, she could see more clearly. The corridor was no longer spinning, and she had a little more strength in her legs.

Then again, she still hurt everywhere, her ribs and

bruised organs an agony. Each step was a small torture, so perhaps she'd imagined the tingle of magic.

But she allowed her enemy to guide her down the hallway. Guards formed up around them, and he issued more orders in his language. Soon, the guards were pushing through a gathering crowd of onlookers. They'd gained quite an audience, she realized. Extravagantly dressed nobles and humble servants alike gazed at her and the man she walked beside.

He didn't look in her direction, nor did he offer to help support her in any physical way. Still, she sensed his intense will silently encouraging her.

Or perhaps she was delusional with pain.

CHAPTER 9

Honryn

The warrior-priestess was stubborn. He'd give her that. Honryn was certain only that stubborn will of hers was keeping her upright. His magic confirmed she had internal injuries. His Fierce One was far worse off than her outward appearance would suggest. And her outward appearance was woeful to the extreme. A lesser being would have been unconscious on the floor, not doggedly limping along beside him.

Yet even she had her limits.

He'd wanted to gather her into his arms since he'd first seen her on the floor, beaten and bloody, but not yet defeated in spirit. He hadn't dared offer more than a helping hand. Even that was pushing the boundaries. To do more would have weakened them both in the eyes of his people. And weakness always brought out the predators… well… more predators.

He already knew many rumors would be spawned by what the survivors had seen him do to the mages attacking the warrior-priestess. That would stir the pot enough for now. He didn't need his enemies to know she was important to him for more than the obvious reasons.

The obvious reasons for his interest would put a big enough target on her back.

But that was a concern for later.

Her healing was his utmost concern at the moment, but first he had to get her somewhere he could perform the healing without an audience.

They left behind the guest wing of the palace and were about to mount the sweeping stairway that led up into the royal wing when he paused, frowning.

After eyeing the long, curving flight of stairs, he knew there was no way she could make it up the stairs under her own power.

With a glance over his shoulder, he scanned the hall-way. But his Elite personal guards had done their jobs and chased away any followers.

"You'll need to trust me," he said.

She made a weak noise in the back of her throat. If she'd been stronger, that noise might have bloomed into a disdainful laugh. But in her weakened state, it was no more than a soft groan.

When he gathered her against his side and placed an arm around her waist to help hold her up, she shoved against him weakly, as if trying to escape his touch.

He leaned closer and whispered in her ear, "Easy. You'll never make it up these stairs on your own."

She blinked at him and then looked up the length of stairs.

He sensed her near despair.

"I've got you," he whispered again. "But if it gives you strength, you can imagine stabbing me once for every step we take."

Then he started up the stairs, supporting as much of her weight as she would allow. When they were halfway up, he sensed she was about to lose the battle to remain conscious.

Scooping her up in his arms with a grunt, he once again marveled at what a large, well-muscled woman she was. When he reached the top of the stairs, he was puffing softly from the climb and her surprisingly substantial weight. He called upon his magic to strengthen his muscles in order to carry her the rest of the way to his quarters.

Gods. She might actually outweigh him.

He traversed this floor of the royal wing swiftly and approached his chambers. He walked through a shimmering shield and mounted the short flight of stairs quickly. As he approached his quarters, more of the spells guarding his private world pulled back, and the outer doors swung open.

The sound of hurried footsteps approaching from behind had him slowing his stride and glancing over his shoulder.

"Your Holiness, please forgive my failure to keep the priestess safe." The captain of his guard jogged forward until she was a step beside him. "I returned to the mountain priestess as soon as the servant brought me the news of the attack. I should never have left her. I accept whatever punishment you deem appropriate for my failure, Your Holiness."

Honryn turned fully to his captain, noting her many injuries. She'd arrived just ahead of him and had clearly battled many of the nobles and their guards in an attempt to reach his priestess. He knew his captain well. The guilt she was suffering now for failing to protect someone important to him was far greater than any punishment he would have doled out had he been inclined to punish her.

But he didn't plan to punish his captain. She was loyal.

"Go," he said, pleased he didn't sound too out of breath. He was growing more certain by the moment that the mountain priestess actually outweighed him by a good amount. "See to your injuries and know I do not hold you responsible for what happened. You were carrying out my orders. I had not expected that number of foolishly suicidal souls existed in all the empire. I overlooked our people's stupidity. That is on me. But after my… reaction," he drew the last word out before continuing, "to the attack, the survivors will rethink going against me and mine in the future."

His captain nodded silently, and Honryn made to enter his chambers.

"Your Holiness," his captain started again, "I would feel better knowing some guards were with you in your quarters if you are going to take the warrior-priestess in there with you."

"Nice try." Honryn snorted, amused. "You're still not getting a peek inside." He'd made it very clear to all that no one was allowed within his private chambers. Not guards, not servants, not his uncle, not would be lovers.

Only his mother, aunts, and twin sister paid him visits upon occasion, using the hidden and warded passageways. But his guards didn't know about those secret ways.

"But your Holiness. She is the enemy. She'll try to kill you the first chance she gets."

"No doubt. But she's in no condition to so much as harm a blade of grass at the moment." He glanced down at the priestess in his arms. That the priestess was about to become a guest in his chambers was sure to fuel more rumors. Not that he could prevent it from happening. After what had occurred, he didn't trust the priestess out of his sight until she was healed and able to defend herself fully.

The captain cleared her throat, her somewhat harsh features turning even sharper in concern. "But you plan to have her healed. For your safety, I must attempt to persuade you to… bend the rules this time. Surely the danger that a warrior-priestess represents—"

"No," Honryn said, cutting her off. He strode the final three paces into his rooms. The shimmering shielding spells snapped closed behind him, blocking his captain and the other guards from entering.

A moment later, the doors swung shut with a soft thump, adding a final note to his command. Though he still caught the sound of his captain cursing softly.

He smiled. His captain was protective and well-meaning and utterly loyal to him, but there were secrets deep within his tower domain that would turn him into a god's cursed traitor in his people's eyes.

He glanced down at the priestess as he walked across the antechamber and made his way deeper into his domain. She looked worse than she had even a few minutes ago. Knowing he needed to begin her healing immediately, he began channeling his energy into her, strengthening her for the coming healing. It would be grueling for them both.

"Don't you dare die on me, my Fierce One. I have been waiting a very long time for an ally such as you."

CHAPTER 10

Honryn

Once inside his sanctuary, Honryn carried the unconscious priestess deeper into his private domain until he came to his bedchamber. After gently placing her on the bed, he stood back and gazed down at her even as he continued to channel his magic into her.

"Gods, you're a mess." He took in the expanse of blood-covered clothing and skin, the cuts and bruises, and the swellings and abrasions. Without hesitation, he set his magic to the task of scanning her body, hunting for the locations of the worst of her injuries.

She'd taken a lot of punishment to her face and

head. But his scan had started there and had already confirmed most of the damage, while ugly, was superficial, little more than cuts and swellings. Her brain had been jostled, but nothing that a touch of his magic and a little rest wouldn't mend. Unsurprisingly, his priestess had a hard head.

While he waited for his magic to complete the scan, he'd clean her up, then begin the healing spells. With renewed purpose, he headed into his bathing chamber to gather the supplies he would need. Shortly, he returned with the first armload. Once he arrayed his supplies on the top of the small table sitting next to his bed, he went back for a large pitcher of water and a washing basin.

Usually, he'd use magic to accomplish the cleanup swiftly. But after building the long-distance portal spell and dealing with all the events that had come after, he wanted to reserve every scrap of his power for strengthening and healing the priestess.

He eyed the task ahead.

"You look like you fought three wars back-to-back, My Fierce One," he muttered. "I'm sorry for that."

He started at her feet and unlaced her boots, gently pulling them off. Next came the finely knitted socks. Eyeing her feet, he thought they might be the only part of her *not* injured.

Moving to her harness and belt next, he freed her of them and began unlacing her sturdy pants. Soaked with blood as the material was, it was a little more of a battle to husk her of them.

Her upper body, with the leather vest and thick linen shirt beneath, proved easier. But he took more time, being careful of her ribs, a few of which his magic had already told him were broken.

The damage revealed to his eyes was as ugly as his magic had promised. Boot-toe shaped contusions ran up and down her sides. She'd taken a few to her pale, toned belly as well. No doubt there were matching injuries on her back. He'd deal with them soon, but first, he had other concerns.

Gently probing her stomach with his fingers and magic, he felt for lumps or hard swellings that heralded the location of her internal injuries. He found the worst injuries along her side, close to her liver.

Hissing softly, he muttered, "I didn't kill enough of them to make up for this. Remind me later to make their lives more miserable."

He closed his eyes and summoned the gentler side of his dual-natured magic, and soon the pale green glow of healing energy was seeping into her side. Delving deep, he took his time and repaired every ruptured blood vessel and expanse of damaged tissue he encountered before moving on to the next area.

It was more important that he used his healing magic on the internal injuries first. The other damages to her skin and muscles he'd treat with stitches and poultices later if he exhausted his magic before he finished this task.

His fingers moved from her abdomen to glide up her sides, probing gently once again to find the cracks and breaks in her ribs this time. After realigning the breaks, he mended them with more healing magic. He'd wrap her chest tightly later if needed.

He moved on to her other injuries.

And she had many.

He frowned unhappily. There was a real possibility he'd have to heal her in two sessions. Either that or call on his mother to aid him. But guilt stopped him. He'd caused this. He'd allowed this priestess to be harmed because he'd not taken the necessary steps to ensure her safety.

It should be his power that healed her.

And...

And he didn't want his mother to see the priestess's condition.

Unfortunately, his healing magic wasn't nearly as strong as his more destructive power. He didn't know if it was just the nature of his mixed bloodline or if his healing magic would grow in strength if he used it more.

It wasn't like he often used this side of his nature. The survival of his loved ones had required him to use deadly force far more than his healing energy.

His hands moved higher, gliding impersonally over

her firm breasts in his search for other internal injuries and broken bones. Her heart thumped strongly, and he paused to check that no damage had befallen that important muscle. His magic confirmed it was as strong and sure as the powerful heartbeat had suggested.

But he soon found a break in her left collar bone for his healing magic to tend. He took several moments to heal it entirely.

She was a fierce warrior, and he wanted to cross swords with her in the practice field one day. He certainly didn't wish an old injury like a broken collarbone to hamper her speed or grace. After seeing her brutal beauty in battle once, he wanted to see more of it.

He continued to run his fingers and healing magic over her, scanning the length of her arms and then back up to her neck and jaw.

Her face was already discoloring with bruises.

He noted the drying blood and bared his teeth. At least most of it wasn't hers. It belonged to Lord Nuran from when she'd torn out his throat with her teeth.

The signs of many blows marked her face.

Both eyes were already swelling shut. Her nose was broken. Her lip split.

He gently probed around her jaw and then inside her mouth. But her jaw wasn't broken, and she wasn't missing any teeth.

Under his protection and care, his warrior-priestess would recover fully.

He set her nose, and then used his healing magic to repair the damage before moving on to the rest of her battered face.

Slowly, the swelling went down.

He ran his fingers through her hair next, physically searching her skull. Not that he didn't trust what his magic had already told him, but he found he needed the reassurance of touch. As expected, her skull was intact. Though he found a large lump forming on the back of her head. His magic made quick work of the swelling. Later, he'd wake her to be sure that everything was as it should be with her mind, even though his scan had found no damage to her brain.

Head injuries were tricky things.

But there was no point in waking the poor woman just to reassure himself, not when he still had lots of scrubbing and stitching yet to do.

"Fear not, Priestess," he said, giving her nearest shoulder a gentle pat. "I will have you patched up and back on your feet before you know it. And I'll do all in my power to arm you for the most vicious of courts."

Once he'd tended the worst of her injuries, he began washing her. It took several trips back to his bathing chamber to empty the basin and refill it with clean water. But after close to an hour, he had her mostly cleaned, stitched, and bandaged.

There wasn't much he could do for her hair. She'd have to deal with that later, but for now, she looked much better than she had. Without the blood of a soul mage covering her, she smelled much better as well.

He inhaled a deeper lungful of her clean scent, liking her natural fragrance rather too much, he admitted. But it was more than just a healthy feminine scent drawing him in—though there was something to be said for a natural essence, free of heavy perfumes and untainted by the hint of spirit rot that always accompanied practicing soul mages. But this was more than just that. The opposing sides of his magic's dual nature both liked her magic enhanced pheromones.

And while his magic sometimes acted like it had a will of its own, it wasn't sentient, but it did resonate with certain persons and their magical essence. As it was doing now with this priestess. He'd sensed the draw almost from the moment he'd laid eyes on her.

His magic was drawn to her because he was drawn to her.

After wiping the rag along her forehead one last time, he set it aside and merely gazed down at her for a time.

She was no classic beauty. Her features were too strong and sharp. There was almost a harshness about them, so too, with the rest of her battle-toned warrior's body.

He moved toward the foot of the bed as he

continued his examination of her form. Defined muscles corded her long, lean build. The term mannish came to mind. Even her hands were almost as large as his. And the warrior priestess was of a height with him, he knew. And he wasn't short for a man, having inherited his mother's height.

He stroked a finger from her knee to her ankle and then along the top of her foot.

It was a little smaller and more delicate than his. Stroking a thumb along the bottom, he grinned when she jerked it out of his grasp in her sleep.

She was ticklish.

His Fierce One was ticklish!

Honryn's grin grew so wide his face hurt. Briefly, he wondered where else she might be sensitive as his gaze moved back up her well-muscled body. His gaze paused at the pale red thatch between her legs. It was neatly trimmed, though otherwise left as nature intended, unlike the women of his people whose current fashion demanded it be shaved bare and sometimes decorated with delicate tattoos inked across the area.

He preferred the tiny thatch of hair.

His gaze moving higher, he studied her breasts. Even though she was toned and muscled, she was still feminine, and from his healing examination, he knew her breasts were full enough to make two very lovely handfuls.

And on her upper chest, she had a scattering of

freckles he found endearing. They ran up the column of her neck to a lesser degree but were still noticeable. She had them elsewhere on her body as well, with the thickest concentration running along the bridge of her nose and over her cheekbones. More of the delicate little spots were scattered across her forehead and disappeared into her hairline.

His gaze was just dropping back down to her pale breasts when the door behind him crashed open. He whirled around to find his mother storming into his private sanctuary.

"Stop ogling the poor woman. I raised you better than that!"

"I wasn't ogling her, Mother." The heat of a very rare but undeniably fiery blush blazed hotly up his cheeks, and his response had come out a little too high and swiftly, effectively telling his mother that she hadn't misinterpreted the direction of his thoughts.

Only his mother still possessed the ability to make him feel like a naughty boy caught at some mischief. Damn his pale, traitorous skin for betraying his thoughts and proving her right once again.

For the first time, he regretted keying her essence into the guard spells protecting his private chambers. But he wasn't about to mention that and merely frowned at her calmly, unwilling to show more embarrassment than he already had.

"I was tending to her injuries," he said instead.

"Something that is a great deal more difficult to do when one's patient is still wearing clothing."

"Yes, indeed," his mother agreed in a clipped tone as she jerked the bedding up over the unconscious woman. "And I've been standing behind that door watching for the last five minutes and noticed you had finished tending to her injuries a good three minutes ago."

He knew why his mother was reacting so strongly.

His mother, also known as Royal Consort Jardeen, had once been a warrior-priestess of Winter Reach. As much as he knew his mother loved him, he was also very aware she took no pleasure in the begetting of him.

"Off with you," his mother said, dismissing him as no one else dared. "I'll use my healing magic to finish repairing the last of the damage."

He hesitated, finding he didn't want to be away from the priestess's side, not after he'd spent time with her, healing her. It felt like a bond was forming between him and this stranger.

And he liked it.

Liked it perhaps more than was safe.

He cleared his throat and then gave his mother a curt nod. "Thank you. Send word if you need my aid for anything."

"I shall." His mother looked at him pointedly. Then, when he still didn't move, she jerked her chin toward the door and added, "She'll likely sleep for a long time yet. I'll stay and then explain a few things to her. It will be better coming from me."

He nodded again, knowing that if he stalled more, he'd earn one of his mother's tongue lashings.

"I'll send a messenger to you when she wakes up and is ready to speak to you," his mother said, clearly adding the last as a concession.

Duly dismissed and mildly disgruntled, he walked from his chambers. But a moment later, a small smile touched his lips.

His mother couldn't guard the new priestess every moment of the day and night; she had nearly as many court responsibilities as him. He'd get his chance to be alone with his Fierce One. He'd make sure of that.

CHAPTER 11

Verdria

aking in a strange bed in an unknown location couldn't be beneficial to her long-term survival, not even a bed that smelled as good as this one, Verdria reflected as she looked around at the lavishly appointed room. She lifted the covers, intending to toss them back and explore the space to hunt for a weapon, but froze when she realized she was naked. While waking in a strange bed couldn't be good, waking up *naked* in a strange bed was even worse.

Her memory was spotty. But she remembered an angry soul mage nobleman named Lord Nuran invading the room the guards had taken her to. There had been a mob.

And a fight.

An unfair fight where she'd been outnumbered and still partly bespelled. She remembered taking a beating, and then the priest-king elect had arrived and massacred his own people. His reasons for saving her were a concern for later. At this moment, her greatest need was to find a weapon of some kind and then clothing.

She took stock of herself. Presently, she should still have been in a lot of pain but wasn't.

She glanced down at herself again.

Clean, unmarked skin greeted her eyes. There wasn't so much as a bruise. She must have been healed and bathed.

And she didn't remember a moment of it. That was disconcerting.

That she didn't remember entering these new rooms must mean she'd passed out and been carried the rest of the way. She'd been in terrible shape. Blacking out, as a result, wasn't a surprise.

The amount of healing done on her was impressive, especially considering she'd been unaware healing magic was part of the soul mages' arsenal of powers.

She got out of the bed and wrapped one of the blankets around herself. Stretching, she discovered she was only a little stiff and sore, mostly around her ribs.

Verdria was striding toward the first of three

wardrobes on the other side of the room when the bedroom door opened, and another woman walked in. Verdria froze.

The stranger was dressed in a long tunic that reached to mid-thigh and loose-fitting pants that billowed around her legs as she walked. The style was oddly foreign and familiar, not unlike something Verdria or any of her priestess sisters would have worn when not out on the trail. But the fabric was much airier than anything suitable for the cooler mountain climate.

The woman looked up from the bundle of clothing she was sorting and saw Verdria. She halted, but a warm, welcoming smile touched the stranger's lips almost immediately. She held her place by a small table near the door and set down her bundle.

But it was what she did once her hands were free, a swift and complex series of motions, that held Verdria transfixed for a moment. Then she sucked in a surprised breath. The stranger was shaping her fingers in the secret language of the moon—signaling that the area was safe, no threats near.

By the other woman's chuckle, Verdria knew her expressive face had just betrayed her again. She needed to gain mastery over her expressions. But in her defense, she hadn't been aware another of her sisters had been captured in the raid.

But this woman was a priestess of the moon. There

was no doubt. She had the size and the musculature of a mountain woman. The frequent mixing of centaur stock in their bloodlines had made Verdria's people larger and sturdier than regular humans. But there was more to it than just that. There was also a certain pride and confidence in her people's bearing. And this stranger possessed both traits.

Verdria studied the newcomer for other similarities and differences.

The woman's thick brown hair was swept up in an intricate style that piled it high on her head in a manner that seemed to defy gravity. Only many ribbons and jeweled pins held it in place. The style and ornaments were decidedly not of the mountains, and the woman was older than Verdria by at least a couple of decades, which was strange. This woman was old enough to be one of the Mothers. The more Verdria looked upon the older woman, the more unsettled she became.

She didn't recognize the woman at all.

While she didn't personally know all the priestesses on the raid, she knew their faces, and this woman had a face Verdria didn't recognize. And more importantly, none of the Mothers ever took part in raids. They stayed behind and guarded the fortresses and protected the few rare males and precious children. One of the Mothers would never leave a mate or a child behind, unprotected.

"Which House are you?" Verdria asked.

"I am Jardeen of Winter Reach."

Verdria nodded. That explained it—sort of.

There had been no priestesses from Winter Reach on the raid.

Jardeen had been captured at some other time and location.

Verdria noted the few streaks of grey in the other woman's hair and mentally adjusted Jardeen's age to that of a Wise-Mother. And no leaders of the House fortresses had disappeared in recent years as far as Verdria had heard.

That could only mean Jardeen had been a soul mage captive for a very, very long time, likely captured when she'd been much younger.

"Here," Jardeen said and handed Verdria the bundle of pale blue fabric, which turned out to be a robe and a matching pair of soft soled slippers that would be useless outside, "I thought you might appreciate these."

Verdria donned the robe and discarded the sheet, then while forcing her large feet into the slightly too-small slippers, she asked. "How long?"

"As you have most likely already guessed, a very long time, my sister." The other woman looked away as if it pained her. "I have lived among our greatest enemy for these past twenty-seven years. I was a slave until the twins came into their powers and granted me my freedom. Thanks to them, I am no longer a prisoner. And if you are reasonable, you need not be a slave. Though you will have to play a part as I do."

Verdria wondered who the 'twins' were. Perhaps the children of a powerful soul mage family Jardeen served? Out loud, she merely said, "It sounds like you have an interesting story."

Jardeen snorted. "This is the Empire of the Soul Mages. There are no 'interesting' stories here, only cautionary tales warning of dangers you would do well to heed."

With that, the other woman launched into her story, speaking of how she had first been captured while patrolling her ocean-side territory with a unit of her sisters. They hadn't seen the ship in the fog-shrouded harbor until they were already within a trap set by a group of soul mages.

Verdria nodded for the woman to continue, believing the tale so far. Or, at least, Jardeen's description of the area was accurate. Her mother's sister had moved to Winter Reach before Verdria had been born, and she had visited it as a child more than once.

"Many of my sisters died that day. But the mages captured eight of us." Jardeen sighed bitterly and then speared Verdria with a look. "I and my surviving sisters had to adapt to survive in this place where life is cheap and treachery hides in every shadow. Assume everyone is trying to kill you or use you, because they likely are if it will somehow increase their standing in soul mage society."

Verdria nodded again, not wanting to interrupt even though she had questions. Better to allow this woman to speak unhindered and later Verdria could begin a subtle interrogation of the other woman.

"Only trust me, my sisters, and our sons and daughters."

"Sons and daughters? You have children here?" Verdria asked, surprised by the news.

"Yes. The twins I mentioned. My beautiful twins," Jardeen smile proudly, and then added, "A son and a daughter. My reason for enduring all these years."

Verdria nodded at the other woman's words, but horror at what she'd heard kept her silent for now while she digested what the other woman had said. The mages must have captured Jardeen along with her entire family group.

Verdria couldn't even imagine half of what the other woman must have endured living here all these years. And to have raised her children in this place?

Moons!

Verdria couldn't hide a wince.

Jardeen's expression turned concerned. "Are you still in pain?"

"What? No. Just stiff." Which wasn't a lie, though it also wasn't the reason for the wince. But she didn't want the other woman to know the depth of pity Verdria felt for her. The woman had been tough enough to endure in this land. She probably wouldn't appreciate Verdria's pity.

"Ah. That's to be expected. The last of the aches and pains and stiffness should dissipate shortly. Let me know if it doesn't go away by tonight."

"Who do I have to thank for my mending?"

"I finished up the last of your healing. However, my son deserves most of the credit for mending the worst of the abuses you sustained. But neither of us expect thanks. If anything, we wish to apologize for what happened to you with Lord Nuran."

Verdria shrugged off the apology. They weren't responsible for that Lord Nuran's actions. And at the moment, she was much more interested in Jardeen and her son. Sons of the mountains were rare. A son of the mountains strong and healthy enough to possess powerful healing magic? That was unheard of in her society. Her mind was already working on ways she could help this woman and her son escape.

Their healing powers must have been deemed valuable enough to keep them alive and gain some standing in the soul mages' society. The rooms the priest-king elect had brought her to were very rich. If these belonged to this woman, it said much about the importance of her position.

As Verdria mulled that over, she realized something about the woman's story didn't add up.

She had said she was still a warrior-priestess patrolling her territory when she'd been captured, but no warrior-priestess bedded a man until they completed their training to become a Mother. And once they mated with one of the few precious males born after the great plague, a priestess would never go back on patrol. Certainly, never with their young family.

As dread slowly churned in her stomach, Verdria felt exceptionally foolish for not realizing something self-evident before now.

But she still needed to confirm her suspicions, to be sure.

"Jardeen, who fathered your twins?"

"I would prefer to tell you a bit about my children before I get to their sire."

Oh, bleeding moons!

Jardeen hadn't conceived the twins back home. They'd been begotten here.

Merciful Mother, a soul mage had sired Jardeen's twins.

Then another piece of the puzzle settled in place. They had discovered recently that the centaurs had had a spy among their number, reporting to the soul mages. Perhaps the priestesses had a leak in the sisterhood far longer than the centaurs, one feeding the mages information about the priestesses' powers and defenses. And Verdria thought she might have been looking at the source of the soul mages' knowledge of Verdria's people.

Verdria couldn't even blame the poor woman. As a slave, Jardeen had likely been beaten and tortured for information. And even if she'd initially resisted the torture, after years of slavery, if they had offered her a better life, she might well have taken it in exchange for giving up what she might see as outdated information.

But to judge by the ease with which the priest-king elect had defeated Verdria's defenses, the mages may have learned far more from Jardeen than what she'd willingly given up.

The more Verdria thought about what that other woman must have endured, the more she pitied her. But that didn't mean she could trust this woman.

She'd need to fish for information carefully. Unfortunately, delicacy and diplomacy weren't Verdria's strengths.

"You said you wished to tell me a little about your children first. Go on. Their father was a soul mage."

A bitter look crossed Jardeen's face. "Yes. But with the Moon Goddess's mercy, he'll choke on a dagger in his throat one of these days. But my son and daughter take after me. They are not like the other soul mages, for all they must keep up the appearance that they are no different. As much as that is possible with their powers."

"Their powers?"

Jardeen nodded. "One thing you may have noticed, or will soon, is that the child of a soul mage and a moon priestess is far stronger than either parent."

Verdria looked around the lavish room once more, dread slowly returning. These rooms were likely a reward earned by one of Jardeen's children because of their potent magic.

Everything Verdria knew about soul mage society suggested power and rank went hand in hand. If Jardeen's children were as powerful as she claimed, they likely held positions of high rank.

"Are these your rooms?"

"No. These are my son's quarters. You were brought here for your protection."

Verdria's mind flashed back to one remarkably powerful male, his bare chest free of the usual tattoos worn by soul mages to augment their power.

"And he was the one to bring me here, your son?" Verdria asked, then added with a harder note in her tone. "The man without tattoos. The one the others called the priest-king. My captor. He's your son?"

"He didn't want to see you captured, but..." Jardeen looked uncomfortable as she continued, "Honryn said his spells were already activated and were going to tear that ship apart. If he'd left you there, you would have died. He couldn't face the thought of killing a Priestess of the Moon Goddess."

None of what the other woman said was untrue,

according to Verdria's magic, but she wasn't simply able to shrug it off and move on.

The future priest-king of the soul mages had saved her, but that didn't mean she'd asked to be saved. She hadn't asked to be made a slave. Or worse, have her will slowly stripped away until she became a puppet to some mage. There were worst fates than death. She was now facing one because of the actions of this woman's son.

And waking up in some stranger's bed put an entirely new and darker spin on what Jardeen had said about the children of a soul mage and a priestess being more powerful than either parent. The future priest-king had been impressed with the strength of her battle and defensive magics. Lord Nuran had said the priest-king planned to make her his consort. Was he planning on impregnating Verdria? It wouldn't work. Regardless, that wouldn't make it any more enjoyable for her. She would prefer to avoid that highly unpleasant business with a soul mage, even if he was half of the mountains.

Clearly, he was a soul mage first. She'd seen enough already to know that.

But she needed to know more about Jardeen's children and their place in soul mage society. And since she was presently more concerned about the son whose bed she'd found herself in, she'd start with him. "I heard your son referred to as a priest-king. What is that?"

"Priest-King Elect," Jardeen corrected gently and

then folded her hands in her lap. "It means he's destined to take up that mantle of power from his uncle this coming dry season because he is the most powerful soul mage. The position of priest-king is always held by the strongest soul mage, and that bloodline has been undefeated for close to three thousand years."

A chill ran down Verdria's back. She knew the soul mage society was old from what her people had been able to glean. But for a single bloodline to have held power for so long…

"And what does a priest-king do?" Verdria asked, simply to end the silence before her mind could spin off into other horrific thoughts.

"He's the spiritual leader of all soul mages."

Of course he is, Verdria mused, her mind snapping back to him—this Honryn—and what she knew of his power and personality and confidence. Jardeen's words fit.

"You need to understand something," Jardeen said, her voice dropping into a whisper as if whatever she was going to speak next was far too dangerous to voice at normal volume. "Honryn has no wish to become the future priest-king, but the position always goes to the most powerful soul mage. He has no choice in his life path. But you should know even if his hybrid nature hadn't given him greater power, he still would hold a high rank among soul mages because of who his father is."

"And his father is…?"

"Emperor Zarkyn sired Honryn and his twin sister, Nadraya. My official title here is Royal Consort Jardeen, but my son has protected me from the emperor for many years now, since shortly after his magic reached its second peak at puberty. You haven't yet met my daughter, Nadraya. But while I've hated Emperor Zarkyn with every bit of my soul from the moment I first looked upon him, I love my son and daughter without equal. They have been my only joy in this hideous life."

Bloody Moons! The news was just getting worse and worse. Not only was Jardeen's son some kind of soul mage spiritual leader, he was also the son of the emperor.

"Honryn will do all in his power to protect you because you are a warrior-priestess of the moon. As will my daughter, Nadraya." Jardeen reached out and took Verdria's hands. "I swear you can trust them. They are good people for all that they are half soul mage."

Verdria very much thought Jardeen was blinded by a mother's love. There was no way a good soul lived inside any soul mage, especially one as powerful as Honryn. She'd already seen him in brutal action.

But it wasn't like Verdria could speak of any of these doubts to this woman. She'd need to feel her way out of this situation on her own. She may still need Jardeen as an ally or to get closer to her target. No point causing a rift by insulting her beloved adult children.

And if Honryn was as powerful as Jardeen claimed —which Verdria was already willing to believe—and if he was evil as Verdria feared he was, then she knew her duty was to see him assassinated or die in the attempt.

She owed that much to her people and the other member races of the five kingdoms.

Besides, there was no such thing as an innocent soul-mage. They were all monsters.

Honryn couldn't be allowed to live.

CHAPTER 12

Verdria

"There is still much to tell you," Jardeen said. "However, why don't we relocate to my quarters? Some of my things may fit you." At her words, both women eyed each other with silent doubt.

While tall and not tiny by any means, Jardeen lacked Verdria's wide shoulders, chest, and hips. The Moon Goddess had been overly generous with her gifts when creating Verdria, and while she had always been proud of her strength and warrior's prowess, right about now, she would have welcomed some properly fitting clothing.

Getting her own boots back would be nice, too.

And weapons.

"Come, even if nothing of mine fits you, I'm sure the servants will be able to round up something in your size."

Verdria nodded and allowed the older priestess to escort her through Honryn's extensive and lavish chambers. While she maintained her vigilance, watching for danger from behind every piece of lavishly carved and richly upholstered bit of furniture, she also allowed herself to take in the grandness around her.

The dark glossy woods of various tables, benches, and chairs were softened by pillows and ornate runners of every fabric imaginable. There were even lustrous fabrics that nearly glowed in the sun, so soft and slippery under her fingers they almost seemed more foreign than the soul mages. Certainly, the fabrics she saw here were far from the cottons, linens, and wools common in her mountain home.

Many of the pillows had bright jewels sewn onto them and she had to arch a brow at that. It screamed wealth and privilege but did not offer comfort. She turned her attention from the furnishings to the struc-ture of the chambers, memorizing them for possible places to hide or hidden exits she might one day have use for.

A mix of landscape paintings depicting lush tropical

vistas and beautiful tapestries adorned the walls between the wide, glassless windows.

That struck her as a bit of oddness.

Without glass or any other barrier that she could see, Verdria wondered what was to stop bugs or larger dangers from entering the priest-king elect's domain.

Seeing the direction of Verdria's gaze, Jardeen gestured at the nearest archway and led them closer. As Verdria neared, a view of blue sky and clouds over-looking a vast city that stretched as far as she could see greeted her marveling eyes.

"Goddess," she whispered. She hadn't known the soul mages' possessed a city anything like this. Her own people no longer possessed the numbers to inhabit great cities, now living in mountain fortresses, but even before the soul mages had attempted to destroy her people, she wasn't sure if the mountain folk ever had the numbers to build and inhabit something like what her mind was struggling to comprehend as she gazed down upon this foreign city.

"Indeed," Jardeen agreed. "It never grows less daunt-ing. But that's not what I intended to show you." She gestured at the open window and stepped closer.

Before the other woman's hand crossed the thresh-old, a shimmering barrier snapped into place and Verdria instinctively jerked back, half expecting an attack. When none came, she eased closer. When Jardeen moved her hand away from the window, the shimmering shield vanished and Verdria realized she could feel the warm ocean breeze upon her skin again.

"As you see," Jardeen explained, "The shield keeps out insects and other, larger dangers, but allows in the cooling ocean breeze."

The way Jardeen had stressed the words 'larger dangers' suggested she meant more than whatever wildlife might call this tropical island home.

Regardless of how powerful his protective shields were, when Jardeen led her from the room, she was still happy to be leaving the male's chambers. Waking up in his bed and dwelling in his chambers had felt far too intimate. It put her on edge.

She gave a mental snort at that thought, acknowledging she would be on edge anywhere in this land. But learning she'd been in the priest-king elect's bed, the most powerful soul mage in existence according to his mother, was just an added jolt of unpleasantness.

When they exited the outer doors, they stepped into the corridor to find a company of twenty guards lining the long hallway in either direction. The guards came to attention and one of them—likely the leader of the group, for he had more silver on his uniform than the others—stepped forward, away from the wall.

He executed a deep bow to Jardeen. "Consort, I wasn't aware you were with the new..." He looked between the two women and then cleared his throat. "With his Holiness's guest." There was a slight stress on his last word. "I didn't see you enter the chamber. Had I been aware—"

Jardeen cut him off. "Yes, yes. Had you been aware you would have tried to come with me to ensure my safety. But I assure you, I am quite safe with another woman of the mountains."

"Of course, Royal Consort."

"And my son's wards would likely have knocked you on your ass for trying, if they were in a benevolent mood," Jardeen smiled at the guard, true warmth in her expression, and he seemed to relax at her humor. "Lucky for you, Hon—" The older woman caught herself before she could say her son's name, "His Holiness summoned me via a portal to finish her healing and see to her other needs. We're going to my quarters to see if anything of mine will fit her. You're more than welcome to walk the length of the hall with us."

He nodded in all seriousness and fell into step behind them. By some unseen signal, three other guards peeled away from their positions and followed at a respectful distance.

But Verdria was distracted by one very big piece of information she'd just discovered. She could now understand the speech of the soul mages. They hadn't been conversing in the speech of the mountains just then.

She desperately wanted to question Jardeen about that, but not in front of all these enemies.

Jardeen glanced at her and then nodded over her shoulder to the guards, seeing and misunderstanding Verdria's concern.

Verdria mentally cursed her overly expressive face for betraying her again.

"They are more vigilant and anxious than normal after what transpired with Lord Nuran," Jardeen explained. "An attack such as that will not be happening a second time, I assure you."

"Good to hear," Verdria mumbled as they started down the hall. She eyed the soldiers lining the walls warily as she strode by them, but they didn't draw weapons upon her, so she kept a tight rein on her battle magic. And while they were soul mages, complete with a few inky black tattoos on their pale skin, they weren't as tattooed or as pale as the other mages she'd seen.

"This is the royal wing," Jardeen explained. "There are always some members of the Elites here to protect against assassins trying to infiltrate the chambers and leaving nasty surprises."

"Elites?" Verdria asked.

"A name that stuck because they are members of the most loyal, most highly trained, and most lethal company of guardsmen found anywhere in the empire. As such, they are tasked with guarding the members of the royal family. You can always recognize an Elite by the tattoo above their right brow."

Verdria made a mental note to learn just how good

those Elites were. Her life might depend on defeating several of them at some point in the future if she had any hope of escape.

Jardeen continued to chat about the various ranks within the Elites, but Verdria only gave the other woman half an ear, her attention on what looked like a balcony at the end of the corridor. The doors were currently open, allowing a cooler breeze to flow in. And unlike the window arches in Honryn's chambers, this one didn't have one of those shield barriers in place, judging by the gauzy curtain fluttering across the entrance to the balcony.

A balcony might be a possible escape route. She needed to find a way to scout it out.

"Here we are," Jardeen said, interrupting Verdria's thoughts of escape. "These are my chambers. You are always welcome here, for whatever reason." The older woman had put more emphasis on the last three words. It was clear what she wasn't saying. These chambers were a place to escape to safety should Verdria need it.

She nodded her thanks to the other woman.

Two guards flanking the large double doors bowed and then opened them for the women. Verdria followed close on Jardeen's heels and found herself in another set of suites that were just as richly appointed as the room that they'd just left.

Once they were inside, a gaggle of what Verdria

realized were servants descended upon her. She tensed, waiting for an attack from any direction.

"Be easy," Jardeen whispered. "These are all trusted servants, loyal to my son."

Outwardly calm, Verdria once again nodded at the older woman. But inwardly, she didn't trust anyone in this land, not even one of her sisters of the moon.

The servants circled Verdria, talking among themselves in their native tongue as they took measurements. But because of whatever magic had been worked upon her while she'd slept, she could now understand every word, but didn't acknowledge as much in the hope they might let slip some piece of information that Verdria might be able to use later.

ALAS, SHE DIDN'T LEARN ANYTHING THAT WOULD HELP her escape. The servants were a tight-lipped bunch, only talking about the business of dressing Verdria. At least in her presence.

One servant, a middle-aged woman with grey at her temples, was gesturing at Verdria's large feet and then down at her own. She placed her foot next to the warrior-priestess's and muttered despairingly.

While the servant fretted about shoes for Verdria's big feet, she mulled over what she had just learned. For one thing, the royal 'wing' was a misleading name. It wasn't a wing. It was three entire floors of the palace.

"Honryn claimed this entire floor for us—me, his twin, and the aunts," Jardeen continued to explain. "He wanted us to be close to his tower so that he could detect any threats to us."

Jardeen smirked suddenly.

"What?" Verdria asked, honestly intrigued by the other priestess's expression.

"To claim this entire floor, Honryn displaced his two older brothers. When they complained to the emperor, he merely laughed at them and told them to learn to fight their own battles."

Verdria arched a brow. She knew Honryn was powerful, and Jardeen had claimed Honryn was the most powerful of all soul mages. But just how much political power did Honryn wield? More than his father, the emperor?

If so, Honryn might be directly responsible for the raid on the five kingdoms that had resulted in the deaths of many of her sisters as well as their centaur allies.

Even as the army of servants worked to make her 'presentable', Verdria wasn't distracted enough to rid herself of that uneasy thought.

And that thought led her mind back to worrying about the fact that the most feared and powerful soul mage had requested Verdria have a midday meal with him.

Lucky me, Verdria thought darkly.

The only blessing was the ridiculous length of time the servants took in bathing and dressing her. The longer they took, the longer it would be until she had to sit across from the priest-king elect.

And she wasn't at all sure if she was ready to see him again.

It wasn't that she feared him.

Though she probably should.

It was that something about Honryn set her off balance, and she didn't like it.

But eventually, the servants were nearly finished with her, even the makeup, which took another ridiculous length of time.

The servants finished at last. Verdria stood and glanced down at a ridiculously elegant skirt, which was too short for her. Then there was the badly fitting corset that was far too tight across the chest.

When the group of servants noticed the shortness of the dress's hem, they frowned with displeasure and then talked at length with each other until one of them disappeared somewhere, only to return a short while later with a length of lace. Speaking rapidly among themselves once again, they seem to decide upon a plan of action and swiftly began tacking on a layer of lace to the hem. Once finished, Verdria noted the material was now long enough to brush her bare toes.

Then there was another lengthy argument about her boots. They absolutely didn't like the boots, but no one had been able to magic up a pair of dainty shoes in a big enough size, so they unhappily presented Verdria with her old boots, which she noticed had been cleaned and polished until they almost looked new again.

When the servants at last stepped back, Jardeen merely looked on and laughed at both scowling servants and scowling Verdria alike.

Verdria ignored the other woman and used the brief reprise from the servants to pull on and lace up her boots. The reprise was brief, and the servants descended upon her once more, poking, prodding, sewing, tucking, and lacing her up some more. That done, they bustled her over to a mirror so she could see the results of their hard work.

Verdria looked at herself and grimaced.

"They shouldn't have bothered. The effort is wasted on me," she muttered low to Jardeen.

"Don't be silly. You look lovely. It will impress Honryn, I'm sure."

Jardeen's statement would have had more believ-ability if she hadn't stumbled over the word 'lovely' before recovering.

Well, the other woman was partially correct.

The servants had worked a miracle with Verdria's

hair and tamed it. And now, it was artfully swept up and pinned to the top and back of her head with only a few soft curls framing her face. They'd left a select few curls to rest on her shoulders as well.

Verdria turned her attention lower to the rest of her attire revealed in the mirror.

Although the skirt was a lovely deep green that complemented her curly red hair, the corset looked just as ridiculous on her as she thought it would. Lacking a shirt, her shoulders were left bare—likely because the servants couldn't find anything big enough to contain them, not even among Jardeen's wardrobe.

That left the ornate corset, bejeweled to outrageous levels but a size too small, to try to cover and contain the rest of Verdria's chest. They'd laced the corset so tight it forced her not-so-meager breasts upward until there was a plentiful amount of flesh spilling over the top.

As for the skirt, in place of the jewels, gold thread had been sewn in delicate patterns along the hem and down pleated sections of the skirt's long panels. Similar to many of the fabrics she'd seen the mages wear, the material was featherlight and almost sheer. Only the many layers protected one's modesty.

On anyone else, the outfit would have been beautiful, even the corset.

"What do you have when you dress an ogre up in a pretty skirt?" Verdria asked Jardeen.

The other woman just rolled her eyes. "It isn't bad at all. You look lovely."

Verdria snorted. "An ogre in a pretty skirt."

The other woman huffed. "Fine. We'll look into getting you more traditional priestess attire shortly. This will have to do for now. My son has sent three runners to inquire about you."

"He's probably starving and tired of having to wait for his meal." Verdria could relate.

She took one last look in the mirror and made faces at herself. She changed her mind. Instead of an ogre, she decided she looked more like a soul-sucking demoness with her blood-red lips and breasts corseted up so tight she couldn't take a deep breath. The lip coloring was truly garish with her red hair. The black lacquer they'd painted on her nails and matching dark stain they'd applied up to her second knuckle of each hand only added to the 'demoness' look. Not that Verdria knew what a demoness looked like if they even existed.

"The guards will lead you back to Honryn's chambers once the servants put the finishing touches on you," Jardeen said. "I'll go tell Honryn that you'll be along shortly."

What? They weren't finished yet? What else was there to do?

But just then, the servants answered her silent question, bringing forward several bottles of what Verdria thought must be perfume.

Ridiculous!

This was not how she pictured being broken by the soul mages.

But it just might work far better than hot irons.

CHAPTER 13

Verdria

$\mathcal{V}$erdria was contemplating how one could commit murder with a perfume bottle when there was a commotion at the outer door. Such things were becoming rather too commonplace, she thought, even as she readied herself for whatever was about to come through that door at her. Somehow, she doubted it was Honryn come to collect her, driven to his breaking point by hunger. She'd pegged him as being made from sterner stuff than that.

One of the guards stationed inside the chambers went to join his unit members outside in the corridor to discover what the disturbance was about. She leaned back in her chair, trying to see past the wall of servants or to catch some snippets of conversation. Though she knew that would be unlikely. The distance was too far and there were entirely too many bodies between her and the door.

But she was alert for any new dangers. She certainly didn't relish the thought of another angry mob of noblemen intent on giving her another beating. She curled her fingers around the hefty, jewel encrusted brush they'd used on her hair. Even the matching comb was large and heavy enough to become a weapon in Verdria's hands.

If some soul mage had come to take revenge on her, it would end much differently than last time. Verdria was no longer under a spell to hold her captive. Even her battle magic had returned to full strength. Not that she planned to attack anyone just yet. She needed to learn more about the politics of this place and the different factions. And she was sure there were various factions. Honryn's behavior and his mother's words had hinted at such.

However, if another noble had come for a piece of her, he'd be shocked as he died.

The commotion outside grew louder.

"Did my brother say she wasn't to have visitors?" the newcomer asked.

Outwardly, the speaker sounded mellow, calm even,

but the touch of annoyance suggested the woman was anything but calm.

"No, Princess, he did not," one guard muttered. "Not specifically. However, he tasked us with her protection above all else. We are under orders to kill anyone who so much as looks crossly at his guest."

"Do I look like I'm dressed for battle? I have no intentions of attacking her. I simply wish to meet her and perhaps have a little talk." The woman fell silent for a moment and then blew out a loud sigh before continuing, as if struggling for patience. "That will not distract you from protecting my brother's newest acquisition. And I promise I won't even 'look upon her crossly' if that sets your mind at ease."

"Very well. But you have been warned. And remember, even you aren't above our future priest-king's wrath."

"Of course. I'm well aware of the type of atrocities my youngest brother is capable."

Ah. She'd said 'youngest brother', not twin brother. That answered one of Verdria's questions. This princess was family, but not Honryn's twin. This must be one of the late Empress Cantonia's offspring. That also meant the woman outside wasn't half of the mountains, which squarely placed her as pure soul mage, an unquestioning enemy. Verdria did so much like when a situation was uncomplicated.

Besides, she already disliked this woman. By the

way she spoke, she came across as extremely superior and entitled; neither were personality traits Verdria tolerated easily.

A moment later, the woman in question came striding in, forcing the servants to scramble out of her path or be run down.

Upon seeing Honryn's oldest sister for the first time, she decided the woman looked nothing like him. She was small and delicately built, with a long face and pointed chin. Her dark brown hair fell like a silky curtain around her face and cascaded over her shoulders and down her back, smooth and perfect. Not one hair strayed from its place. The word elfin came to mind.

While the woman crossed the chamber, Verdria scrounged for Honryn's oldest sister's name. Jardeen had mentioned it in their earlier conversation.

Ah, yes. Princess Kuyan.

Verdria stood as the other woman approached.

Kuyan stalked a circle around Verdria. She made a humming sort of sound before she spoke.

"The rumors said you were the tallest woman in the empire. For once, they weren't wrong."

Verdria said nothing, just stared the other woman down. Eventually, the soul mage royal would get to the reason she'd come.

"Who knew my littlest brother liked the tall ones."

Verdria didn't so much as blink.

"Aren't you a talkative one?" Kuyan huffed, sounding more intrigued than annoyed. "I'd heard that Consort Jardeen had been talking to you. I thought you should have a more rounded picture of the court politics and just how very ruthless it can be for a newcomer."

Verdria's lips quirked against her will. So much for keeping a blank expression and not betraying any emotion to the enemy. Oh well, she knew she was never good at being subtle. Might as well go straight at this opponent and see what happened.

"I assume you're not here to make friends," Verdria drawled as she picked up the heavy silver brush the servants had used on her hair earlier. "If you heard Jardeen has been to talk to me, you've also likely heard what I did to the nobles who attacked me while I was partly immobilized. You're either here to stab me in the back or to forge an alliance. Which is it?"

"An alliance," Kuyan answered swiftly and without derision. "One that can benefit us both."

"Good," Verdria said as she smashed the brush back on the ornate table hard enough to dent the wood. "I'd have hated to smash your skull. Would have gotten gore all over me again. Then I would have had to stand still while the servants poked and prodded and sowed me into a new dress."

"My, aren't you a savage one!"

"Yes." She smoothed a hand down her dress and added, "You mentioned something about an alliance."

Verdria glanced up when the silence stretched longer. Meeting the mage's eyes, she nodded for the other woman to talk.

While Kuyan was a soul-mage and not to be trusted, that didn't mean she couldn't provide information Verdria might use.

"Did Honryn's mother tell you all his wicked deeds?" Kuyan asked at last.

Verdria snorted. "What doting mother would?"

Kuyan grinned suddenly, but it didn't reach her eyes. "I see you've figured that out about Jardeen, but then she isn't subtle."

"Neither are you. Or you wouldn't be here so soon," Verdria mused aloud.

"True. You'll learn that soul mages of substantial power are seldom subtle. We don't reach such positions by holding back or reining in our natures. The royal line is no different. If anything, we're the worst. The royal line has a long history of bloody and brutal successions, and I know one day my littlest brother will put all past royals to shame in the most glorious of bloodbaths as he takes out anyone he perceives as a threat to his loved ones."

Verdria arched a brow.

"My other brothers are ambitious," Kuyan explained. "They'd both like to see the twins dead. They will foolishly force Honryn's hand. I plan to be blood-drenched but alive at the end of it, standing close behind Honryn as his greatest supporter."

"Fascinating." And if the two brothers needed a little push to start the bloodshed, Verdria was certain Kuyan would be the one giving the required nudge at just the right time.

Verdria added this female to her too-evil-to-live-needs-to-die list.

"Indeed, it will be a fascinating event to watch." Kuyan sounded equal parts gleeful and proud of what she expected Honryn to do one day. She was speaking of the death of her half-brothers. They might not share the same father, but they shared their mother's blood.

Did family mean nothing to the soul mages?

"Why are you telling me all this?" Verdria asked instead, to get the woman back on track. Her gaze had taken on a distant and hungry look when she'd mentioned standing close to Honryn as he murdered his kin.

Princess Kuyan gave her a wintry smile. "Since you've proven to be a relatively unflappable woman, I've decided to give you the respect you are due. I intend to be Honryn's priestess-queen."

Didn't see that coming, Verdria mused. So, the future priest-king's not-actually-a-sister-but-still-too-close-for-comfort family acquaintance wanted to marry him. Or maybe just marry his power?

Verdria kept her face neutral, but she wondered what Honryn thought about his oldest almost-sibling's plan. Did he even know of Kuyan's schemes? She almost felt pity for the poor man, and now understood why his chambers were warded up to the hilt. Otherwise, he might wake with that power hungry viper in his bed.

"You don't have any comment, Warrior-Priestess?"

"Don't know enough of this land, its court, or its politics to make any judgment yet." Which was a partial lie. She'd already formed judgments aplenty.

"Well then, here's another piece of the puzzle you'll hear from some other source before long, so there's no harm in me telling you myself. Like many other powerful noblewomen, I'm barren. While I plan to be Honryn's future priestess-queen and later empress of all, I can't carry the next generation. Any great legacy I create will die with me." Kuyan paused, as if just thinking of something else now. "And Honryn is so great in power; it would be an injustice to our great Serpent God to deny him the chance to produce future priest-kings as great in power as he is. That is why you will align yourself with both Honryn and me. You will be his breeding concubine, and I will be priestess-queen and co-ruler of the empire."

And just like that, Kuyan answered another one of Verdria's unasked questions. Kuyan wasn't just looking to make Honryn her husband. It confirmed she was looking to make herself empress.

"While it will be an unusual arrangement for me, it should seem normal enough for you." Kuyan continued as calmly as if she was speaking about the weather. "As I understand it, all your women must share their mates since there are so few males."

Verdria ignored the insulting tone and arched a brow at Kuyan. "You and Honryn aren't blood relatives, yet you call each other brother and sister; I assume you were raised together, and he thinks of you as a sister? Doesn't that create a bit of a problem for your plan?"

Kuyan smirked. "True brothers and sisters have been co-rulers in the past. Rulers need not share a bed. They merely share their power against any threats to the throne. And as you say, Honryn and I aren't actually related, so that isn't an issue. And he is easy on the eyes. Taking him to my bed would be no chore. But as I said, I am barren, so I am willing to share him with a powerful and loyal ally."

Verdria snorted, doubting the part about the allies. Kuyan's plan likely also included doing everything in her power to see Verdria dead after she produced the next generation. But Verdria wasn't about to show her hand to this enemy just yet.

"I don't think I'm Honryn's type," Verdria hedged, instead of stating what was on her mind.

Kuyan looked her over. "I would normally agree,

and I do not claim it is logical, but you've done something no other woman or man has managed. You have stirred my brother's interest. Even as big and brawny and crude as you are, you're female. With a little guidance and polish from me, you might keep my brother's interest long enough for him to plant his seed in you."

It was a testimony to Verdria's swiftly improving skills at diplomacy that she didn't reach out and snapped Kuyan's neck.

"Perhaps it's because you're a lowly Priestess of the Moon," Princess Kuyan continued, unaware of how close she flirted with death. "Blood calls to blood after all, even if that blood is of a lesser line."

If Honryn's older sister would have instilled more insults, Verdria never found out as another woman stormed into the room, anger etching her features into something harsh and yet familiar.

The newcomer looked like a prettier, female version of Honryn. And the family resemblance was so remarkable between Honryn and this woman, she could only be his twin sister, Princess Nadraya.

"Kuyan, what are you doing here?" the other woman asked, her tones holding a sharp snap of command.

Kuyan smiled indulgently. "Just having a chat with the newest member of the court, Little Nadie."

Nadraya's jaw clenched, and she drew herself up. Verdria half expected to see blood at any point. But Honryn's twin schooled her expression and said in a calm, reasonable tone, "There is no way Honryn granted permission for you to talk with her before even he has."

A cold smile full of calculation graced Kuyan's lips. "And I suppose our brother has granted you the great privilege you say he has denied me?"

The younger princess snapped her teeth together.

Ah, so Honryn's twin wasn't supposed to be here either. Verdria added rebellious to Nadraya's nature. From the little she'd already gathered about Honryn, the twins likely shared that trait.

"I didn't think so," Kuyan said with a smug little smile. "Child, you should learn to keep quiet when you're among your elders so as not to embarrass yourself."

Verdria eyed Princess Nadraya and guessed her age to be at least early in her twenties. Hardly a child. Honryn seemed older, but that must be more about how he carried himself, his behavior, confidence, and actions.

To judge by the tension in the room, things were about to go downhill between the two sisters. Verdria waited until they were firmly focused on each other, and the guards were focused on them before making her escape.

It was easy to slip away from the distracted women.

The guards were another matter, and she noticed half of them were following her as close as her shadow.

Oh well, an escape was too much to ask. And honestly, she needed to know much more about her surroundings before making plans of that nature, but she continued marching determinedly down the corridor, knowing there was no avoiding dinner with the future priest-king of the soul mages.

She slowed, stalling as her battle magic tingled with warning. There was someone of great power nearby. While her magic was trying to hunt out the unknown mage's location, she glanced over her shoulder, briefly giving the guards a cold smile and asked, "Which room belongs to your future priest-king again? His mother suggested he was getting hungry and cranky."

"Have you forgotten that the priest-king elect lives in a ridiculously ostentatious tower at the end of the hall? You can't miss it," whispered a voice from the shadowy alcove to the immediate left of her. "And I never get cranky from something as inconsequential as a late meal."

Doing her best to hide her reaction at his nearness, she followed the voice and found His Holiness, Priest-King Elect Honryn, standing in the deep shadows between two large potted palm trees. He stood with his muscular arms crossed and hip cocked, looking anything but holy at the moment with a glimmer of mischief in his eyes and a sexy smile on his lips.

Unlike earlier, he wasn't wearing the long dark robes. A knee-length loincloth, sandals, and leather wrist bracers were his only items of clothing. If he wasn't dressed like he had seduction in mind, she would have allowed herself a moment to enjoy the sight of a young and healthy male body in its prime.

But seeing so much of him, and the knowledge he might have plans she didn't like, pushed her earlier unease from mild to outright battle readiness. But this wasn't an opponent she could best in a magical fight. And she likely couldn't beat him in a battle of words either, but her bravado was all she had to call upon.

"Were you trying to spy on me or hide from your sisters like a coward, Mage?"

"Hiding from my sisters. I don't have the patience to deal with Kuyan and her intrigues. And Nadraya would manage my life for me if given half a chance. Besides, mother promised to keep them out of our hair for a few days until you've settled in."

An arm sculpted with firm muscle and smooth, unmarked skin reached out of the shadows, hand palm up, open in invitation. She studied the leather bracers covering his wrists and wondered what kind of tattoos lurked under them. But that was a curiosity to solve at another time.

Just now, she found herself in a situation where she could once again snub him, or she could be gracious.

It went against every fiber of her being, but she took the mage's offered hand.

He laughed softly and squeezed her fingers. "Your face is very expressive."

"I've had greater insults tossed at me."

He only laughed harder. "What did you have to promise yourself later to take my hand just now?"

"That I'd get to kill lots of soul mages at some point."

His grin grew broader, and that look of mischief intensified. "Come, my warrior-priestess, let me lead you to my lair, and we will talk about that very thing."

His tone was pleasant, playful even, but Verdria still couldn't help a shiver that slid down her spine at the thought of being alone with him over something as intimate as a secluded dinner.

Honryn

As he ushered Verdria farther into his quarters, Honryn glanced around with a critical eye. He allowed no one besides his mother, aunts, and twin within, not even members of his trusted army of servants, which was reflected in the room's general messiness. He now regretted not attending to a bit of tidying while he'd waited for the warrior-priestess to be made presentable.

But it was clean and relatively free of dust, at least. His arsenal of purifying and protection spells saw to that, removing dirt and dust, along with any foreign magic that attempted to invade his private rooms.

Verdria followed close at his heels without comment, though he watched her reflection in the large mirror that took up much of the west-facing wall's surface. She gazed around at his chambers with a calm ruthlessness, studying every window and door and alcove even though she'd already been this way when leaving for his mother's suites. Was the warrior-priestess already plotting her escape? Or looking for unseen dangers?

Likely a bit of both, he mused.

He guided her to the main sitting area, where he'd already set out the food the servants had left with the guards outside his chambers.

At least the food was predominately fruits, cheeses, biscuits, and fancy little cakes. Nothing that would congeal when cold.

He pulled out a chair, breaking just about every rule of royal etiquette, and waited for her to sit. She regarded the chair in a fashion that suggested she thought it might be venomous before she stepped closer. Once she was seated, he skirted the table and took his own chair.

When he looked back up at her, she'd transferred her glower to him.

"Be at ease, Priestess. No harm will befall you tonight."

She pointedly glanced down at the food next.

"It isn't poisoned," he said in a serious tone. "That's

one thing my household spells always search for when food is brought to me."

"Not a well-loved priest-king elect?" She countered, before making selections to fill her plate. He could see her body was still tense with distrust for either him or the food. Maybe both.

"Well-loved?" He bit the corner of his lip to keep from laughing. "In this empire, fear will get you farther. Rivals attempt to poison various members of the royal family no less than fifty times a year. That's just with poison, not other assassination attempts."

She eyed their food, a question clear in her gaze. "How many times have people tried to poison you?"

"None in recent years. No one is foolish enough to attempt that with me. Not anymore. Mere poisons alone are not enough to kill one of my strength. A spell to take down the victim's natural defenses must always be inserted with the toxins, and that spell is what allows me to track down the would-be assassin." Honryn shrugged. "I may have gained a reputation for being a little like a vengeful hound on a scent. Once someone makes a move against me or someone I love, I track them down and relieve them of their souls for my trouble."

Her face far from expressionless, she chewed one of the biscuits and then washed it down with juice from the tender-sweet vine. After she made a face at the sweetness of the drink, he made a note to make fewer sweet selections for their next meal.

After another sip of the fruit juice, she asked, "When was the last time someone attempted to assassinate you by other means?"

"Two years and eleven months ago." He grinned suddenly, realizing something. "Until you. Back on that boat, you seemed determined in your attempts to get me to cross over to you. When I wouldn't, that only seemed to fuel your need to take my head. So, I suppose I now need to reset my calendar since you tried to end me."

Her bark of laughter was both loud and harsh, but he found the way it lit up her face and eyes endearing.

"What do you find so funny about that?" he asked, wanting to hear her answer almost as much as he wanted her to laugh again.

"You're going to be resetting that calendar a great deal if you plan to keep me close. I'll make a very dangerous pet, Mage."

"I shall keep that in mind."

Her laughter brought more color to her face, which helped offset the vivid, garish red the servants had painted her lips.

He'd been doing his best to ignore her attire.

A feat made more difficult now that she was laughing so hard her chest heaved, making her breasts jiggle in a way he was finding far too enjoyable. He forced his gaze elsewhere before she noticed.

After a bit, Verdria got her laughter under control, and she returned to eating her food. He did the same but couldn't help from stealing glances at her.

The longer he sat there across from her, silently studying her, the more he acknowledged he was both fascinated and mildly appalled by what the servants had done to his warrior-priestess. Verdria wasn't comfortable in the dress; she kept tugging at the top circumspectly, trying to get it to cover more, which only made the upper swell of her breasts jiggle in that way he found enticing.

Honryn chewed his food and picked up his goblet, using the excuse of sipping his drink to peer over the rim and gaze at her every chance he got.

The corset top left the entire expanse of her powerful shoulders bare to his gaze. Only a few locks of her fiery red hair were left to curl artfully against her shoulders, softening all that strength.

When she reached out to pour herself a goblet of water, he marveled at the contrast of defined muscle, soft skin, and an elegance that only came with confidence and hours and hours of training with a sword. There was supple strength in every one of her motions.

Soon his gaze crept back to the generous cleavage on display, and his thoughts strayed to what it would be like to press kisses along all that lovely skin.

He glanced back down at his food, selected another of the tiny cakes, and took a bite. When he looked back up, both her hands rested over her breasts, her fingers digging into her corset and tugging it up with a little more force. When that didn't work, she gave it a couple more savage jerks.

He could only watch in a helpless sort of fascination as his logical, reasoning mind seemed to halt all function.

Amid taking another bite of the cake, he accidentally inhaled it when her index fingers pointed straight up.

"My face is up here," she bit out. "Do I need to draw you a map?"

Honryn choked and sputtered, then grabbed for his drink to help wash the bit of dry cake down, but he coughed and inhaled that too.

He clutched his chest and gasped as the sweet drink burned its way down into his lungs. His entire chest spasmed, and he fought for breath as his body continued with its attempt to cough up one of his lungs.

He looked at her face to see both her brows arched over her green eyes. She rolled them at him and then got up. He thought she was leaving until she came around to his side of the table and hit him in the back hard enough to jar loose the errant bit of seed cake.

The juice still burned, though, and he sputtered and wheezed.

"I told them an ogre dressed up in a pretty dress was still an ogre in a dress. They all looked at me like I'd lost my mind. What I didn't know was that you have a thing for ogres and would be so distracted by the sight that you'd almost kill yourself with food and drink."

His embarrassment at being caught staring, made worse by nearly choking to death in front of her, warred with humor at her words. In the end, humor won out, and he laughed, which turned into more coughing and wheezing.

She rolled her eyes at him a second time and gave him a few more thumps on the back.

"Breathe, Mage. I don't want the blamed for your death when I haven't caused it." She paused and then looked down with a frown before giving her dress another tug. "At least not intentionally. There's no honor in that."

Forcing his eyes to remain on her face, he said, "I'm sorry. You're no ogre, and I should not have been staring, but the servants *do* have you laced up so tight, if you bend over, you're going to fall out of that corset."

"You think I don't know that?" she muttered in disgust.

"Here," he said hoarsely, rising and gripping her elbow, urging her to turn around. When she resisted and snatched up the butter knife, he explained, "Let me fix it. At least you'll be able to breathe. We don't need two of us suffocating today."

"Fine," she agreed with a grumble, but the distrust he felt radiating off her was nearly hot enough to burn him.

He didn't miss how her fist tightened on the butter knife.

"You're safe. I'm no beast. But take this," he said, drawing the dagger from its sheath at his waist. "Might as well have a real blade. And if I do something you deem inappropriate, you have my permission to stab me in the leg."

"Which leg?" she asked as she held out her hand for his dagger.

He hesitated for only a moment before placing the hilt in her hand. "Your choice. But if you attack me without provocation, I'll be forced to defend myself."

"We'll just have to wait and see what happens, won't we?" she said in a falsely sweet voice.

He grinned at her tone. Then he stepped around behind her to get a look at the laces. It didn't look too complicated. He sighed in relief.

Dressing women in fancy clothing, or undressing them for that matter, wasn't one of his skill sets. His previous partner had been many years ago now, an older, experienced servant, one willing to endure his youthful fumbling and teach him a few skills.

But he'd never had to peel her out of complicated dresses.

"Did I frighten you off, Mage?"

He grimaced as his body stirred, her tone having the opposite effect on him to what she'd likely intended.

After giving the small bow at the bottom of the corset a sharp tug, he leaned forward and breathed in her ear. "No. Just figuring out the lacing."

His magic could read the tension in her body, telling him he'd just made a misstep. If he wanted her to learn to trust him, he needed to give her reasons not to feel threatened by him. This idea of his wasn't a good place to start, but he would try to salvage it.

He talked of his island home as he loosened her laces, telling her of its gardens and beaches and rain-forests. "Once you are more settled in and my people have time to adjust to a new Moon Priestess, I will show you this island's most beautiful places."

"Sounds like a nice prison."

His fingers froze. She didn't know how true her words were. His home was a prison. A prison he'd never be free from, but he was working on a plan that would see all his loved ones and loyal allies freed from this place, free from the dark society of the soul mages. And he hoped Verdria would join his secret rebellion once he'd gained her trust.

When she glanced over her shoulder at him, he returned to loosening her laces. His fingers accidentally touched the silky skin of her back in places. It wasn't a caress, he told himself. Although he found his fingers stroking over a birthmark near her left shoulder blade.

He ordered his fingers to behave, and then, sensing he'd been silent for too long, he said the first thing that came to mind. "I'm not up on the most recent of fashions; however, doesn't one usually wear a blouse or some other top under a corset?"

"Ogre. Remember?" Verdria said with a huff. "They couldn't find something on such short notice that was ogre-sized."

Honryn knew he shouldn't be grinning like an idiot, but he couldn't stop.

"I'm sorry," he said to soothe her. "I shall order the servants to return your clothing to you and then have one of the royal seamstresses make you a wardrobe befitting a warrior-priestess."

"Good. I wasn't looking forward to stomping around naked."

His fingers paused in their work at the image, and he had to force himself to focus on the task of loosening laces.

Really. It shouldn't have been an arduous task. It was just that his mind wandered down other tangents every time his fingers brushed her skin, or she said something that had him picturing her naked.

He cleared his throat. "I'll instruct the seamstress to make something similar to your warrior leathers to wear daily, but I'll also have her and her apprentices create something that's a cross between battle attire and elegant court dress. Items that will go well with my own attire."

She tensed under his fingers once again.

He winced at his choice of words and the fact they sounded like he planned for her to be nothing more than one of his ornaments. "If we dress in similar colors and styles, it will be a constant visual reminder that you are under my protection and off-limits."

"You mean it won't be to signal to all that I'm to be your slave?"

"Slave? No. And the court gossip must be flying very fast indeed. You are my guest." He finished loosening the corset. "There. How's that?"

She hoisted it up higher. "Better. I forgot how nice it is to take a deep breath."

"Good. Just hold it in place while I redo the laces."

Verdria did as he asked. And soon he was retying the bow at the bottom of her corset.

"There. All done."

She turned to look over her shoulder at him. "And I didn't even have to stab you."

"I told you I'm not a beast." However, even now, he was having to fight the urge to press his face into the curve of her neck and inhale her clean scent.

"You didn't even sneak a peek. I was watching." She pointed to the mirror along the west-facing wall. Sure enough, the angle was such that she would have been able to watch him as he'd worked.

He was suddenly glad he hadn't leaned forward to appreciate the view as the corset had loosened.

Returning to his seat, he continued his meal. He was silently debating what topic to approach next when Verdria cleared her throat and speared him with a severe look.

"This banal small talk is useless. There are more serious topics I'd prefer to address."

He nodded. "Of course. What is on your mind?"

"What are your intentions toward me?" She asked. "I've already heard various scenarios from other people, but you haven't enlightened me to what *you* expect."

He froze with his goblet halfway to his lips. "What have you heard, so I can tell you if it is a mere rumor or has a kernel of fact?"

"Well, for one, I've heard from more than one source that I'm to be your 'breeding concubine.' I believe those were the words Lord Nuran and Princess Kuyan used."

Honryn cursed.

CHAPTER 15

Honryn

"**D**amn them to the farthest reaches of the void," Honryn cursed at what Lord Nuran and Princess Kuyan had told Verdria. His breeding concubine indeed! He supposed that there was irony in the situation, but he did not find it funny and slammed down his goblet. "I'm sorry. We should have had this conversation as soon as you woke up to put a few of your worries to rest."

He sighed, searching for the least alarming way to say what needed to be said. "I couldn't hide your arrival, and I needed to protect you, which as you've likely noticed, my attempts at such haven't been the most stellar of my accomplishments, but I had to tell my people something, so I claimed you for myself and let them read into it what they would. Without my claim, you would swiftly find yourself at the mercy of one of my older brothers, or perhaps even my father. I couldn't allow that to befall you. However, I also can't show what others would perceive as sentiment toward my mother's people. If I expressed any kindness toward you simply because you are of my mother's people, the rest of court would see it as a weakness. And weakness in the emperor's court is a death sentence."

He paused, hoping Verdria would understand his meaning.

She made a non-comital grunt.

"So," he said, "I must pretend my interest in you is rooted in the fact you and I would spawn fearsomely powerful offspring. Rest assured, I have zero interest in bringing a child into this world, but I must pretend to tame you, and you must pretend to be tamed. You understand that we both will have a part to play while we are in public?" He waited for her answer.

At last, she nodded, though her expression was still one of deep distrust.

He released a breath he'd been unaware he was holding and gave her what he hoped was a reassuring smile. "In private, you are free to be yourself."

When she didn't immediately respond, he arched a brow. "Do you understand my meaning?"

"That would be a 'yes' about the play-acting, but a firm 'no' about the reason you are offering me protection and some semblance of freedom. It can't be something as simple as the fact I'm one of your mother's people." She narrowed her eyes at him again, her jaw tightening slightly. "You're a soul-mage. I'm a warrior-priestess of the Moon Goddess. We are natural enemies in every sense of the word. That gulf is too wide to bridge, Mage. Why are you granting me even a hint of freedom? You could put me in magical chains, and there is nothing I could do about it. What is your purpose? What do you gain?"

"After meeting my mother and my twin, I thought you would already have figured out my reasons. I mean no ill-will toward you or any other member of your sisterhood."

Her eyes were still narrowed as she watched him. "And yet you're a powerful soul mage—the most powerful in existence, according to your mother. And you had to be involved in the raids on our lands."

That accusation was bound to come up. He'd expected it to come sooner. Still, he winced.

He wouldn't even try to deny it. To do so would be a lie, and he'd promised himself that he wouldn't lie to her. But he couldn't reveal his reasons for his involvement. He didn't yet know if he could trust her, and if trustworthy, whether she would prove capable of keeping his most dangerous secrets. That did not mean he had to hide all. He could share with her what was common knowledge.

If she were as calm, cunning, and logical as he hoped, in time, she'd figure out more on her own. Perhaps by then, he would know if he could trust her with the rest of his secrets.

But he couldn't tell her everything now, not even when his instincts, highly honed instincts that were seldom wrong, were telling him she could be trusted. It wasn't just his life at risk. He had to think about the others depending on him.

But he could tell her what was public knowledge in the hope it put her somewhat at ease.

Decision made, he forged ahead. "The plan to journey to your land was one my father, the emperor, set into motion. One I couldn't stop." Then silently, he added, *as much as I tried to unravel his most ambitious plan in decades, it failed.*

Verdria remained silent, her green-eyed gaze as intense and piercing as before. Honryn refused to look away as he continued his tale. "His council and many of the nobles were so strongly behind the plan, I feared they would send many ships on their own in secret to acquire some of your sisters, starting another bloody war no one needed. I suggested to my father there were more peaceful ways to achieve what we needed and convinced him to send only three ships, led by a man I trusted."

"Three ships," Verdria said suddenly, her expression turning to a look of horror.

"Rest easy, Priestess," he assured her. "It will put your mind at ease to know we lost two of them in a hurricane. The surviving ship, and fastest of the three, had set out five weeks before the other two, intending to find safe harbor and make initial contact with the five kingdoms."

"Make contact? You say it like it was supposed to be a peaceful expedition."

He sighed and topped up their drinks, and then said, "It wasn't supposed to become the bloody mess it did. It was to be a trading mission of a sort. From my mother," Honryn said even as his distaste for his father coiled strongly within him, "the emperor learned your people still could not breed robust males, and since my people have now suffered a similar issue with our women—"

Verdria smirked at him. "Yes, we heard you mages tripped over your egos and somehow unleashed your own plague on your populous."

"It wasn't quite like that," he said. "But, yes, there was an accident. However, after seeing how blending mage and mountain women's bloodlines produced such powerful offspring, my father was obsessed. He wouldn't be put off, but I convinced him to offer the mountain women something they needed, and in return, we could ask for the same." He stared at Verdria to see if she was following along.

Her eyes widened in understanding. "Slaves. You planned a slave exchange. Some of your men for some of our women." She bared her teeth at him as if she wanted to tear out his throat. "You and the rest of your brethren know nothing about us. While we and the centaurs take part in honorable Hunts, we never traded in slaves. Our captives were always treated with kindness and respect and eventually willingly joined our Houses."

"Not slaves," Honryn said in a soothing tone. "The young men on the other two ships were all volunteers. They were willing to give themselves to your priestess sisters as husbands if your sisters were willing to give the same number and volunteer to become mage brides." He gripped his goblet harder as unpleasant memories rose within him. "The leader of the expedition, a nobleman known for his intelligence, patience, and diplomatic savvy, and a man I considered a friend, died enroute. A freak accident, the reports from the ship said."

Though Honryn doubted very much it was an accident. However, he'd never know, since none of the soul mage crew had ever made it back for him to interrogate.

Verdria's expression turned slightly less cold and harsh, curiosity sneaking slowly in.

"Once that first ship realized the other two weren't coming," she asked, "and then the leader of the expedition was lost, why didn't that first ship return to your lands instead of commencing raids?"

He barked out a bitter laugh. "My father saw the expedition's failure as a personal affront against him, that it somehow disgraced the throne since it was ultimately his decision to send the ships." Honryn took a sip from his drink, thinking back to how everything might have turned out differently had he been there. But of course, the future priest-king elect, spiritual leader of all the empire, could not risk himself in such an endeavor. "The emperor told them not to return home without something valuable in the ship's hold. After they attempted to capture some of your people and were repelled, they found themselves in dragon territory."

"The three Hunts that were massacred," Verdria said, her tone biting and her look deadly. "I lost friends and acquaintances in that battle."

Honryn's meal was suddenly a lump in his stomach. "I am sorry. I did not learn of that massacre until after the fighting was over. Same with the dragon eggs. They had not set out to hunt the dragons, a far too difficult prey, but they found the nest..." He took another swallow of his drink. "You know what unfolded."

"Yes, because of your meddling ass, I ended up captured. And here we are. Both unhappy with the outcome of events."

Honryn didn't speak aloud, but he disagreed with

her last comment. It surprised him how pleased he was to have her sitting here across the table from him. Until now, his existence had been rather bleak. Oh, he wasn't happy with the fallout from the raid, the wasted lives, the destroyed families, too many good people dead because of the greed and ambition of powerful men. Still, he wasn't unhappy that Verdria had leaped into his life, her sharp axes flashing in threat.

Verdria seemed to mull over his words silently. He gave her as much time to digest what he'd said as she needed. Eventually, she sighed and looked him in the eye again.

"So, you had originally intended the expedition to be a friendly dialogue between our peoples?" She said, her tone incredulous.

"Friendly? By the Serpent God, no." He snorted. "I hadn't expected it to be friendly or easy, but I had hoped it would be relatively peaceful. I know your people have sound reasons to hate mine, but I had hoped that something could be worked out for our mutual survival that didn't involve more war and death and heartbreak. Once we made contact, my mother wanted me to create a portal so she could oversee the negotiations herself. I wasn't ecstatic about the idea of my mother going, but the benefits could have been great. But that won't be happening now, not after the expedition ended in catastrophe."

There was a long, intense silence.

"And now what comes next?" Verdria asked, breaking the tension at last, but her tone, full of suspicion and accusation, put him back on the defensive.

She trusted him no more now than when they'd first sat down. Honryn bowed his head, feeling suddenly tired and perhaps a little defeated, thinking she'd never see him as anything other than a soul mage. At least not for months or maybe even years. Years were a luxury he did not have. If only the other two ships hadn't sunk, and had achieved peaceful negotiations…

But that hadn't happened. Now he had to pick up the pieces and pacify this priestess's suspicions. It wasn't a straightforward task with what soul mages had done to the people of the mountains centuries ago, and again more recently.

"You suddenly run out of words, Mage?"

"I'm sorry. What were you saying?" He asked, deflecting her question with one of his own to give him a moment more to mull over what he could say to alleviate her concerns about him.

"I said, 'And now what comes next?'"

"Dessert?" he blurted out before he could think further on the topic.

Verdria adjusted her seat, tugged unconsciously on her corset, and then speared him with another glower when his gaze dipped down to her cleavage.

Being celibate really wasn't terribly rewarding, he mused as he took another sip of his drink.

"Am I to be your dessert?" she asked bluntly.

Honryn nearly choked to death a second time in one evening.

"Dessert? N-no," Honryn said, nearly tripping over his tongue in his haste to get the denial out.

What was it about this priestess that made him lose all his calm, cool reserve and left him sputtering like a youth looking upon his first courtesan? Worse, he could feel the heat rising in his face again and cursed his pale skin.

"If your words are supposed to reassure me, I should point out that your expression and tone just now, not to mention how you nearly choked to death earlier, twice," Verdria jiggled her corset for good measure, "have done little to convince me your plans for me are noble. To go by what I've seen so far, I suspect your thoughts and plans are anything but wholesome."

"Ah," he said, understanding her concern and wanting to smack himself for his uncouth behavior.

"Ah?" she echoed him but somehow laced that single word with a threat.

"You need not worry about me bedding you and stripping away your battle magic," he explained. "I would prefer you to keep that power. It will serve you well, here in the court, where danger is ever-present."

"The direction of your gaze earlier told a different story, Mage," her voice came out edged with frost and steel.

"Fine. Listen carefully, my Fierce One. I am about to share with you a secret I haven't shared with another soul."

Verdria tilted her head in his direction, a small crease forming between her eyebrows. "And I should put faith in this secret of yours? Why?"

Against his will, his lips compressed in a firm line. He couldn't expect her to trust him already, but he'd hoped she'd at least hear his secret before tossing it away as false. He leaned back and crossed his arms, giving her nothing but his intense gaze and icy silence. If she wanted to play this game, very well. He was a master at outwaiting his opponents.

"Fine," she muttered after silence stretched by for several moments. "Speak."

"Maybe I no longer feel like confiding in you." He winced again. His words, intended to be humorous, fell flat, sounding whiny instead. A spoiled child would have been hard-pressed to outdo his tone.

"Your expression!" she said and then snorted in laughter, unable to say more, but gestured for him to continue.

Only after she had her mirth under control did he relent.

"It should put your mind at ease that I haven't bedded a woman since after my power reached its third plateau. I'm now in my power's fourth plateau." He drummed his fingers on the table and did some mental math. "It's been over a decade since I've been able to perform the act."

Verdria's laughter died, and now she raked her gaze over him, her shock evident in her wide eyes and elevated brows.

"Yes, yes," he muttered. "Now you know you are safe with me."

Her expression, that face which was usually so expressive, became shuttered, and he couldn't read what was going on in her mind.

She remained silent for a time and then cleared her throat and asked in a soft voice, "Is it that you're afraid you'll lose your magic if you sleep with a woman because you're half of the mountains? Like one of my sisters or I would lose our battle magic if we bedded a man and became one of the Mothers? It isn't like that with our men, if that's what has you concerned. Our moon goddess does not change what types of magics she gifts our men throughout their lives." Verdria snorted suddenly, a bitter bark of laughter. "She rarely gifts them with magic at all now. The plague that your people released upon our lands weakened our men and stripped away their ability to receive her gifts. The healers have never been able to pinpoint the exact cause. You may be born of a mountain woman, but you need not worry about our goddess stripping you of your powers."

"That isn't what I fear," he muttered.

She huffed again. "Good. Because it's a moot point anyway. The Moon Goddess would never gift magic to the reprehensible get of a soul mage."

"Hold nothing back," Honryn muttered. "Make sure you tell me exactly what you think of me."

Verdria snorted again, her earlier humor restored. "Always happy to tell you what I think of you and your kind, Mage."

It was Honryn's turn to grunt his dissatisfaction about how the conversation was going. Well, at least when she was laughing at him, he supposed, she wasn't likely afraid of him.

He'd been silent too long, and Verdria had grown impatient with him. "So," she asked sharply, "if you're not afraid of losing your powers, why haven't you bedded a woman in over ten years? Prefer other men?"

He smirked suddenly. "Would you like to watch if I did?"

Once again, Verdria's face expressed her shock, embarrassment burning hot upon her cheeks. Her freckles stood out in sharp contrast.

Point for me, he thought to himself.

"No," she said, nearly stumbling over her tongue. "No, of course not." Her pale skin turned an even brighter, fiery red as he watched.

"You may be one of the best warriors I've ever crossed," Honryn drawled. "But you're a terrible liar. The thought of watching me with another man intrigues you? Or perhaps it's just the thought of watching me?"

"You! You cocky—" For a moment, he thought she was going to reach across the table and grab him by the throat. But she calmed herself, carefully took up her drink, and sipped from it before looking him in the eye and saying, "Only a soul mage would find being a good liar an admirable quality."

"A survival trait is always to be admired."

"Whatever you say, Mage. But if it's not one of my other suggestions, what is the true reason you're celibate?"

Honryn picked up his goblet and leaned back in his chair. "Since we've both concluded you're such a terrible liar, I'm not sure if I should trust you with this secret. You might expose it without even meaning to." Which was true, but that wasn't the reason he wouldn't tell her about the real cause for his celibacy. As fierce as she was, she *wasn't* ready to hear that truth, likely not for a long time. And he silently prayed to the goddess of the moon that Verdria never saw him when he was fully in the grip of the serpent god's power.

Verdria took his silence better this time. She tilted her head to one side the barest bit, her expression turning thoughtful and inward. After a few moments, her eyes came back into focus. All humor was gone, her expression far more solemn and sympathetic.

"I think I understand now." She leaned across the

table, and he tensed, thinking she was trying to trick him, perhaps to grab his head and slam it against the table. That seemed like something his warrior-priestess would do. But instead of all the nasty things he could envision, she patted his hand. "I will spread no rumors. Your problem is common among the men of the mountains. There's nothing to be ashamed of. Perhaps you're more of the mountains than I realized. Many of our men can't perform. It's why we have so few children."

What?

She thought he couldn't get it up?

"That's not what I...." His ego rose, and he nearly blurted out a denial and corrected her mistaken assumptions, but then he realized as much as it stung his male pride, it was better his priestess thought he couldn't get a cockstand than be afraid he'd attack her. Besides, wasn't this better than her digging until she learned the true reason for his celibacy and have even this stoutest-hearted of warrior-priestesses running from his side?

"Shh. No shame," she said in a reassuring tone. "Your secret is safe with me. And I now understand why you said we'd need to act, to play a part." She patted his hand a second time. "Honryn, your secret is safe with me. I promise."

Damnation! He could see it in her eyes. She liked him better now that she thought he wasn't able to get it up.

Thus is my life, Honryn thought to himself, and groaned softly.

"But to get back to my original question. What's next?" Verdria asked as she settled back in her seat, seeming much more relaxed now. "How do you spend your days? What am I expected to do on a day-to-day basis?"

This time when he met Verdria's gaze, her expression was thoughtful and kind, which, he supposed, was better than her glowers and distrust. Any kind of improvement was better than none, he told himself.

"First," he explained. "I'll show you where you'll be staying while you're my guest."

CHAPTER 16

Verdria

"*P*lease tell me you're jesting," Verdria barked out without turning around to glare at Honryn, even though he had earned a good long glare. When he'd said he'd show her where she'd be staying, she'd expected him to lead her somewhere outside of his chambers. "We're still within your suites."

He stepped up beside her to peer into one of the side chambers that he'd said would be hers. "My living quarters are large enough for ten people. I'm sure the two of us can get along without killing each other."

She grunted in answer, not trusting her voice at the moment. Her earlier and very brief feelings of comradery had evaporated. Yes, he might be more of the mountains than she'd first thought, but he was also a powerful soul mage, a master of deception.

"It's for your protection, as much as keeping up appearances," he explained. "My people won't think it's unusual that you're sharing my rooms now that rumors are spreading about my intentions to make you my consort. They'll think I'm working on taming you."

"Find a different word, Mage. I assure you; I am not tame. Never will be."

"I'm aware of that." He gave her that disarming smile of his, the warm mirth transforming his face from the ideal of masculine beauty to something even more breathtaking. "But as I've mentioned before, we have parts to play. You'll have to adapt to yours even as I have mine."

Worse, there wasn't so much as a hint of deception or cunning in his look. And her battle magic didn't consider him a threat. As far as she could tell, he was being honest with her. Had been all through dinner.

"Great," she muttered in response to his words without a hint of excitement. She already knew she'd be miserable 'play acting', whatever he meant by that. She was a terrible liar and play acting sounded like the next level up.

"The hottest season is still some months off," Honryn said as he tried and failed to coerce her into the room for a tour. "Which is good for you. It will give you time to accustom yourself to our way of life. We split our waking hours into two segments, sleeping during the hottest part of the day and again toward the middle of the night."

"That's preposterous," she muttered, while actually eyeing the room beyond his shoulders. It was large and well-appointed from what she could see, with a large bed, chests, tables, wardrobe, and a tall mirror. Carpets softened the stone of the floor and tapestries served the same purpose on the walls.

"You won't find it so preposterous once the dry season is upon us. Trust me. Our days are sweltering during the summer months. That has led us to adapt our sleep cycle to cope. You will wish to nap now if you can, so you're fresh for tonight's feast."

She turned her attention back to him and arched an eyebrow, then asked, "How do you get anything done when you sleep away the afternoon?"

Honryn's expression took on the look of a mother explaining the simplest situation to a toddler. She wanted to swat him upside the head. Her question wasn't foolish or naïve.

"Most court business takes place in the mornings," he explained calmly, clearly unaware of her thoughts in that moment, "leaving the evening for military and magical training. Afterward, there are entertainments. And late-night walks along the ocean can be exquisite."

"Lovely for you and your walks along the beach. But I'm not sleeping in the daytime. It's unnatural."

Even as she said the words, she admitted she sounded like a petulant child.

But for whatever reason, the future priest-king of the soul mages found her intriguing and wished to keep her close, like one would a cherished ally. She didn't fool herself. She'd seen the way he looked at her with hunger in his gaze. Had he been able to act upon that lust, she knew her situation would be very different.

But perhaps the Moon Goddess was still looking out for Verdria because as much as Honryn's eyes and quick mind might lust after her, his body could not carry out those desires.

At least she didn't have to fear rape and losing her battle magic, not with an impotent and possibly possessive Honryn guarding her night and day. Perhaps living in his chambers was the wisest choice.

After all, she'd been captured without her supplies, and that left her in a bit of a bind without her fertility suppressing tea. Her brows knit together with her unhappy thoughts. She'd never been without the herbal hormone suppressant while out on a patrol and hadn't experienced its withdrawal symptoms before, but she would notice them in the coming days if she couldn't find a source here. Jardeen might know where to find the plants.

She'd need to guard herself well until she could

speak with Jardeen again. While Honryn might not be able to get it up, neither of them would enjoy it if she lost her sense and attempted to seduce the poor man when her hormones ran amok.

Or worse, she shuddered as another thought came to her. What if she started lusting after some other soul mage man? The idea turned her stomach. But she'd heard rumors about what suddenly going off the tea could do. And as much as she appreciated the tea suppressing her normal monthly moon bleeding and other symptoms, making her duty as a border guard easier, she now regretted she'd ever started taking it.

But neither had she expected to find herself in the empire of the soul mages.

She hoped Honryn's mother knew where she could find the herb if it even grew in this climate. If not, she hoped the other woman knew something Verdria could use as a replacement.

"I swear you are safe," Honryn said as he reached out and placed one hand on her right shoulder, probably having seen something in her expression. "No one else may enter my private domain, not even servants."

Verdria fought off the urge to swat his hand from her shoulder while she mentally cursed her expressive face and the mage's keen attention that missed nothing.

"If you were as noble as you claimed," she muttered, "you would allow me to have one of my axes for protection."

Verdria didn't need her axes to protect herself. She still possessed her battle magic, and her training allowed her to turn almost any object into a weapon. But she was feeling out of her element here, and in the days to come, with her hormones out of sorts, she wouldn't be able to trust her own feelings. That insecurity must be why she found herself wanting to trust Honryn.

She desired an ally in this place. But she also feared there might be more to this sympathy that she felt for him. There might also be a touch of admiration.

That couldn't happen. Better to keep their relationship more antagonistic. She dared not soften toward him. Earlier, when he'd talked of his mother and twin sister, his love for them shone from his animated face. Then she'd been taken aback by the discovery Honryn suffered impotence, just like many of the men of the mountains. She'd responded as if he was one of her people, related with him, feeling protective toward him. But Honryn was a soul mage, and she couldn't allow herself to forget that.

When she blinked and brought her inner thoughts and her eyes back into focus, she discovered Honryn's expression had taken on a hint of sadness and something else. Determination maybe?

"I thought you understood you were safe from me," he said. "I wouldn't force you, even if it was possible for us to be together in that way."

"I'm not actually afraid of you, Mage," she reassured him, even though she was sabotaging her attempt to get her axes returned to her. "I just want a reason to have a weapon in my hands again."

"I grew up knowing what my father did to my mother," Honryn said in a harsh voice, ignoring her words, his gaze leaving hers and turning toward the room before them, unseeing. "I loved my mother; it killed a part of me that I wasn't strong enough as a child to stop it. It wasn't until after I hit puberty that my powers manifested in strength enough to rival my sire in strength. And as I grew to adulthood, even he learned to respect me. When I was fourteen, I first taught him to fear me. I had come upon him and my mother…."

Honryn's nostrils flared, and his features took on a harsher look, his eyes going cold and dead. Magic, barely seen, coiled and twisted in the air around him.

Goosebumps raced across her body, and the hair at the back of her neck stood on end.

"I lashed out," he said in a voice as forbidding as his expression. "But because I hadn't killed him outright, and my power was more than enough to have accomplished that feat, he believed me when I said it escaped my control and that I would learn better mastery over it." He grinned savagely. "I have never lost control of my magic. Not once."

Verdria suppressed the urge to whistle. "I'm surprised you're still alive to tell me this story."

"He learned nothing. A year later I again found him with my mother…" Honryn flashed his teeth at her. "I summoned his soul and held it in my hand. I told him that if he ever touched her against her will again, I would destroy his soul."

Verdria's one eyebrow arched nearly to her hairline. Really, she wondered, how was he still alive to tell her all this?

Her face must have betrayed her again because he gave her a tight smile, one devoid of humor. "Why do I still live, you're thinking? That's the question the entire court wants to know. Both my father and I know he isn't strong enough to kill me. And if he tried, I'd take his life, his throne, and his whole fucking empire. But he also knows I'm not ambitious and wanted no part in ruling the empire. He thought I was weak for loving my mother. He still thinks he uses that weakness to control me and keep me in line, but I am just bidding my time, looking for a way—" he ended suddenly and looked up, startled.

She knew then that he'd said more than he'd meant and nearly spilled some closely guarded secret.

"You are far too easy to talk to, Verdria of High Rock."

"You should see people around me once they've been consuming fermented drinks."

Her comment broke the tension in the room, and he laughed. "I can only imagine."

But soon his smile vanished. "I only meant to explain that you need not fear me trying to rape you, as my father did my mother. I could never do that to a woman, not even a most hated enemy. I am not capable of such and under no circumstance would I wish to be."

Verdria nodded, his statement needing some response, but she didn't have any fancy words.

He sighed suddenly. "Still, I imagine no woman enjoys being ogled. All I can do is apologize for my behavior and promise to do better in the future."

"I accept your apology and believe your words, Mage," she said, conceding to him. "But it doesn't mean we are friends."

"No," he muttered as he walked farther into her rooms. "That would be too much, too soon."

Then he went to an enormous wardrobe and threw open the doors. He bent, presenting her with the nicest ass she'd ever seen. What would he look like without that knee length loincloth obscuring the view?

"Eyes up," she reminded herself, more than mildly horrified she'd admired a soul mage's ass. Apparently, Honryn wasn't the only one who needed to work on not ogling. And she really needed to ask Jardeen about the hormone suppression tea the next time she saw her.

A moment later, Honryn turned back to her. In his hands, he held her axes. Verdria inhaled sharply, joy blooming in her chest. She'd feared she'd never see her beloved axes again.

"I kept these for you," he said in a quiet voice. "Perhaps they'll help if my words alone aren't enough to allow you to sleep peacefully."

Verdria took them, stunned he'd given her back her goddess-blessed weapons, axes that could kill a soul-mage. Perhaps even kill a soul mage as powerful as Honryn if she could strike him before he could immobilize her.

"That door," he said, gesturing toward a closed door she'd thought was storage, "leads to a large, shared bathing chamber. There you'll find another smaller room to attend to any bodily needs. If you have any questions, feel free to ask."

As she hefted the familiar weight of her axes and looked back toward him, she found him retreating from her sleeping chamber.

"Rest well, Warrior-Priestess Verdria of High Rock," he called back over his shoulder to her. "I will wake you this evening when it is time to practice our skills in the sand ring."

After she watched him go, she glanced back down at her weapons, feeling entirely befuddled by the Priest-King Elect of the Soul Mages.

He was nothing like she'd expected.

Ruthless, yes.

And yet he seemed to have a gentler side as well.

If that wasn't just more acting on his part.

She didn't think it was. And her battle magic didn't consider him a threat,

But he was half soul mage and she could not—would not—trust him yet.

If ever.

But the bed did look comfortable, and she wouldn't mind resting her eyes for just a moment as she processed all she'd learned.

CHAPTER 17

Verdria

A light tapping at a door woke her. She jerked upright, tossing aside the lightweight cover and looked around. The soft tap came again, followed by a muffled masculine voice.

"Verdria, we should be leaving for weapon's practice soon," Honryn called through the door, his voice fading as if he was walking away. "I'm just finishing…"

Whatever he said was too soft to hear.

She reached for her small axe and got out of bed. Instinct from years of living on her skills and battle readiness had her scanning the room for threats before going into morning stretches even though it wasn't morning.

Several minutes later, she headed for the door that Honryn said led to a bathing chamber. She turned the handle and shoved the door with her hip. He hadn't lied. A large bathing chamber filled with every luxury one could ever dream about greeted her vision.

As she walked farther into the room, past a tall screen, she remembered belatedly he'd said the bathing chamber was shared by both suites.

Verdria stumbled to a halt, all sleepiness vanishing.

The room was already occupied.

Honryn was standing in front of a tall mirror.

Naked.

Absolutely naked.

If asked, she'd deny the little feminine gasp that escaped her.

She froze in place, helpless to stop herself from admiring his very, very fine form.

Her gaze drifted lower, following the elegant curve of his spine.

And like she'd noted the night before, he had a very fine ass. Muscled and firm and perfectly formed.

It took her a moment or two more to realize he was actually shaving in front of the mirror—not standing naked for her perusal.

Who actually shaved while standing naked in front of a mirror?

The future priest-king of the Soul-mages, apparently.

"I suppose we need to work out some kind of visual communication method," he mused aloud. "Maybe hang something from the doors when one or the other of us is using the room?"

She snorted to cover up her embarrassment at barging in on him mistakenly. "Don't worry, Pretty One. I'll be more careful in the future. But I need to piss…" She intentionally aimed for crass, hoping it would rub him the wrong way. She had the uneasy feeling that this soul mage liked her for some strange reason known only to him.

Under no moon could that be a good thing. Maybe if she became a thorn in his side, he'd send her off to another keeper, a less powerful mage where she'd have a better chance at escape? Or maybe she could convince him to assign her to his mother?

But Honryn wasn't falling for her attempt at 'rude guest' and chuckled good-naturedly. "There is a room in the back. The levers feed water from the roof to flush away waste and there is a basin with more levers for washing."

"I'm not an animal. I'm sure I can figure them out," she muttered.

His rich laughter gave chase as she stomped toward her target.

"I am very aware you aren't an animal, my Fierce One."

Goddess! Now they were exchanging terms of endearment. While hers was meant as an insult, he sounded far too delighted for his term to be an insult.

When she was finished in the room, she returned to the main bathing chamber to find him still standing in front of the mirror. Though this time, he wore another pair of those ass-hugging black pants he seemed to favor.

"So, no tattoos anywhere," she said to break the silence. She hated feeling awkward and decided if something about his person was making her feel flustered, then it was time to face it head on and crush it.

"No," he agreed. Though he didn't offer an explanation as to why.

Though she thought she already knew why. It tied into why he'd been bare chested yesterday and again today. His lack of tattoos was a status symbol, telling all the other soul mages he was so powerful he didn't need the added help of the stored power normally contained in a soul mage's tattoos.

"What's on the agenda for this evening?"

"I informally introduce you to the court out on the practice field."

"You trust me not to go on another killing spree?" She grinned at him. "Or punch holes into that pretty body of yours."

"I trust you to be cunning enough to not do something foolish that will force me to punish you. Whether you like it or not, you are my guest for the immediate future. And while I have no interest in harming you, as I said this morning, you will soon need to learn to play the willing consort."

"How convincing are you expecting me to be?" His earlier casual nudity hinted that soul-mages might be rather uninhibited. That could be dangerous to her battle magic.

Verdria's hand tightened on her axe's handle.

Honryn either didn't notice or didn't care. "It would be natural for you to be feisty at first. Though later the court will expect some public showings of…"

He seemed at a momentary loss for words.

"Lust?" she supplied for him.

He surprised her by wincing. "I was going to say affection, but yes, lust would work, too. Once you have had a few days to study the court, you'll better understand how to act."

"If you expect me to be some simpering fool, you're going to be disappointed."

He made another face. "You are a warrior-priestess. I'll expect you to continue to act like one for today. Later, we can talk more about your taming."

She snorted.

"Easy. This will all be an act to convince others to think what we want them to think." He paused and frowned at her. "But I see it is still too early for you to trust me yet. But for your own good, you need to play along for now. When I'm certain I can trust you not to betray me or accidentally reveal my secrets, I will tell you the rest of my secrets so that you'll be able to trust me or use them against me, Verdria of High Rock."

Verdria could only shake her head and guess at what was going on behind his beautiful eyes with their sinfully thick lashes. One thing was certain, he was cunning beyond measure and a master at manipulating people.

CHAPTER 18

Verdria

True to his word, Honryn led her from his chambers where a unit of the Elites were awaiting him. As a group, they made their way through the halls of the vast palace complex, and on out into the sultry late evening air. If it was still this warm now, Verdria hated to think what midday must feel like in the height of summer.

Probably almost hot enough to turn rock molten.

Good thing she planned to escape before then.

When they reached a lush tropical garden, Honryn gestured for his Elite guards to give them space. The female captain looked like she wanted to rebel but merely gave Verdria a warning look to behave and then bowed to Honryn before she led the guards to set a perimeter somewhere out of sight. And just like that, Verdria was alone with Honryn once more. Feeling uncomfortable, she chose to study the land around her.

What would have been a steep grade to the sloping ground of the island was tamed by terraces and retaining walls and gleaming white stone stairs. The sweet scent of night blooming flowers was just beginning to fill the air. Tropical ferns and palms and vines grew on either side of the stone stairs. Brightly colored songbirds dipped and darted through the vine-laden trees.

Verdria even had the opportunity to study three different kinds of parrots in the short time she'd been outside. Plates of seeds and fruits had been set out for them. One great blue parrot with the biggest beak she'd ever seen flew to the Priest-King Elect's hand, where he magically presented it with one of the small cakes from their midday meal.

She wasn't actually sure if it was magic or if he'd just managed to hide it on his person somewhere.

Eyeing his bare chest and tight-fitting pants, she thought it more likely he'd used magic than found a place to hide the treat in his clothing.

Once the parrot had eaten the treat and flown away, Honryn ushered her forward once more.

Verdria followed Honryn deeper into the garden

filled with a myriad of flowers and large foliage plants, the like she'd never seen before.

It was beautiful, but there was still something about it that made her uneasy. She nearly snorted out loud at that thought.

What about this island kingdom full of soul mages didn't make her uneasy? Knowing it was better to hide her emotions from Honryn, or any other enemy, she unclenched her hands and joined Honryn where he'd stopped under a tree, seeming to be talking to said tree.

Verdria squinted, but she still didn't see the person he was talking to. Frowning, she stepped closer. Only then did she realize what he was talking to.

"My lovely, lovely boy," Honryn crooned as he held an arm out to the largest snake she'd ever had the misfortune to gaze upon.

Immediately, her chest felt tight, and her heart began to race. Clammy sweat coated her skin moments later. A fine tremor raced down her body even as her battle magic responded to her fear, rising within her.

She probably couldn't have screamed even if she'd wanted to. Her jaw locked as tight as her chest felt. The enormous snake, a great beast of a thing decorated with bright blue scales, stretched his head toward Honryn's hand, and then began crawling up his arm and over his shoulders.

He allowed it to coil more of itself around him until he was liberally covered from head to toe in the snake.

The snake's head was near his own, as if it were whispering in Honryn's ear.

For his part, Honryn seemed completely unconcerned he was in danger of being swallowed by a snake of monstrous proportions. Honryn actually appeared happy as he continued to croon loving words to the snake. She didn't have a clue what he was saying. A high-pitched ringing filled her ears, drowning out all else.

Even as she fought to hold her battle magic in check, she briefly wondered if she was going to pass out. Honryn was suddenly standing closer to her, his stance protective as his gaze scanned their surroundings as if searching for danger.

It occurred to her that he was responding to her, thinking she sensed some threat he had missed.

"Verdria," he shouted as he reached for her. "What's wrong?"

"Don't touch me!" she screamed, her voice breaking. Leaping backwards, she stumbled away from him and the monstrous snake.

"Verdria?" He paused and glanced down at the snake in sudden understanding. "He's a pet. Cobalt Shadow won't hurt you."

Honryn continued toward her, his hands held out before him in a pacifying manner. Verdria wasn't in any kind of state to be pacified. It didn't matter that her logical mind knew the big snake was a pet.

It was a big monster of a snake. And that was all her illogical fear cared about.

She managed to hold back her battle magic.

Barely.

"You're afraid of snakes?" Honryn asked in gentle understanding. "A phobia?"

"Yes," she bit out. "Don't come any closer."

"Easy. I'll stay right over here." Honryn paced away from her and then began urging the snake to move to a nearby tree branch. The snake seemed reluctant to go, but Honryn persisted.

Once he was free of the snake, he turned back to her and took a step toward her before halting.

"May I approach?"

She shook her head. She wasn't ready to allow any soul mage near her when her battle magic was still so close to the surface. Not even Honryn.

"No." Her voice came out sharper and higher than normal, the panic still evident.

"Everything will be fine," he soothed, crooning to her as he had the snake a short time ago.

He glanced above her head and his eyes widened a fraction, probably seeing her magic.

"Verdria, please come to me."

She shook her head. "No. I'm good where I am."

Honryn just held his hand out to her. "Come with me. We'll discuss this little problem elsewhere."

"Not a problem. Nothing to discuss. I just don't like snakes."

"That *is* the problem. We worship the Serpent God. All snakes are sacred. The city and surrounding islands are teeming with snakes."

Teeming. With. Snakes.

Those three words sounded like doom to her. An island of snakes. Verdria moaned softly. Of course it would be.

Soul Mages were all that was evil. Of course their most beloved pet would be the one thing Verdria feared without reason or logic.

Verdria moaned again, still far beyond the ability to act rationally. In truth, Honryn was lucky she had not tried to vaporize the snake while it was still wrapped around him. He was still talking, she realized, and put more effort into understanding him.

"Verdria, just step to the left three paces. Come on, you can do it. Everything will be fine. I'll take you down to the beach. There are no snakes there usually."

A place with no snakes?

That sounded good, so much better than here.

"Okay." She nodded sharply.

"Good," Honryn nearly sighed out his obvious relief. "That's good. Now you just need to trust me, and I will—"

He stopped mid-word and then cursed. Even as he was leaping forward, instinct drew her gaze away from him and up into the tree canopy directly over her head.

She saw the movement as the first thick coil dropped down around her, the strange dry scraping sensation of its scales and its firm body full of a muscular strength drudging up the familiar horror from deep in her memories. Verdria screamed then, her battle magic rising up to destroy the threat even as she froze in terror, all her training gone, her mind as frozen as her body.

She screamed a second time and directed her magic at the snake, but Honryn was suddenly there, freeing her from the snake and blocking her magical attack at the same time.

"It's alright. I'm here. You're safe." Suddenly she found herself in Honryn's arms, one of his hands gently stroking her hair.

Her body still shaking with tremors, Verdria shoved away from him and took several steps into the open area, uncaring of the sun's oppressive heat. It was better than being under the tree canopy where a snake could drop down upon her at any moment.

Slowly, she gained control of her breathing. Her body's trembling would take longer.

Honryn stepped into her line of vision. "Verdria, I'm sorry. If I'd known, I wouldn't have brought you to the gardens."

"It's fine," she barked out. "I'm fine."

Honryn shook his head at her words. "Clearly it is not fine. You have an extreme phobia of snakes."

Verdria laughed bitterly. "So now you know how to break me, Mage. Just toss me in a pit and dump a bunch of snakes in with me. You'll have me mewling in terror in no time."

"My Fierce One, I would never…" He fell silent and then placed a hand on her shoulder.

She looked up as the silence lengthened. Honryn was staring down at her with a look of sadness and regret. "I have no interest in breaking you. Your secret is safe with me, but we will have to work on this flaw in your armor. It's a weakness anyone could exploit."

"I'm aware of the flaw. Do you really think I haven't tried to conquer and vanquish this unreasoning fear over the years?"

Honryn's brows furrowed. "Perhaps that's why you've failed up until now. You don't conquer or vanquish a phobia. You must first accept that it's a part of you and then slowly learn to function despite the fear. The fear may always be a part of you, but you can adapt and slowly it will lose its power over you."

Verdria snorted derisively. "How does one do that, Mage?"

He shrugged. "Everyone's path is different. But you might start by allowing me to guide you with the snakes. I can hold them while you study them at a safe distance."

Verdria felt her one eyebrow arch and a sarcastic retort danced on her tongue, but she held it back. She could feel Honryn's honesty. He really seemed to wish to aid her. But could she trust him—a mage?

Never.

Honryn, unaware of her thoughts, continued, "It might also help if you told me what first caused your fear. Sometimes speaking about the root of our fears can help us in the long run."

Verdria rolled her eyes at him. "Because reliving a trauma sure sounds like a fun way to trigger nightmares and flashbacks."

"At first, yes," he nodded. "It might stir up memories one would rather forget, but in the long run, those same memories will slowly lose their hold on us."

She glanced down at her hands where they were clenched and then back up at Honryn's compassion filled gaze.

Some part of her wanted to trust the honest concern she saw there in his eyes, but she could never trust a soul mage. Though he was likely correct about her needing to accept and adapt. She absolutely couldn't let more of the enemy see her weakness and exploit it. She needed to master it enough to prevent others from finding out she had this phobia.

"Fine," she agreed at last. "Your words make sense. We'll work on my snake problem."

"Good." There wasn't a hint of humor or superiority

in his expression. He looked relieved. "Why don't you tell me more about how it started on our way to the beach? Once I know the source of the trauma, it might give me some idea how best to proceed."

"What makes you such an expert on trauma?"

Honryn huffed. "I'm not sure if I'd call myself an expert, but I and my loved ones have all suffered much trauma. As a youth, having to watch my mother and her aunts and my cousins suffer at the hands of their soul mage masters was traumatizing. It scarred me as well."

"Aunts? Cousins?"

"Mother said she mentioned the other mountain priestesses captured with her. Those women I call my aunts. Their children I call my cousins because they are like my twin and I. Half soul mage. Half of the mountains. And we have never been allowed to forget that."

Verdria knew her face was showing way too many of her emotions when Honryn's brows scrunched over his nose.

"Yes, yes," he muttered. "Evil Mage for only just clarifying that now. In my defense, there is a great deal I still must tell you. But while we're on the topic of my extended family, I'll mention that you are welcome to spend time with my aunts. And if you prefer, you can ask them to aid you with this phobia of yours."

Honryn fell silent and seemed so still, she wondered if he breathed.

She hardly knew what to think, but his words required a response.

"Thank you. I'd appreciate a fellow priestess aiding me with this issue." For a moment, she thought she saw a hint of disappointment flicker across his expression, but it was gone so fast, she may have mistaken it.

He gave her a courtly bow. "Tomorrow I will make sure you have a chance to meet some of my aunts. Two of them are returning early. They will be here tomorrow. The others are away with my cousins, brothers, sire, and uncle."

Verdria nodded, suddenly realizing her 'introduction' to soul mage society would likely have been much bloodier if his older brothers, sire, and uncle were present. Though so far, she'd learned nothing about Honryn's uncle beyond the fact he was the present Priest-King.

"In the meantime," Honryn said and gestured with his arm, "let us go to the practice rings on the beach."

Verdria nodded once again and followed Honryn willingly enough when he turned and led her in the direction of the beach. But her thoughts were on his aunts. There were other priestesses here, which meant they might be allies.

THE PATH TURNED SHARPLY AND SUDDENLY THEY WERE standing on a balcony overlooking a wide beach. Spreading off in either direction down the beach were a series of practice rings.

The training areas were surrounded by benches and open sided tents that provided shade but allowed the ocean's cooler breeze within. The tents were filled with finely dressed and bejeweled nobles watching the fighters in the rings.

Besides the men and women training, she noted an army of servants and food preparers with little stalls all along the waterfront.

Closer to the water's edge, there were blankets spread out on the sand and adults and children playing in the surf. She tried her best to hide her surprise at seeing so many children. She'd never dreamed such a bounty of precious little ones existed in all the world.

And it infuriated her that such a wealth of children belonged to this most hideous of enemies. But her rage turned to shock when she realized most of the swimmers playing in the surf were as naked as the day they'd been born.

But they were just playing or swimming, trying to beat the heat of the day. It had a kind of innocent wholesomeness about it that, try as she might, she couldn't really find fault with their actions.

But it did reinforce her earlier assumption that the soul mages had less inhibitions when it came to nudity.

"If you expect me to skip through the surf naked, we're going to have a problem," Verdria muttered without glancing in Honryn's direction. She kept her voice lowered, since they were no longer alone. As soon as they'd exited Honryn's personal gardens, several of the Elite had materialized from out of the shadows and flanked Honryn as they left the palace grounds for the city.

Honryn looked in the direction of the beach and chuckled. "My mother holds much the same outlook. I don't really understand why. The human body is beautiful and need not be hidden."

She rolled her eyes. "I'll keep my scars to myself. Thanks."

His gaze tracked back to her. "You have very few scars, but you need not worry. The public beach below is for all the residents of our empire. However, the noble Houses have their own private beaches in other locations around the island. The royal family also has its own beach. You might be more comfortable swimming there. And trust me, after weapons practice, a cooling soak in the ocean is always welcome before dinner."

His words were very logical and informative, but she was still hung up on his first line.

"How do you know how many scars I have?" she asked with growing suspicion.

He turned his gaze back down to the beach before

he spoke.

"Don't go into a rage and attempt to stab me," he said with a chuckle, suggesting he didn't think she would actually do it.

She frowned at him harder.

Sighing, he chanced a look in her direction, a boyish sort of smile graced his lips, and she was struck again by how handsome this particular soul-mage was.

"My mother said she'd told you that I was the one to do the majority of your healing. Surely you realized my patient needed to be naked for that? And I needed to bathe you to tend some of your minor wounds. I didn't have the magical resources left to heal you fully all at once. While I was tending your newest round of injuries, I saw evidence of older damage. Not much, which doesn't surprise me having seen you fight."

Her frown still didn't diminish. She'd known he'd been the one to heal her, but it hadn't occurred to her that he'd been the one to strip and bathe her. She'd just assumed it had been his mother, or maybe a royal healer, who had tended to her afterward. But Honryn's words now enlightened her to the truth.

"Come," he said, holding out one hand, unaware of her dark thoughts. "It's time I introduced the royal court to my warrior-priestess. And I can think of no better way to do that than in the practice ring with the high nobility looking on. If you can hold your own against me, it will increase your status among my people."

"And what happens if I beat your ass into the sand?"

He chuckled. "Then they will fear my warrior-priestess consort as much as they do me."

"Fine. Let's go do this."

But afterward, she still wouldn't be swimming naked in front of others, especially this particular soul-mage. He'd already seen enough of her hide.

CHAPTER 19

Verdria

The crash of the surf drowned out the sound of their panting. Barely. Sweat poured down her skin and Verdria knew she needed to pace herself better if she wanted to be the last opponent standing.

And she very much did, even though she wasn't back up to her old strength yet.

It didn't help her plans that Honryn possessed far greater martial skills than she'd first guessed. She'd assumed because he was a royal with entire armies to protect him, not to mention his formidable magic, that he wouldn't be her match in the practice ring.

But he most certainly was her match, to her great dismay.

She was still going to beat him bloody with the wooden practice sword, though.

They'd started out with edged blades. A bold move on his part, as well as practically shouting to his people that he'd already tamed her enough that he trusted her not to attempt to kill him in the practice ring.

That had rubbed her the wrong way. But it was part of the act, so she let him set the scene to whatever best suited his plans.

Partway through their third round in the ring, he'd called a halt and switched to lighter weight wooden practice swords, laughingly saying he didn't want either of them to slip and mortally wound the other.

Which was a legitimate worry.

They had both been tiring at that point. The risk of them accidentally getting impaled or lopping off a limb was a real possibility. And as much as she didn't trust Honryn, and as strange as it was to admit, he was also currently the greatest ally she had here, deep in enemy territory.

They had switched to wooden practice swords over an hour ago now. The sun was almost touching the ocean, and she was more exhausted than she had been in a long time.

But by the Bleeding Moon, she wasn't going to give in!

"Come at me," she shouted at Honryn where he was slowly circling her.

He was sweating and panting as hard as her. His entire body glistened in the light of the setting sun, his muscles rippling in a contrast of light and shadow caused by the sun sinking into the ocean in the west.

Magnificent, she found herself thinking as she looked upon him. Which only annoyed her more and fueled her will to best him in the ring.

Honryn chuckled, then said, "If I come at you, it's just going to be to lean against you."

The image of them leaning against each other, both too stubborn to quit, made her laugh, which likely utterly destroyed her fierce warrior-priestess persona she'd been going for.

"Concede the fight, Pretty One."

"You first, my Fierce One."

"Never!" Verdria shouted with gleeful defiance.

"Oh, just fuck and get it over with," a surly voice said. "You know that's the only reason you're letting her match you in the ring, brother."

Across from her, Honryn's humor bled away, replaced by a harsh, cold glint. Here was the ruthless priest-king elect of the soul-mages, Verdria found herself thinking as she looked upon him.

It was eerie to watch how easily he slid into that personality. Not for the first time, she wondered if this was the true man before her now, and the hints of the gentler male with a boyish smile was the deception.

But she had another, more pressing concern. One named Princess Kuyan.

Verdria's eyes darted to the edge of the ring where a crowd of nobles had gathered to watch. It didn't take long to find Honryn's older sister. The nobles to either side were slowly putting distance between themselves and the woman.

"When, where, and how often I fuck my future consort is none of your concern," Honryn said in a cold tone. "However, for the slight toward Verdria's skills as a warrior, I'm of a mind to allow her to drag you into the practice ring at some point in the future, Sister."

Princess Kuyan almost managed to keep the sneer off her face. "Perhaps I will cross blades with the priestess from the mountains one day."

Honryn drew himself up, all traces of exhaustion and merriment gone from his face. "Sister, was there something in particular you wanted? I know you didn't come here to pick up a sword."

His sister snorted. "Great Serpent, no. I don't know why you would wish to practice such a barbaric form of combat. Our magic is much deadlier," she paused to take in Honryn's sweat and sand covered form, then added, "and doesn't leave the user in such a state of dishevel."

"I like to have mastery over every form of combat."

Honryn motioned one of the servants forward and accepted the towel he held out. After a moment, Honryn snapped up a second towel and handed it to Verdria with a little bow.

It wasn't intended as an insult. The exact opposite, she realized. A moment later Verdria returned the gesture, matching the depth and form of the bow exactly.

They were both acknowledging the other was their perfect equal.

When she straightened, Honryn turned to his sister. "Now. What was the real reason you came all the way down to the beach?"

Kuyan laughed in delight. "You forget, many from the lesser noble houses have already been arriving for the upcoming festival of the Concubines in two weeks."

"I have not forgotten." Honryn sounded very annoyed about something. The festival?

"With Father and our brothers still away, if you don't make it to dinner tonight, there will be a lot of disappointed nobles."

Honryn barked out a sharp laugh. "And we mustn't disappoint the Lords of the Houses jostling for position within the court."

"Exactly," Kuyan purred.

Honryn finished mopping the sweat from his thick dark hair. "Now tell me why you're really here."

"Ah, your blunt honesty is always refreshing, little

brother," Kuyan said, then added, "I was wondering if your new priestess had yet mentioned my generous offer?"

Honryn's lips thinned. "You mean how you want to become my priestess-queen and rule beside me? While Verdria becomes my…" He turned to Verdria suddenly. "What title did she bestow upon you again?"

"Breeding concubine, I believe were her words," Verdria supplied helpfully.

"Ah, yes." Honryn turned back to Kuyan. "Verdria as my breeding concubine and you as my priestess-queen."

Honryn fell silent, using the towel to brush sand from his skin. When he was finished, he looked back up at Princess Kuyan. "But you've made a great miscalculation in your plans, stepsister. Your destiny will never be to rule. You will have no great legacy."

He held out a hand to Verdria. She hesitated for a moment, but then she stepped up to him and placed her hand in his. His fingers closed around hers and he tugged her gently closer.

Verdria knew this was some of that 'play acting' he mentioned, but that didn't mean she liked this.

"Warrior-Priestess Verdria of High Rock is powerful and ruthless. Though not as powerful as me, she is stronger in magic than you, stepsister, or any full-blooded soul mage woman, and I have already chosen Verdria as my future Consort. My Priestess-Queen. We will birth a new line of hybrids with immense power."

"Naïve!" Princess Kuyan growled. "You may be powerful beyond measure, little brother, but you are not invincible. But with my alliance, you would have been as invincible as a mortal can come. And you spurn my offer for what? To elevate this great fire-headed horse of a woman to your near equal? You should have taken me up on my offer, at least that way you still could have begot your spawn upon her. Now she won't even remain yours."

She laughed when Honryn remained silent. "Or do you really think the emperor or our brothers will just allow you to keep her? No, father already has too many houses vying to marry a daughter to you. As for the new warrior-priestess," Kuyan drawled, giving Verdria a good once over, "our brothers have made it no secret that they, too, want a warrior-priestess as their plaything. Though they might change their minds once they see this horse. They'll certainly need a mounting block..."

"Go." The single word snapped in the air with power, energy rising like the sensation just before a great crack of lightening hits the ground.

Princess Kuyan twitched but held her ground.

Honryn ignored the reactions of those nearby and directed his next statement at the princess. "Announce that I'll arrive to dinner shortly with Verdria, my future priestess-queen, at my side. If I learn you haven't done exactly as I've said, I'll see you exiled to one of the outer colonies."

Honryn's stepsister jerked back like he'd slapped her, and her eyes narrowed dangerously. Clearly, she didn't like being dismissed, but she must have sensed she'd toed the line as much as she dared, because Princess Kuyan bowed and muttered low. "I shall carry your message to the gathered nobles."

With another bow, she left to carry out his command.

"Come with me, Priestess," Honryn said, his voice still cold and distant.

Verdria wasn't a fool. She knew his displeasure wasn't with her and she wasn't about to turn it toward her. Walking a step behind him, she followed him meekly from the practice ring and crossed the beach, heading back to the stair that would lead them back into the palace.

He didn't acknowledge her or his personal guard, who followed as closely as his shadow.

Verdria had become used to the silent, competent royal guards. They weren't chatty, nor particularly friendly, but they hadn't yet looked down upon her or whispered snide remarks. Certainly, none of them had called her a horse, at least not to her face.

Once they were within the corridors of the palace, Honryn signaled the royal guards to give them some space.

"Be careful of Kuyan. She has been testing me this last year and thinks she can push me further than I'll allow others. If she threatens you, tell me at once and I shall remind her that I am the one with the ultimate power. It's the only thing she understands or respects." He fell silent, his expression dark. "Just be careful of her."

Verdria glanced sidelong at him. "You should take your own advice. Me, she just wants to dominate. You, she wants to marry and fuck. That would be in whatever order you're willing to grant her wishes."

Honryn turned so swiftly, he nearly stumbled into a wall. When he'd recovered his balance, his expression was still locked in a grimace. Breath hissing between his lips, he said, "Don't ever mention that in the hearing range of the council. They might actually think it's a good idea."

He shuddered.

"Sorry. Just repeating what she said. She's got it all worked out. You as Priest-King, her as Empress, and me as your breeding concubine."

He grunted. "Kuyan hasn't tried to hide her ambition, but the rest is a newer development."

"You mean your pseudo sister hasn't tried to crawl into your bed before?"

"No. And until she mentioned it to you, I wasn't aware I was that large a part of her plans."

"Well, she was pretty clear about what she wants and she's willing to wet your dick to get the title."

"Stop," he said a little weakly. "Or you're going to see the Priest-King Elect wretch his guts out in front of you."

"In all seriousness, what she said about your father and older brothers, is that true? Will they fight you for me?" Verdria wasn't fishing for a compliment. This was serious information she needed for her immediate future. As much as she didn't want to play the part of Honryn's concubine or consort or whatever, she very much didn't want to live the part with one of his other male relatives.

She'd attempt to kill them first, of course, but seeing how powerful Honryn was, she feared the rest of the male line might also outclass her in magic.

His expression turned serious at Verdria's questions. "My brothers are both ambitious and no doubt they will try to take you from me or cause you harm in an attempt to harm me if they think I've come to care for you. However, they are no match for me in magical or political power, marshal training or cunning."

"The emperor?"

She glimpsed a slight hesitation before Honryn continued. "He's a more difficult obstacle. As things stand now, if I must fight him, it will be a battle against not just him, but my two older brothers. Not to mention half the Elite Royal guards." He turned to her then, his gaze intense but showing no fear. "But it likely will never come to that. My father is wise enough not to test me in this, not over a new warrior priestess. Allowing me to have my way will be far less costly to him than forcing my hand. And I gave you my word I would protect you. I will not dishonor my word."

Verdria halted, suddenly understanding she didn't have weeks to figure out an escape plan after all. She had days. Honryn might be powerful, but he was only one man. If she was still here when his extended family returned, Verdria's life was going to get very, very difficult, very quickly.

CHAPTER 20

Verdria

They returned to his chambers to freshen up and change before dinner. To Verdria's surprise, the royal seamstresses had already managed to put an outfit together for her without even measuring her. At first, she'd thought it must have been some strange magic, but then she discovered from Honryn that the seamstresses had merely borrowed her cleaned mountain gear before they'd been returned to her.

However, he need not have laughed so hard while he'd explained the more mundane methods they had used to get her various measurements.

Now, in a grumpy mood, she stood in front of Honryn as he looked over her outfit.

Verdria ran a nervous hand along the billowing fabric of her skirt. It was made of separate panels of a black fluttery fabric with silver stitching. The fabric was intentionally light and airy for the hot climate.

The top half of her outfit was made of the same airy fabric. Its design left her shoulders bare. The material pulled tight across her breasts where a large knot clenched it together but still allowed the remaining length to fall open naturally. The sides of the top were long and fluttered in the breeze, revealing glimpses of her midriff and sides. Tiny silver chains linked the front and back panels of the top, keeping it from flipping high in the air on the stronger gusts of wind, but still managing to leave her sides mostly bare.

Sandals of the same matching black and silver as her outfit laced up to her knees.

"That will do nicely," he muttered, a good bit of appreciation showing in his gaze.

His own outfit was a close fit to hers, just in a more masculine cut. Once again, he was wearing black pants that showcased his muscular form. His shirt was long, more like a tunic, but open down the front. Silver chains decorated the shoulders of the shirt, and a large silver medallion rested on his chest. His customary bracers had been replaced by fancier black and silver ones, but they still covered most of his forearms, hiding whatever rested beneath. He was never without them, so she concluded he was hiding something under them. In place of sandals, he was wearing knee-high heavy black boots with silver buckles running down them.

"I have boot envy," she told him as she took in his attire.

Honryn chuckled. "Fret not, I have put in an order for both practical and more fashionable shoes for you. Unfortunately, footwear takes longer than making adjustments to clothing already partly designed."

She nodded as her gaze reversed back up to his face, pausing only briefly at his chest and momentarily admiring his shirt's design that intentionally revealed more than it hid.

Strangely, seeing only part of his magnificent chest was more tantalizing than seeing it all at once. Which, she reflected with a scowl, was likely what the seam-stresses had planned and Verdria's wandering eyes had been all too happy to gaze upon.

"Since we're both appropriately prettied up, do we get to go eat now? I'm starved." She infused her tone with the needed degree of grumpiness.

He chuckled again. "Yes. Let us go."

She started to follow him toward the outer doors when he halted suddenly.

"Wait," he said, just as he pulled a small vial from his pants. "You'll want to apply this before we leave. The great hall isn't like being outside."

He thumbed open the small vial and poured a little bit of liquid out onto his palm. "If you don't want to lose your appetite, you're going to want to lose your sense of smell. I'm sure you've come to notice the unpleasant scent of the more powerful of the soul-mages. It's the odor of a soul's corruption. Only other magic wielders can smell it. And it will be much more noticeable in the hall than it was out on the beach. And tonight's dinner will have many of the most powerful Houses present."

Verdria knew what he was talking about. And she'd wondered more than once why he didn't carry the odor, but she hadn't asked and didn't want to tip him off that she'd already figured out something was different about his power. She was certain it had to do with his mixed heritage. Perhaps being the son of a moon priestess somehow offset the spiritual rot that set in from feeding on other souls?

"Most soul-mages and those living with them day to day are born without much sense of smell or swiftly become nose dead," he explained. As she watched, he took some of the liquid and dabbed it in each nostril.

When he made a face, she knew whatever the liquid was couldn't be pleasant.

"This will kill your sense of smell for a few hours."

She took the offered vial and then did as he had, seeing no point in postponing the unpleasantness.

The first inhalation burned out the inside of her

nose. She gasped and it continued on down her lungs. She wheezed and choked and sputtered, cursing him, the gods, and all three moons.

"I'm sorry," he muttered in apology as he thumped her on the back. "I should have warned you to breathe in through your mouth and out through your nose until the tingle subsides. Breathe like me."

She noticed that's what he was doing, but she'd been in too much of a hurry to follow his example.

"Bloody moons," she hissed as she attempted to follow his gestures and slowly managed to breathe in time with him until her lungs stopped burning and the spasming subsided. "Warn me next time you try to kill me. At least then it would be a fair fight."

"You'll thank me later. The herbal ointment is good for several hours. It will get you through tonight's dinner and the dancing afterward."

"I don't dance," she managed in a hoarse tone.

"Well, aren't we just a matched pair in every way?" He laughed at her expression. "I dance no more than I absolutely have to."

Verdria

The more she learned about Honryn, the more Verdria reflected he was nothing like she'd expected. She was actually coming to almost like him, she admitted. Almost.

But he's still a soul-mage, she scolded herself. *Just because he hasn't done anything to remind you of that fact in the last few hours doesn't mean he isn't the enemy.*

She was still mulling over her unsettling feelings when he at last led her into the great hall.

The large area was like no great hall she'd ever seen in her life. This was a great open-air structure. Arches lined each of the walls, allowing in the glorious sight of the still fading sunset.

The many arches also allowed in the cooler air of evening.

Since it was still hot enough to raise a sheen of sweat on her skin, she was grateful that she wasn't still wearing her heavier leathers and cotton and wool.

Honryn led her up to the front of the room where a raised dais waited. Upon it stood a long table of polished dark wood. Cups, goblets, pitchers, and platters covered its surface. A quick count showed settings for five.

His mother, twin, and older stepsister were already seated, leaving two seats in the middle. Honryn ushered Verdria up the dais and gestured her to take the seat next to his twin while he took the one next to his stepsister. Verdria didn't miss how he placed himself between his viperous stepsister and the rest of his family.

Princess Nadraya leaned forward and tapped her on the shoulder, interrupting Verdria's glower aimed at Kuyan. "I thought Honryn was going to make us all starve away to nothing before he decided to bless us with his company."

"It certainly wasn't me holding him up," Verdria said to the other woman. "I'm famished."

Princess Nadraya laughed in delight. "I think I already see what my twin likes about you. You're so refreshingly blunt compared to others. No one ever speaks their true thoughts around us."

"Then you can always come to me for a breath of fresh air," Verdria said with a hint of humor. She turned to Honryn. "And as I said earlier, I'm starving. You're treading close to becoming a poor host."

Princess Nadraya laughed in delight.

Verdria already knew she liked Honryn's twin sister much more than the older, almost-sister.

"If it will mean you two will stop bellyaching and give me peace for the immediate future, I'll have the servants begin serving the meal," Honryn said to them without glancing in their direction.

True to his word, he signaled the servants to begin the meal.

Verdria's gaze skipped over the servants carrying trays of food, and instead studied the nobles still milling in the center of the room, moving between the tables as they socialized. But even they didn't hold her interest for long.

She wasn't interested in the threats she could see. She was hunting for the ones hidden, noting the thick screen of palms and vines that grew along the walls. It was as if the outdoors had grown right into the hall. But upon closer inspection, she spotted the large urns and troughs.

The wildness was artfully created and also provided

the perfect places for hostile watchers to observe their targets.

Verdria scanned the walls and the hundreds of plants until she was confident no one hid within them, at least no one planning to stick a blade in her. Many of the guests wandered into the concealing greenery for private conversations, and maybe some other more intimate activities.

As she scanned for threats, she noted how the jewel bright parrots came and left on their own, the tamest of the large birds strutting down the long tables to steal whatever treat they wished.

If she'd been somewhere she could let her guard down, she would have smiled at the bold birds. As it was, she merely dismissed them as the one living creature in the room that likely wasn't a threat.

Servants carried food to the high table, serving Honryn first, and then her to Verdria's surprise, followed by his mother and then two sisters. Once the high table was served, more of the servant army moved through the hall below, bringing food to the close to three hundred nobles taking their seats.

One of the first things she noticed, now that she wasn't actively hunting for threats, was how very overdressed she was compared to the rest of the assembly.

Many of the nobles were only wearing scanty loincloths and beads to show off their tattooed bodies. And their soul crystals.

Hundreds of soul crystals were on display.

The sight sickened her.

She'd only seen her first soul crystal in the battle to take the ship.

At the time, she'd been too busy rescuing dragon eggs. Now she had time to think about the horror of the soul crystals. So many innocent souls trapped and enslaved, all to empower a soul mage to perform even greater feats of horror.

There were so many on display this night, she wondered where they had all come from.

She turned to Honryn for answers.

"The soul crystals… Has your empire conquered so many lands?" She kept her voice as calm and free of judgement as possible, knowing there would be many ears listening in on any conversation she had with the future priest-king.

After looking up from his meal, he gazed first at her and then out into the room, unseeing. At last, he spoke. "Some are very old, passed down through families for generations. Although many are newer, from prisoners and slaves and criminals who attempted to escape. Others come from shipwrecks and raids. Still others from duels between rival Houses."

"Winner takes the loser's soul? Lovely," Verdria muttered.

Honryn nodded. "There is also a merchant trade in soul crystals."

"How does that work?"

"When a family member is dying, they will sometimes contact a merchant's reaper to harvest their soul in order to give their loved ones a better life."

Verdria pushed her food away, no longer hungry.

Then another thought occurred to her.

"How many do you have?" she asked with growing horror.

Honryn sighed, his gaze seeking hers out. He looked into her eyes without flinching. "I possess far more soul crystals than most other members of the royal court or the richest of merchants. Only my uncle and the Temple possess a larger collection."

Verdria's hand dropped to the hilt of her dagger.

Even as she'd known she was starting to like the man, she'd been waiting to be reminded that he was the enemy. And here was that first harsh reminder. He was one of the monsters.

He continued like he didn't know she was thinking about stabbing her dagger into his heart. The only thing that stopped her was that she didn't know if she'd be able to take his head swiftly enough before the guards were upon her.

Soul mages were incredibly hard to kill, and to be certain of the kill, one had to take their head or burn their body to ash.

"Most of the...collection came to me as part of the priest-king elect's inheritance, passed down through the generations, grown in number by each new priest-king elect." He paused and looked away. "Yes, I have added to it. I have many rivals. The collection has grown by several dozen more soul crystals this day. The souls of the men who hurt you are now part of my collection. I feel no sorrow over their fates…"

His voice trailed off to silence a moment later, and he picked up his goblet and took a big drink.

Verdria was still horrified by his news about owning one of the largest collections of soul crystals long after the meal was finished and servants came to push aside the tables.

Even as music began to fill the air with a pretty melody, Verdria was still cold down to her soul.

Honryn seemed to sense her unease, for he cut their evening short and escorted her back to his chambers. He'd hovered at the threshold of her sleeping chamber, as if he wanted to say something, but she stepped farther into her bedchamber and then woodenly closed the door on Honryn's face without saying a word.

Then she stumbled to her bed and curled on her side, her fingers clenched around the shaft of her throwing axe.

CHAPTER 22

Verdria

*S*he'd survived her first day here in the heart of the enemies' territory. Now to see that she survived the second day, Verdria mused as she silently watched servants clear away the dishes and leftover food from the morning meal, seeming to make everything vanish in one trip. She marveled at their efficiency and then worried that the poor servants likely had to do everything with utmost efficiency and perfection to avoid punishment.

Verdria made another mental note to look into that later, but just now a different group of servants were approaching the high table bearing large clay pitchers glazed in bright floral patterns. She recognized a few of the flowers from her time in the garden before the incident with the snake. While Verdria was internally wincing about the snake and the fact she would have to face snakes again later this afternoon, the servants came forward and filled cups with the bright red liquid and a few pieces of ice.

Having come from the mountains where it was relatively cool even in summer, she hadn't understood at first why anyone would go to the trouble of making or harvesting ice to put into drinks. It seemed like a waste of time.

But after only one full day on this island with its relentless tropical humidity and heat, she was coming to understand the benefit of ice. She was actually tempted to shove some under her arms and between her breasts, but she didn't want to give Honryn something else to laugh at her about. Or worse, draw his attention to her breasts. She'd already caught him looking a time or two this morning already. While he might not be able to perform, that didn't mean it wouldn't enter his head to order her to touch herself while he watched for his enjoyment or…or…

Her imagination failed her at that point.

However, she did not need the complication of an amorous…or something…Honryn. He was still her most powerful ally and she'd hate to have to bust his balls and ruin their young alliance.

Beside her, Honryn stared off into space. On his other side, his mother and sister were having an animated conversation about some kind of soul mage spell, but Verdria could only follow some of what they said, the terms they used unfamiliar to her. But she'd learned that not all soul mage spells needed souls to power them.

She added learning all she could about soul mage magic to her mental list of things she needed to look into. If she had a chance to study their magic, she might be able to find weaknesses to exploit.

"What are you thinking, my Fierce One?"

"How to better destroy my enemies," she replied with cool honesty.

Honryn chuckled. "That is good. You'll need to harness every advantage when you face off against your future rivals." He leaned forward suddenly and whispered in her ear, his warm breath washing over her skin. "Though I think you were going to say 'soul mages' instead of 'enemies' at first."

Verdria turned her head to meet his eyes, and then said, "I don't differentiate between enemies. Makes things simpler. I like simple."

"I assure you there is nothing at all 'simple' or uncomplicated about the empire or its people. I'm the most complicated of all." He winked at her and then turned his attention back to his food and tossed the last slice of fruit into his mouth, chewing and swallowing swiftly.

"Come," he added as he pushed aside his plate, "we should be going. My uncle is expecting us later this morning and it isn't wise to keep the Priest- King waiting." Honryn stood then and offered his goodbyes to his mother and sister. Then he was striding down from the dais with Verdria once again his great big hulking shadow.

She'd learned upon waking that Honryn had contacted his uncle to update him on everything that had happened with a more in-depth account than the hasty report he'd sent earlier yesterday while Verdria had still been asleep after her healing.

With this new update, apparently his uncle had immediately ordered Honryn to create a portal so His Holiness could return to the capital swiftly.

Honryn had already obliged.

All that had happened while Verdria was still asleep and now His Holiness, the Priest-King of the entire empire, wanted to see Honryn and Verdria in person.

For his part, Honryn was as cool as ever, seemingly not concerned at all that his uncle wanted to meet the newest warrior-priestess.

Verdria held her silence so as not to betray her nervousness.

They continued walking until they had left the

palace for a rather fancy stables complete with dark polished wood and ornate torches.

As they crossed part of the city she'd never seen before, she attempted to memorize the roads, stores, fountains, and statues. But the task was made more difficult by the high-strung, hot-blooded giantess of a mare Verdria had been assigned. The beast was a lovely, dappled grey, but that's as far as Verdria's compliments went. The mare shied at every little shadow and perceived threat, both real and imagined.

"She's playing you," Honryn said after Verdria cursed at the horse for going sideways instead of forward.

"She's welcome to stop at any time," Verdria muttered.

"She'll make you a lovely partner once you two work out who's the leader."

"She's stubborn, you mean?"

"No. She's a free-thinking horse. That means she's intelligent, cunning even. She out thinks and out lasts most people."

"Great. As I said, she's stubborn. Couldn't you have given me a stupid, placid, and completely obedient horse?"

"There is no such thing."

Clearly, he'd never met a mountain pony.

Well, she mentally corrected herself, mountain ponies weren't stupid. They were loyal and steadfast mounts and Verdria would give up one of her axes to trade this nightmare of a mare for a mountain pony.

They eventually made it to the temple. Though Verdria still thought they would have made it there faster on foot.

"Was that so terrible?" Honryn asked as stablehands came forward to take the horses.

"Yes. That took twice as long as needed."

"Oh, stop being so grumpy. No one is perfect. You'll develop a connection with that fine mare one day."

"No, I won't. I'm walking back. There won't be a next time on that temperamental nightmare."

"As the lady commands." His words practically dripped with humor, and he placed one arm behind his back and dipped into an elegant little bow that was anything but gracious. And his accompanying smile?

Pure mischief.

After a moment more, the humorous glint in his eyes vanished and he sighed, pulling his deadly priest-king elect persona back around himself. "We shouldn't keep my uncle waiting."

Verdria nodded, but her thoughts were focused on the fact she missed the mischievous Honryn, even if it was an elaborate act to gain her trust.

And that was a personal flaw she would need to fix.

But she had another soul mage society obstacle to navigate first. Honryn's uncle. And going by what she'd learned so far, he was Honryn's direct superior. She didn't want to do anything that would lead his uncle to question Honryn's judgement in allowing Verdria to remain free from the normal controlling spells they used on magic wielding prisoners.

That meant she needed to be on her best behavior to prove to His Holiness that she understood her situation and was already loyal to Honryn.

Mistakes could not happen, which meant she needed to know as much as possible about what to expect inside the temple.

Another reason she hated her assigned horse. She'd wasted so much time fighting to keep the horse in a straight line that would have been better spent questioning Honryn about his uncle.

"How should I address him? Your uncle, I mean. And does one bow and how deep and for how long?"

Honryn paused where he had started up the long ramp that led up to the temple. Verdria noted the stairs to either side and briefly wondered why they weren't using those. Then decided it was likely because walking up a ramp was more difficult than stairs and the Serpent God probably enjoyed punishing his worshipers in the name of making them stronger.

"This will be an informal family meeting," Honryn explained. "As such, there will be no bowing or strict adherence to the social norms while meeting one of such power and position as my uncle. But still address him as Priest-King or His Holiness. The position always requires the candidate to surrender his name before ascending to the title."

"I understand. Still think it's horrible to have to surrender so much of oneself for a title. But got it. Keep it to Priest-King or His Holiness."

Honryn nodded. "Though he still likes for me to call him uncle in private. If you make a good impression on him, he might ask you to call him uncle as well. If so, go with it. It will strengthen your standing in the eyes of high priests and priestesses of the temple."

Verdria didn't get to ask why the Priest-King of all soul mages might want her to call him uncle. But they'd reached the top of the long ramp and three soul mage clerics were awaiting them.

An older priestess was flanked by two priests. All three were robed and hooded, but Verdria spotted some grey in the end of the braid that snaked out of her hood. And while she could see the priest's faces, nothing of their hair showed, but the skin of their hands was young looking, unblemished by wrinkles or age spots. But she couldn't guess their age going by the glimpses she'd seen of their faces. Not that Verdria was particularly good at judging a man's age anyway, since she'd seen so few in her life.

"Greetings, Priest-King Elect Honryn. We are to take you to His Holiness.

Honryn merely nodded and indicated for the three clerics to lead. "His Holiness is not still doing morning rituals in the altar room?"

"No," the priestess said, her tone giving nothing away that Verdria could detect. "His Holiness started the morning rituals early."

The priestess paused and then turned her head in Verdria's direction and added, "I believe he's eager to meet the new moon priestess. He has sent for refreshments in the sacred garden."

"Excellent," Honryn said, but Verdria thought she detected a slight hesitation. If they'd been alone, she would have asked if the change in routine was good or bad. There was nothing to it but to steel herself for either possibility. And she was relatively confident that her features were well schooled, and she was ready for anything.

As they walked into another lush tropical garden full of the songs of birds and insects, Verdria realized how wrong she was.

Snakes.

Her heart began to pound.

Snakes everywhere.

Bright jewel-coloured snakes curled on stones along the path.

Dark olive-green snakes hanging off the branches of tidy ornamental trees.

Large black snakes swimming in an ornate, stone-edged pond.

So many snakes everywhere.

Her breath came faster, attempting to keep up with her pounding heart.

Honryn grasped her hand and tugged her after the retreating form of the priestess and her two flanking priests.

Verdria realized she'd frozen in place, her fear having taken her over again. She held back a curse, squared her shoulders and nodded to Honryn.

"Stay close to me. I'll make sure none of the snakes can reach you. The center of the garden is an open sitting area. There are no trees at that spot. You need not fear having any unwelcome visitors drop down on you."

Verdria only had time to nod in understanding and then they were walking into a sunny garden surrounded by vine-draped trees.

A man with long, pure white hair and dressed in the most ornate, gem studded robes Verdria had ever seen turned at their approach.

He smiled and held his arms out in welcome.

"Honryn! It is always a delight to see you, my boy," he said in greeting, genuine pleasure glinting in his eyes, but his gaze quickly switched to Verdria. "However, I must confess to calling for this meeting for the sole purpose of meeting the female who has at last caught my favorite nephew's interest."

Honryn released Verdria's hand and stepped away from her, making room for the Priest-King.

His uncle took advantage by circling Verdria to study her from all angles. He poked and prodded at her, testing the flex and movement of her muscles while humming softly.

Verdria endured being looked over like a horse at an auction.

It could have been worse, Verdria supposed. He wasn't hurting her or leering at her with sexual interest.

He genuinely seemed interested in her musculature for some reason.

"She's a strong one, both physically and magically," he said at last.

After he stepped back, she felt a spell disintegrate and flow away. It was a subtle working, barely any power to it. Nor was it hostile in nature, which may have been the reason she'd missed him working it upon her.

"She'll easily win in a fair fight against any of your enemies."

Honryn snorted. "I'm not concerned about her ability to win a fair fight. It's the unfair ones that concern me."

"Wise," Honryn's uncle mused, his look growing

distant before sharpening again after a moment. "You should take her to the assassin's guild for training. They'll be better able to train her in what to expect."

The younger man nodded. "I had been planning a visit. I'm told they miss their training sessions with me."

The Priest-King suddenly leaned closer to Verdria until he was nearly nose to nose with her, his penetrating gaze attempting to look beyond her eyes and read her mind it seemed.

"Is it true you tore out Lord Nuran's throat with only your teeth while still being partly under Honryn's binding spell?"

"Yes. And I would do it again."

He laughed in delight at her bold tone.

He glanced away to take in Honryn with an amused look. "She's an absolute delight. And you haven't needed to spell her in any way?"

"She is delightful. And, no, I haven't had to force her compliance. My Fierce One is as intelligent as she is strong. She knows that her future will be a great deal less pleasant without my protection."

"And I've got eyes," Verdria barked out. "I've seen how you protect your mother and twin. And while I haven't met your 'Aunts' yet, your mother and sister both said you treat them just as well. You might be a mage, but you have some redeeming qualities. And that's not something I expected in a soul mage."

The priest-king arched a brow. "You're truly loyal to Honryn? Already?"

She had a suspicion His Holiness had woven another spell of the truth-sensing variety. Lying now would likely end badly for her. And she was a terrible liar. The blunt truth it was.

"You're getting ahead of yourself, your Holiness," she said, then to take the sting out of her words, added hastily, "I'm far from ready to fully trust any soul mage. Not even Honryn. But he's gained my respect, and I know he is a very powerful and worthy ally. I'll have his back for as long as he has mine. But as soon as I detect a hint that he plans on betraying me..." She let the threat hang there.

The Priest-King laughed boisterously and turned his attention back to Honryn. "You've picked well, my nephew. I had my doubts when I first heard the rumors, but she is delightful in her blunt honesty. You won't have to fear her stabbing you in the back some night. She'll come at you from the front, loudly announcing her intentions." He grinned again, the slight winkles around his lips and eyes deepening. But as swift as it had come, his humor fled, replaced by a calculating glint in his eyes.

Verdria was instantly on edge, but her magic didn't sense a threat emanating from the Priest-King, at least not one directed at her.

"Verdria shall receive the Serpent God's blessing,"

the Priest-King said, surprising not just Verdria, but Honryn too.

"That is…" Honryn cleared his throat, "Very generous."

"Indeed." More of that secret humor danced in the older man's eyes.

"You've seen something," Honryn said, drawing himself up. "Tell me."

His Holiness chuckled and then countered, "And are you already the priest-king?"

Honryn huffed. "No, of course not."

"Exactly. What secrets our God tells me are not my secrets to share."

While they talked, she focused on what was to come. She wasn't at all certain she wanted to receive the Priest-King's 'blessing'. Actually, she was pretty certain she did not want to undergo anything involving serpents—gods or otherwise. But going by the intense looks Honryn was aiming at her, this was required and since she was not yet ready to attempt to battle her way free, and likely die in the attempt, she would just have to endure this 'blessing' from her goddess's enemy.

She wasn't sure what to expect, but as the Priest-King began a soft chant in a language she didn't know, a soft grey power, one that reminded her of mist, rose up from the ground.

She battled with her instincts and forced herself to remain still. Honryn had gained her trust by not using magic to enslave her, so she was trusting him, and he seemed to trust his uncle.

Honryn's uncle circled her as he continued to chant, his words spoken in a monotone. He circled her twice more, the mist rising to her waist and then to her shoulders.

Verdria kept her expression blank as she battled a rising urge to strike out, but one glance at Honryn and his subsequent shake of his head and a silently mouthed 'easy' reminded her she wasn't ready to start a war with the second most powerful soul mage in the empire.

The chanting stopped and the mist suddenly swirled around her the exact number of times the Priest-King had.

Creepy.

Then Honryn's uncle stepped away, the mists disintegrating into nothing. "There, that should give you an added layer of magical protection. I'm not so arrogant to pretend my spells are equal to my nephew's power, but a second layer of protection never hurts."

"Thank you, your Holiness," Honryn said, then bowed deeply to his uncle. Verdria swiftly murmured her thanks and copied Honryn's deep bow.

The Priest-King laughed. "It was not entirely a self-less act." Then he directed his next words at Honryn. "I wish to aid in the shaping of our blood line in whatever way I can. You and your priestess will breed strong sons and daughters to inherit both the title of Priest-King and Emperor or Empress."

"May the Great Serpent make it so," Honryn murmured in a ritualized, lilting tone and bowed swiftly to his uncle again.

Verdria wasn't about to enlighten uncle dearest that she was barren. She'd need to keep that hidden. While Honryn might keep her secret if he found out, no other soul mage would. Then the position and protection that came with being the Priest-King Elect's chosen mate would vanish as soon as the truth was discovered.

Honryn's uncle gave him a solid clap on the shoulder. "I look forward to watching your warrior-priestess navigate her way through the court. She's going to leave a glorious number of corpses behind. I can feel it."

Verdria kept her lips firmly sealed, utterly baffled how she should respond to his obvious pleasure at the idea.

What kind of kingdom enjoyed watching their own people get murdered?

Honryn merely grinned. "I must admit, I'm looking forward to watching my Fierce One navigate the court and put my enemies in their place."

"As would I, were I younger and in your position," the Priest-King said and then turned to Verdria. "And as to my earlier comment about leaving corpses behind, I'll shed no tears if you start with Honryn's two older brothers. And that venomous stepsister of his."

Verdria's mouth gaped as she scrambled to understand the older man's thinking, but Honryn came to her rescue since his uncle was already walking away. "He just gave you his blessing to kill my two older brothers and is also offering you the protection of the Temple." Honryn fell silent for a moment, seeming to think upon something, then said, "I had not expected him to do either of those things."

Verdria's mind was still spinning, going over various reasons for him to wish to see two of his nephews dead and what he could gain by it, but she didn't know enough to come to any conclusions other than it might be a trap.

"Why would he say such a thing about his own nephews?"

"Revenge."

Verdria stared harder at Honryn until he explained.

"As the Priest-King, it is deemed below his station to partake in the various political blood sports common in the court. A Priest-King is only supposed to react to threats or slights directed at his person, the wisdom of the holy temples, or the Great Serpent. My uncle had three daughters and a son. My older brother had all four of them murdered because they were a threat to his ascension to the throne once our sire is dead. And the second oldest helped him. As for my uncle's children, the youngest was a child of five. The oldest was thirteen."

Cold horror wrapped her chest in tight bands.

"Moons," she breathed at last.

"Indeed," Honryn agreed. "And because none of his children were old enough to be ordained as a priest or priestess yet, they didn't fall under the protection of the holy temple. A loophole my brother used to accomplish his plans with no punishment. My uncle could do nothing without breaking the ancient rules and starting a civil war. My father would not have stood by and done nothing while his brother killed his two sons."

"That's certainly a reason for your uncle to hate your brothers."

"Yes," Honryn agreed, then added, "I loved my little cousins and would have challenged my brothers, but I was still young when it happened, still growing into my powers. My uncle stopped me. He didn't want to lose another boy he viewed as a son. And there was my sister, mother, and aunts to worry about. If I was killed, they would lose my protection."

"That's..." Verdria found herself speechless and enraged once again.

"Terrible?" Honryn supplied.

"Yes. I can't even comprehend not taking revenge, no matter the rules of the temple."

"Oh, my uncle planned his revenge the very day he discovered what my brothers had done."

"You are his revenge," Verdria said in sudden understanding.

"Yes. And a most willing tool in this case. He also plans for my twin to play a part. But the advantageous time he's waiting for has not yet come. Now things have changed with your arrival. I have a new, powerful ally in you."

He gave her a little bow. "One blessed by the Great Serpent. As my future mate, with the full support of the Priest-King and the temple, that gives you a great deal of political protection. It's complicated and I'll explain it in more detail later, but you can act without fear of punishment. It would be seen as you are honoring my uncle and the Great Serpent God. Weakness is not permitted to inherit the throne. If you are able to kill my two older brothers, then they were too weak. But I do not expect you to fight my battles for me. I have already instilled fear in my brothers by my other actions. They know I have no love of them or of tradition. I've intentionally made myself into a wild and terrible force within the court. You will not need to kill my brothers to secure your place at my side." He grinned suddenly. "However, don't be surprised should you hear rumors that you are my personal assassin who dispatches my enemies for me."

"What if I want to kill them for you?"

He hummed, "Their heads *would* make a lovely wedding gift." Then he said in a voice so low it was almost a purr, "Now I must think of a gift to you that would bring you as great a joy."

Verdria laughed as she caressed the handles of her axes. "Now you're flirting with me again, Pretty One."

"Perhaps a little," he said before his tone turned serious once again. "But never doubt, there is no family more bloodthirsty anywhere under the three moons than mine."

"I would expect as much from the top level of leadership within the land of the Soul Mages."

But I just never expected one such as you, Verdria thought to herself.

CHAPTER 23

Verdria

*O*nce again Verdria found herself following Honryn through the maze-like corridors. If not as docile as a lamb, as close as she could come. Though this time, it wasn't a projection of her mediocre acting skills. This eagerness to follow him was real.

She didn't want to do anything that might cause Honryn to change his mind about meeting his 'Aunts.' Or at least the two women expected to arrive in the city today. Ahead, the corridor they were following ended in a large archway and beyond that she could see the lush greens of tropical foliage and the jewel bright splash of colourful flowers.

Soon they exited what she thought may have been the servants' quarters and walked into another manicured, though more subdued, stretch of gardens compared to the riot of colors and streams and stonework she'd seen last time. Just as they left the cool shade of the building, the sound of soft giggling followed them. She turned back and glanced down the corridor and spotted two servant girls darting into a side room.

When she arched a brow at Honryn, he explained. "It's not every day they see a new warrior-priestess walking the halls of their home."

Honryn's words confirmed they were indeed traipsing through the servants' quarters.

"They're not used to seeing red-haired ogres?" Verdria quipped.

Honryn rolled his eyes. "You with that again? The truth is that rumor of you, and my plans for you, has already spread throughout the empire. The servants merely wanted to get a look at you. Don't fear the servants spreading news I don't want spread. They are loyal to me. There will be no whispers of our meeting or this training session with my aunts."

"You're so certain the servants are loyal?"

"Yes." His one-word answer was so certain it left no room for questions. Besides, she could hear other voices drifting through the greenery from somewhere deeper in the garden. She left the mystery of Honryn and the loyal servants until later. There had to be more to it. Honryn was not one she'd peg as the trusting type. If he'd somehow enslaved the servants to ensure their loyalty, Verdria would find out.

She didn't want to believe Honryn would bespell some innocent, but she'd only known him a few short days.

The sound of arguing voices coming closer, drew Verdria from her worries.

"Just what are you hags bickering about this time?" Honryn shouted to be heard over the voices and the distance.

Two enraged squawks came from the same direction as the earlier sounds of arguing, followed by rapidly stomping footsteps.

"I hear a lippy young male who needs his bum swatted," growled an older, red-haired woman as she stormed up to Honryn. "Bickering hags indeed!"

"Sondrena," Honryn said with a laugh and held out his arms wide.

The newcomer took him in a swift hug—a punishingly strong one to go by Honryn's wheezing grunt. After a few thumps on his back, the tall woman shoved Honryn off to the side hard enough to make him stumble, and then she turned to Verdria.

Her steps stumbled.

Verdria froze as well, studying the tall redhead. Hair the same red as Verdria's. That shade of red, while not confined to her House, was most common to Verdria's own home fortress.

She noted the newcomer was tall and strongly built. But that wasn't what held Verdria frozen. It was the older woman's eyes. The green was almost an exact shade as her mother's eyes. And that long face. That shape of jaw. Even her nose and mouth had the same familiar curves and angles.

The older woman cleared her throat, finding her voice first. "Child, from what House do you hail?"

"High Rock."

She nodded, then asked, "Your mother's name?"

"Sondria," Verdria answered, and then asked her own question. "Honryn called you Sondrena. What year were you born?"

But Verdria was certain she already knew. She had watched her mother place gifts on the family altar each year on the anniversary of her older sibling's death."

"I will have seen fifty-three cycles around the sun this coming year."

"My mother thought her sister died in an avalanche." Verdria's voice was soft in her shock, but she already knew that while Sondrena and her hunting party might have been caught in an avalanche, they had not died there.

This woman was her mother's older sister. Her aunt.

An aunt she'd thought died before she'd been born. Moons. Verdria didn't know what to think. Or what to feel.

So much had happened in the last day.

Sondrena, unaware of Verdria's swirling emotions, just shook her head and said, "I didn't die in the avalanche. A few of my fellow huntresses survived as well. In the early days I had wished we had all died in that avalanche, but Fate had other plans. We were rescued," Sondrena said, bitterness colouring her words. "Rescued by Soul Mages."

Honryn glanced between them. "I had a suspicion you and Verdria were family. The resemblance is there."

Sondrena turned on Honryn and did something a warrior-priestess would never do to a mountain man. She punched him, catching him in the shoulder, holding nothing back.

"You! You mischievous little whelp!" She punched him a second time and Honryn darted out of her reach. "You should have told me!"

He danced a few steps farther away from Sondrena. "I didn't want to get anyone's hopes up and have them crushed later if I was mistaken. You were born of the same House certainly, but I couldn't be sure how close the blood relation might prove to be."

Sondrena glowered at Honryn before turning her attention back to Verdria and grinning. "He just likes his little mysteries. You'll get used his secrets. He really is a sweet boy under all that calculation and cunning."

Verdria turned to glower at Honryn and noticed another woman now standing behind Honryn. Verdria gave him another glower. "We'll talk more about not telling me that your 'aunt' was actually my aunt, and she's been alive all these years and I didn't even know it!"

"I suspected the connection since you arrived, but as I said, I wasn't certain, so it's not like I've been keeping a secret from you for years."

She grunted, still unhappy, but let it rest for now.

From what she'd asked her mother over the years, she knew Sondrena was a superb Huntress, skilled in various magics and a master of the hunt. Certainly, good enough to become one of the mothers, had House High Rock had any available males at the time, but pickings had been slim, so Sondrena had moved to a new fortress closer to centaur territory where she'd hoped to be able to capture and tame herself a husband. Clearly it had not turned out like that.

But Verdria had another warrior-priestess to meet and glanced at the other newcomer.

It made sense that if all or some of Honryn's aunts were captured at the same time, they were likely also from Sondrena's adopted house of Winter Reach. The same House as Jardeen.

Sondrena placed a hand on Verdria's shoulder. "I

can almost see what you are thinking. A few of my fortress sisters survived. This is Arannia, our Leader."

"No one ever asked me if I wanted to be our leader," the woman said with a shake of her head that made her mop of blonde curls bounce.

But her tone wasn't angry or upset, so clearly, she'd settled into her role as leader.

Verdria took in Arannia's appearance, a woman of medium build with a pale complexion and pleasant expression, she seemed nice enough, like she'd be open and easy to talk to, but Verdria didn't see what it was about her that made her leadership material.

But then again, Verdria hadn't even known her for an hour yet.

"So," Arannia said with a little frown, "Honryn's letter said you had a snake phobia. He didn't go into details, only saying that between the lot of us, we should have enough time and skills to help you get past this fear."

Sondrena interrupted Arannia. "Or at least control your responses so you don't reveal your terror to anyone with a pair of eyes and a brain."

Arannia speared the older redhead with a sharp look and Sondrena snapped her teeth together and fell silent.

Then the blonde beamed at the taller woman before turning back to Verdria.

"Good. Let's get started," Arannia said and looked

around, scanning the trees. "Honryn, where did your big pets slither off to now? They're usually somewhere close when you're in the gardens."

Verdria's spine straightened, and her hands went to her axe handles.

"Easy," Sondrena said. "Arannia is just testing you. She wanted to see how you react to just the mention of snakes." Sondrena leveled a glower at her fellow warrior-priestess. "Great way to build trust with my niece, Leader."

Arannia looked a touch embarrassed. "It was the quickest way to discover the level of her fear. I won't do anything to trick you again, Verdria."

Verdria grunted in acknowledgement, but she would not take her at her word.

"Honryn," Arannia called him over, "I think we'll start with just letting her watch you play with your snake. We'll see how she does with that and go from there."

"Watch me play with my snake?" Honryn managed to say between laughter and gasps. He snorted a few more times.

"Well," Sondrena began, a smirk on her lips, "I see Honryn needs a lot of practice at flirting. You're never going to get to bed Verdria at this rate."

Honryn sputtered out something else as he tripped over his tongue in his haste. Either that or he was gripped by a brain fever.

Though the shade of red he was turning was rather entertaining, Verdria thought.

Sondrena grinned evilly. "Yeah, I still haven't forgotten that little 'bickering hags' remark. You might be too old for me to take you over my knee, but I'll get you back in other ways, Your Holiness."

Honryn, the scariest Soul Mage in the entire empire, winced. "Come on," he pleaded. "It was a jest meant in good humor."

"Hmm. Not sure if I care," Sondrena barked back.

Honryn groaned again but seemed to rally. "Fine. I await my punishment, but don't we have more important items to attend to at the moment?" He tipped his head in Verdria's direction.

"He has a point," Arannia said. "You'll have to wait to get back at Honryn later."

With that, Arannia began directing events, with Honryn and Sondrena acting as her underlings.

THE AFTERNOON GREW HOTTER AS EVENING APPROACHED. Halfway through the afternoon, Honryn stripped out of his long black robes, leaving him in sandals and a long loincloth. If it wasn't for the snake crawling all over Honryn's sweat-slicked body, Verdria might have enjoyed the view. But the snake kept moving, jarring

Verdria out of any enjoyment she managed to eke out of this cursed plan of his.

"I think that's enough for today," Arannia shouted from where she'd been sitting on a garden bench, calling out orders.

"Yeah. Honryn must have had his fill of playing with his snake for today," Sondrena drawled.

Honryn chuckled at his aunt's words, but he directed his next comment at Verdria. "Come. We'll head back to our chambers to wash up before dinner."

Thankfully, before he approached her, Honryn released the snake and sent him up a tree to hunt or rest or do other snakish things. Verdria didn't care as long as the snake did it far from her.

Before Honryn had said his goodbyes to his aunts, he'd invited them to dine with him, but they both gave rather weak excuses and left Verdria in Honryn's company.

"Why do I have the feeling I was just intentionally abandoned by your aunts as part of some plan they've set into motion?"

Honryn only shrugged.

She frowned at him until he huffed out a laugh and held his hands up in surrender. "I fear my aunts are in matchmaking mode."

"Matchmaking? Haven't you already basically announced to the realm that I'm going to be your consort or priestess-queen? Or whatever? How much more matchmaking is needed?"

"They are well meaning, and I love them," Honryn explained as he walked with his arms behind his back and head down, studying the path. "But my aunts can also be a great pain in my ass. I imagine they see us as a potential love match and want to give us more time alone together to see if feelings… bloom."

"They're in for a long wait. I didn't come here to flirt with a half-blood soul mage."

Honryn chuckled. "Are you sure about that? I remember our first meeting was rather like flirting."

"Only so I could get closer to try to take your head."

"And here I was trying to save yours." He swung an arm around her shoulder and urged her back into motion. She tensed for a moment but forced herself to relax as Honryn continued the conversation in an amused tone. "We can discuss the finer point of a bloodthirsty flirtation over food. I'm starved."

Verdria was hungry, but her mind had trouble focusing on anything other than the sensation of Honryn's body pressed close to hers. His warmth, his scent, the soft caress of his skin against hers left her feeling off-balanced once again.

As they made their way back into the palace compound, Verdria battled the urge to curl her right arm around his waist. Of course, that led to wondering what that lovely muscular ass of his would feel like if she brushed her palm across it. Accidentally, of course.

Even the arrival of his Elite guards, as they materialized around them from the shadows where they'd been hiding along the walls of the building, wasn't enough to distract her from Honryn's overwhelming presence filling all her senses.

A moment later, Verdria mentally scolded herself. *'Don't be foolish. Lusting after a soul mage will only distract me from my goal.'*

CHAPTER 24

Verdria

The return to Honryn's chambers was uneventful. There were the customary complaints from the captain of his guard, begging for Honryn to see reason and allow a dozen Elite guards to protect him while he slept, since he was still sharing his suite with an enemy warrior-priestess. But as usual, Honryn waved off his captain's concerns, much to the older woman's frustrations.

Once alone inside his chambers, Honryn gestured her forward, deeper into his private domain. They crossed the main chamber, bypassing her bedroom and the large, shared bathing room, and soon entered a room she'd seen only briefly before. They were in Honryn's bedchamber.

"I want to show you something."

"In your bedchamber?" she asked with suspicion thick in her voice.

Honryn huffed. "I didn't think that out very well. What I meant is I want to show you my tower. This is the closest entrance. There's another out by the glass door that leads out into the gardens, and another just off my study, but this is the closest."

Honryn went to the far wall of his bed chamber and pulled a tapestry to the side, revealing the stone of the wall.

"Here. See?" He gestured at the wall, counting six stones down from the ceiling and ten from the east corner of the room. When she nodded, he summoned his magic until a little bit of velvet darkness flowed between his fingers and then he drew one long digit in an intricate pattern along the stone.

"Your battle magic will work just as well, but in case one of my enemies ever found this, there needs to be evidence of a soul mage's magic, not just power gifted by the Moon Goddess."

Her breath froze in her lungs.

Did he mean he could summon her people's magic?

She knew he was half of the mountains, but he'd never shown a hint of that power in her presence. But would he? He hadn't known her long enough to trust her with all his dangerous secrets.

A slight hum from the stone drew her attention back to what Honryn was doing. A moment later a flash of magic rippled across the stone and suddenly the entire section of wall shifted back. Honryn stepped into the darkness and took a torch from the wall. A snap of his fingers lit it and then he was gesturing her forward into the secret passage.

She hesitated only a moment, weighing the danger of going into a darkened tunnel with the Priest-King Elect of the Soul-Mages, but then decided he'd had lots of opportunities to harm her and hadn't. He probably wasn't about to start this evening after a long day of trying to cure her phobia.

He also hadn't hidden the spell from her sight, and she'd carefully watched, mimicking the pattern of the spell by drawing it against her thigh with one finger. She'd need to find a way to test it, but she thought she had it memorized.

"Are you coming?"

As usual, he'd put a minor challenge in his voice that spurred her into motion and she stepped to his side so he could draw the pattern a second time, triggering the wall to shift back into place.

Verdria stood at the bottom of the tower, looking up at the twin white stone stairways that spiralled up level by level, and whistled.

"When you said 'tower', I wasn't picturing something almost the size of one of our mountain fortresses. And this is all for just your use?"

"Yes. It used to be for storage. There are hundreds of rooms contained inside."

She studied the structure, squinting to see the very top. The soft blue-white glow of magic flickering in the sconces lining the stairs didn't provide enough light to see all the way to the top. Either that or the ones at the top two-thirds of the tower hadn't yet lit.

"How far up are you taking me?"

"The very top."

"You going to toss me from the battlements?"

"No." He rolled his eyes at her.

"That's a lot of stairs," she said with a huff of laughter. "I might want you to put me out of my misery by the time we get to the top."

"Moons," Honryn uttered, and then chuckled. His use of one of her people's swear words caught her attention, but he either didn't catch her look or ignored it and clarified, "I never walk the entire way. Not even when I'm most stressed and need a physical outlet for my emotions."

Now it was her turn to roll her eyes at him. "What? You just fly to the top?"

"In a matter of speaking."

She swallowed back her laughter, looking first at him and then up the stairs. Surely, he couldn't actually fly?

Seeing her look, he burst out laughing. "I know what you're thinking and no, I can't fly. But this is the next best thing to it."

He gestured at a large disc imbedded in the floor. If she was to hedge a guess, she'd say the stone disc on the floor was the same type as the stairs. But unlike the unadorned stairs, the disc had runes carved around the edge, circling the entire circumference.

A spell, she realized. A very powerful and complex one. Still dormant, though. She wondered what it did.

But just then, with a flick of his wrist, he sent a small thread of magic racing toward the disc. When it connected with the nearest rune, the spells engraved in the stone ignited with a soft glow. One after another, the runes all along the disc's edge burst to life, the spell waking.

Was she seeing how he created his portals?

But once the glowing circle of runes was complete, the disc began to rise, and she realized her guess was far off the mark.

The disc was floating!

"Not as impressive as it might have been for me to sprout wings and fly—a power I don't possess, by the way—but I am rather proud of this spell. It's one I came up with all by myself when I was only a youth and had recently put my brothers out of this floor of the palace." He gestured up at the vast tower. "It was partly because I wanted the tower for a place to protect all my secrets. Booting my brothers out of their chambers was only a bonus. Did I mention I turned into a bit of a destructive force during my adolescent years?"

"You've changed?" Verdria mused, remembering back to how he had killed half a roomful of mages without a speck of remorse when he found them beating her.

"I'm more refined now. Less flash and posturing and empty threats. I just get straight to the point now."

"Except when you have some secret up in your mighty tower that you want to show me but won't tell me what it is, yes?"

He tucked his hands behind his back, gave her a little half bow, and then strode toward the floating disc. "As my aunts would say, I do love my little mysteries. Are you coming?"

He didn't tell her more, and she didn't want to reveal her curiosity, but she also wanted to discover what it was he wanted to show her. Hesitantly, she followed at his heels until he half turned and motioned for her to step up onto the floating disc.

"Under no moon am I getting up on that thing until I see you do it first. I'm giving you the benefit of the doubt, Mage. But I'm not an absolute fool."

He merely laughed and then stepped up onto the disc. It didn't tilt under his weight, not so much as a little dip. When she still hesitated, he added, "It would hardly be useful if the rider had to maintain perfect balance or get dumped off. I assure you it won't rock under your weight."

"Fine," she barked out, purposely stomping harder than normal as she joined him. But as promised, it didn't so much as quiver under her added weight. With another flick of his wrist, the runes glowed slightly brighter, and then the disc was rising smoothly and swiftly, carrying its passengers faster than they could ever walk up the steps.

For a moment, the strangest sensation assaulted her stomach, and she braced her arms against her abdomen and glowered at Honryn.

"I'm sorry," he said, and turned his hand the least little bit, somehow slowing the disc's rate of ascent. "It's a little disconcerting the first few times."

Verdria only gave him a sharp nod and braced her legs farther apart. Even though her head said they were standing on a solid surface, her body disagreed.

Honryn didn't comment further, likely sensing he wasn't her favorite person at the moment.

As they rose higher, they passed many landings with great ironbound doors, but he didn't so much as cast a look at them as they continued their ascent.

Just when she thought the tower might be endless,

they reached the top landing. The disc came to a halt, and her stomach and body tried telling her she was still moving upward for a moment. With a grumble, she stormed past Honryn when he waved her to disembark. Once he'd joined her on the landing, he waved a hand at the door in front of them. Black magic rippled in the air directly above the door's surface. It stilled a moment later, and the door swung inward. She didn't know what it said about her that she was swiftly becoming used to seeing the black magic of the mages. Even though she'd never seen Honryn draw upon a soul crystal to power it, it was still a clear reminder that he was a soul mage.

And she just…what?

Was okay with that?

No. She very much wasn't okay with soul mages or being here in this empire, but Honryn wasn't… completely bad. She could see more and more glimpses that he was a good man. Or would have been a good man if he'd been born anywhere but this land.

"Come," he said after the heavy door swung open under its own power. Self-opening doors had grown less strange each time she saw them, too.

As for what was on the other side of the door, she wasn't sure what she expected, but a large open-air room with its twelve carved stone arches holding up the ceiling wasn't it. Taking a few steps toward the arch directly ahead, she looked out beyond the stone balustrade with its balusters carved with a motif of beautiful flowering vines and crescent moons. Beyond that was the midnight sky, its velvet darkness broken by hundreds of stars shining in the moonless expanse.

None of the three moons were out yet, it being too early, and the sky was breathtaking.

Behind her, she sensed Honryn approaching. When he came alongside, he handed her a goblet of cool fruit juice.

"Where did you magic that up from?"

"From cold storage," he said and pointed behind him.

She looked back and saw an alcove housing a large stone box with glowing runes etched into the sides.

When he walked back over and opened the hinged front of the box, her brows arched. Inside was enough food to feed a person for a week.

"The spells keep the food cold and preserve it until I might find myself in need of time by myself and enough food that I don't have to go face the court or my Elites for a day or more."

"And your guards must love that," she muttered with a good bit of sarcasm.

"Actually, my Elites love it. They know the tower is impenetrable and when I lock myself in alone, it's like a rest day for them."

"And your uncle, sire, brothers, and the rest of the court?"

"Hate it," he said with a laugh. "But they know I'm working on my projects, and everyone besides my uncle is too afraid to make an issue of my occasional disappearance for fear they will become my next personal project. There's a rumor that some of my enemies get an up-close and personal look at my tower and various secret projects before becoming a project and vanishing forever."

"Good reason to leave the priest-king elect alone," she agreed as she sipped at her drink. If he'd been going to harm her, he'd had plenty of time to do so already, so she doubted she was about to become one of his projects. Eyeing some of the food in the storage container, she took a step toward it and then stopped and glanced at Honryn.

"Go on," he said. "Eat however much you like. And if you need to relieve yourself at any point, there's a small chamber beside the entrance." He pointed toward a smaller door beside the heavier, ironbound one. "When you have what you want, come join me on the western facing side of the tower."

With that, he turned and vanished around the central curving wall that must act as a support. She knew nothing about engineering, only knowing it took an impressive feat to keep a structure like this standing against the workings of time and the environment.

She hesitated only a moment and then grabbed a plate with what looked like sweet treats upon it, and the pitcher of the cool fruit juice in case they wished to refill their drinks. With her prizes balanced in her arms, she hurried after him to find out what secret he wanted to show her.

He hadn't gone far.

A wide, low bench sat facing the ocean. Honryn was there, one leg propped up on the bench, while he reclined with his back braced against one of the seat's curved and padded armrests.

"Come sit with me," he said and then took a sip out of his own drink. "Enjoy the beauty of the night, my Fierce One."

"You can stop with the terms of endearment. We're alone. There's no one to hear." At least she didn't think so.

He shrugged. "It's become habit. As for this place, as I said, this is where I come when I wish to be alone. Though my mother, twin, and aunts also have access and visit regularly in secret. You are welcome to come here whenever you like." He nodded to the panorama of the night sky all around them. "This view always brings me peace, to look out at the stars and think how free they are, traveling their own paths out there. Powerful and eternal. Or, at least, eternal as a mortal might view such things. Though it is theorized that stars are born and do die, just on a grand scale that our mortal minds can barely comprehend."

Verdria scowled out at the stars. They were as

eternal as the moons and the ground this tower sat upon. Where did he get such a strange notion that stars died?

Soul mages. So odd.

She gave her head a shake and stood and looked out over the tall railing and down into the brightly lit city below. She couldn't deny that the great island city was pretty by day or night.

It was lovely and yet steeped in the evillest of taints.

She cast a glance over her shoulder at him to find him watching her, his dark eyes unreadable in the dim light of the softly glowing sconces. She looked back out over the view, beyond the city, toward the ocean and the star filled sky.

Perhaps that was why he liked it up here. It was as far from the taint as he could get and still be within this city.

Her eyes narrowed thoughtfully. Was he befriending her for the same reason? She was as far from the rest of the corruption that clung to all the other soul mages as it was possible to be.

Did the Priest-King Elect of the Soul Mages crave purity to offset the horrors he lived daily?

That fit with her theory that he was actually a good man, twisted into something darker, trapped in an impossible situation.

That was a horrible thought. To be half of her own

people and yet also be their greatest enemies. Did he battle his dual natures?

If so, she hoped his Moon Goddess heritage always won out over his soul mage side, that it kept him from tipping over some internal precipice and descending into something wholly evil.

Eventually she tired of standing and looking out over the city and walked over to his bench and stared down at him in silence for long moments. When he merely smiled at her, she huffed.

"What was it you wanted to show me? It has to be more than the view?"

Knowing how much he liked his little mysteries, she was certain there was something more than the view, beautiful though it was.

"I thought you would have sniffed it out already," he said with an amused chuckle, then turned his head and jerked his chin to a slightly more shadowy section.

Her gaze followed the direction of his. She froze, her mouth dropping open in shock. Then she bolted forward, covering the distance in a few long strides before skidding to a halt in front of an altar. Three statues sat upon the altar, their feminine figures elegant, their arms raised above their heads, holding aloft spheres that represented the three sister moons.

Here in the heart of the Serpent God's unholy empire was an altar to Verdria's Moon Goddess, the three statues representing her three phases—Maiden, Mother and Wisewoman.

She touched the three statues reverently, her magic rising within her, responding to the closeness of her goddess's altar. She scanned the long stone slab with its edges carved in a motif of the three moons in their various phases. Running a finger along the carvings, she marveled at the workmanship.

Sitting upon the altar were all the other bits one would need to perform any of the usual rituals. Bowls, incense, oils to anoint the statues, candles, herbs, mortar and pestle, and even a long, sharp knife for slicing up ingredients or drawing a few drops of blood.

And most surprising of all, the bowls, candle holders and mortar and pestle all looked well used. This wasn't some decoration Honryn had installed in his tower. This was a living altar. She could sense every item was steeped in the Moon Goddess's power.

"Honryn?"

He walked up beside her and ran a finger along the altar, his touch loving. "I made all this with my own hands for my mother and aunts shortly after I acquired the tower. I tried to make everything as accurate as possible, piecing the design together over a two-year period from things my mother and aunts had mentioned. I kept it secret until it was ready and then surprised them with it." He paused and picked up a stick of incense. "Out of all of it, these little devils were the hardest to recreate. The plants that grow here are not the same as what grows in your mountainous homeland, but after a lot of trial and error, my mother and aunts all agree this is very close to the sacred incense commonly burned at the Moon Goddess's altars."

Verdria took it from his hand and inhaled deeply. It wasn't an exact match, but it was close enough to bring on a wave of homesickness.

"It's very close," she agreed, her voice hoarse with emotion. "Thank you for doing this for your mother and aunts. May I…"

She gestured at the altar.

"Of course. It's why I brought you here. I wanted you to be able to worship your goddess. My mother and aunts gather and perform the great rites here. They will welcome you into their circle."

"Thank you. If you don't mind, I'd like to take a moment." She gestured at the altar.

"Of course." He nodded toward the bench he'd recently vacated. "I'll wait there. Take as long as you like."

CHAPTER 25

Verdria

A quarter hour later, she finished up at the moon altar. She padded over to Honryn where he was reclining on the bench. He glanced up at her when she reached his side. They both were silent for a moment, as if acknowledging that he'd just looked the other way while she prayed to an enemy goddess. His actions would be deemed treasonous if any of the other soul mages learned of it. He'd endangered his position and standing—his very life—by creating the Moon Goddess's altar and was now compounding that treason by allowing them to worship at it.

"Honryn," she started and then faltered, swallowing

hard. "This altar and the gift of my free will are two things I'll never be able to repay. Thank you."

He nodded wordlessly and then shifted his leg aside, making room for her wordlessly. She settled next to him. The bench forced her close enough she could feel his body heat, but she soon relaxed.

As if sensing her awkwardness, he broke the tension by holding out the plate of sweet treats she'd snatched from the storage container earlier. When she didn't immediately take it, he gave it a little jiggle. "I saved half for you. Sweets are my weakness. You're lucky I left you half."

She laughed and took the plate, selecting one of the little cakes made of a soft creamy cheese sweetened with honey and topped with a fruit sauce. It was one of her favorite treats.

Eating in silence, she cast a sidelong glance at him. He wasn't paying attention to her. Instead of looking out into the night sky, his unfocused gaze suggested his mind was somewhere far off.

"Would you leave this place if you could?" she found herself asking.

He blinked, coming back to himself but remained silent for so long, she thought he wasn't going to answer, but at last he sighed and then words fell almost reluctantly from his lips. "Your word you will never repeat what I say to another living soul?"

"You have my word."

"Then… yes," he said simply.

She thought that was the end of it until he continued. "Yes, I would leave this place, this prison, if I was ever given the chance. I would trade all my power, all my position, simply to be a good man." His jaw flexed and he looked down into his hands. "But I have never, and will never, have that opportunity. So, my role has turned me into a man of darkness and power."

Not knowing how to respond to that, she held her silence and then reached out her hand, offering him contact, a lifeline to another living soul not yet corrupted by this place of beauty and wickedness.

From the corner of her eye, she saw when his head tilted to look down at her offered hand. There was a slight hesitation, and then he took her hand and closed his fingers around it.

Sighing like a great weight had been lifted from his shoulders, he turned to study her profile while she looked out at the night sky.

"Thank you," he whispered and then tugged her hand up to his lips and pressed a kiss to her fingers.

With his free hand, he reached out and cupped her cheek. A look of intense longing crossed his face, and then his hand moved from her cheek to cup the back of her head. Was he going to kiss her?

Confused as to his plans, she stiffened.

He must have picked up the new tension in her muscles, for he loosened his hold and brought his other hand up to rest one on either side of her head, and then he brought their foreheads together. After a moment, his hands slid from her head and down her shoulders to capture both her hands.

"I'm sorry. I seem to have forgotten myself." He sighed and leaned back. "All I can say in my defense is that you remind me of what I cannot have, no matter how much I might want it."

She'd seen his looks of hunger before, but this was the first time she'd seen tenderness, a deep longing. Was he touch starved? She thought he might be. His position and his condition setting him apart.

What a pair they made. A barren warrior-priestess in possession of near unparalleled battle magic from one of the most powerful lines with no hope of passing that power on to the next generation, and an even more powerful impotent priest-king elect.

The more she thought about it, the more curious she grew about his condition. Clearly the mages had healing magic that far surpassed her people's. But whatever ailed Honryn had to be something beyond his or any healer's ability to fix.

He said nothing, nor did he press for more from her after that aborted kiss, though she was starting to think he wanted more. His body just couldn't provide it.

And that probably was a mortal wound to his male pride and also further alienated him from others, intensifying the loneliness his position as future priest-king must force upon him.

Not for the first time, Verdria felt pity for Honryn even though he was a soul mage, one of her sworn enemies. And while she certainly wouldn't have willingly bedded him, even if he'd been capable of getting a cockstand, that didn't mean she couldn't give him some other simple solace, one human to another.

There was also the fact she wanted to further gain his trust, to better enable her to survive this place so that she could one day escape and tell the elders all she'd learned about the soul-mages and their home.

And sometimes situations just called for a simple act of kindness.

Decision made—be it foolish or not—she shifted closer to him and curled her arm around his waist before leaning against his chest, using one of his pectoral muscles as a pillow.

"Don't take this the wrong way," she muttered, "but it's getting cold and I'm tired. If you plan to keep me up here with you, the least you could do is help keep me warm."

It was mostly a lie. She wasn't cold, but the ocean breeze was blowing cooler than it had all day, and she might grow chilled… eventually.

"We can't have that," Honryn said, his voice nothing more than a rumble in her ear.

A moment later, muscular arms encircled her and

Verdria decided being held in strong male arms wasn't bad at all. She relaxed farther and simply enjoyed breathing in his scent.

After a time, his hands started running up and down her back rhythmically. It was almost like being petted.

She'd never been petted in her life.

Normally she'd be inclined to punch someone for taking such liberties, but she'd started this and Honryn's hands were otherwise well mannered, never dipping below her waist, so she just closed her eyes.

And if there was a silly grin on her face, no one was around to see it.

CHAPTER 26

Honryn

She'd fallen asleep against his side. His Fierce One had surrendered to sleep while in his arms. When he'd brought her up to his secret place of solitude, he'd never dreamed she'd curl up against him and fall asleep. He'd deemed it a great win just for having her sit willingly on the same bench with him. Then she'd reached out a hand, an offering of friendship and companionship, one lonely soul to another.

But this?

The trust she was showing him was humbling.

Goddess of the Moon! He wanted to kiss his

warrior-priestess. Nearly had kissed her earlier, but realized it was a terrible idea.

His body, already semi-hard for her, stirred to full rampant life at the thought of kissing her, of feeling her hard muscles and feminine curves pressed into him.

His body's reaction didn't come as a surprise. It was always eager for her.

Normally he had to pretend to be a healthy young male, just as lustful as the next. The irony was that as a youth, he'd never been interested in any of the soul mages. And while many a pretty young servant would have willingly bedded him, he never approached them because of his position. He'd learned that with his first lover, an older trusted servant. Still, his oldest brother had learned of it and Honryn had only barely rescued her in time.

Anyone close to him was in danger, was a target for his brothers' bloodthirsty schemes.

But Verdria was to be his consort, and she was not a helpless victim. With his aid, she would become very powerful indeed.

And he wanted her. Both sides of his magics coveted her. Their mating would be superb. But it was impossible. The universe's great jest. Verdria thought he couldn't get a cockstand when, in fact, he had two very potent cocks. Worse, she was terrified of snakes. And once a month, when the moons abandoned the sky, he shifted to become half snake.

He could never let Verdria meet the lustful, raging monster he turned into on that night. No one could see that. In those times he was a danger to everyone, be they loved ones or enemies. It didn't matter. They were all prey. And even if he could control it, Verdria was terrified of snakes. She'd run from him and never look back. Or he would traumatize her beyond her ability to heal.

Grunting in frustration, he shifted himself farther down on the bench until he was reclining more comfortably with Verdria asleep in his arms. With his head resting on the padded armrest, he looked up at the carved ceiling with its night vine and moon motif.

He inhaled a deep breath of her scent and nuzzled her hair.

Verdria hadn't stirred awake while he'd shifted himself into a more comfortable position. She must be a heavy sleeper.

Grinning, he pressed a kiss to the top of her head. "Sleep well, my Fierce One. I'll keep you safe and warm this night, and any others you will allow me this same glorious privilege."

He shifted again, attempting to relieve the pressure of her thigh pressing against his groin. Which probably wouldn't normally be an issue except that his primary shaft was hard and aching for her and his secondary was even now prodding at his seam as it sought freedom to expand. The persistent throb refused to abate.

But he'd stab himself in the leg before shifting out from under her completely. It felt too good to have her cuddled against him, her soft damp breath washing over his chest.

She shifted in her sleep. One of her hands splayed open across his abdomen, then moved lower. It was nothing more than an innocent twitch in her sleep, but his overeager body had other ideas and his members strained harder for freedom.

"Fuck."

Muttering other curses, he spread his legs slightly farther apart.

It still didn't help.

"Verdria, are you still awake?" He was certain she wasn't, but he wanted to check first before dealing with the persistent problem that showed no signs of going away.

He gave her a little shake, but she still didn't wake.

Goddess bless heavy sleepers, he thought with a grin as he pushed aside his robe and unlaced his loincloth.

Then, just as he was reaching to free his aching members and give them some much needed attention, Verdria shifted. Her one leg curling over his calves and her entire weight shifted until she was resting with more of her body on top of him.

A position he would have enjoyed immensely if they'd both already been naked. But as it was, his members were now firmly trapped under the weight of her hips and two layers of clothing. There was no way to free himself without pushing her to one side, which might wake her.

And there was no way he wanted her to wake up. If she did, she'd likely move away, and he very much wanted to hold her in his arms for a while longer. As long as she'd allow. All night if he could manage such a feat.

"Fine," he muttered and pressed another kiss to the top of her head. "Apparently I shall not be indulging in the deviant behaviour of jerking off my two cocks and marking you with a double load of my seed this night, my Fierce One."

With a huff, he relaxed back against the bench and looked up at the ceiling once more. Besides, what was a case of blue balls compared to being able to hold his Fierce One in his arms for the first time?

A GENTLE SHAKING OF HER SHOULDER WOKE VERDRIA. She blinked in confusion for a moment, but two things became apparent. It was dawn. And she'd spent the night sleeping on top of Honryn.

Oh Goddess. She'd only meant to give him a little comfort, not turn him into her pillow. A very nice pillow, she admitted. And then noticed the fingers of her right hand were splayed low on his abdomen, as if she'd been stealing caresses in her sleep.

Could it get any more embarrassing?

She'd only meant to give him some comfort. He'd seemed so lonely. But somehow, she'd ended up falling asleep with him on that narrow, uncomfortable bench.

"As much as I'm enjoying holding you, my Fierce One, I really need to piss," he said with a chuckle.

"I'm so sorry." Verdria was sure her traitorous cheeks were a bright fiery red and she wouldn't look at him.

Once she'd freed him from under her weight, he vanished into the small side chamber for a couple of minutes before returning. She shuffled into the chamber and attended to her own needs.

Then together they stepped upon the disc and slowly dropped many floors until they were once again in his chambers. An awkward silence stretched between them until they both vanished into their bedrooms to freshen up for the day.

Cleary neither of them were morning people, Verdria mused. Either that, or Honryn didn't want to talk about the night before. They'd both let down barriers and she didn't think that had been his plan and now he was likely uncomfortable with all she knew about him.

Well?

So was she.

But she damned well better work on getting all her barriers back into place because she'd get eaten alive in the mage's court otherwise.

CHAPTER 27

Verdria

*V*erdria had seen little of Honryn all day. His uncle had summoned him for some kind of priest-king training shortly after dawn. As a result, Verdria ended up spending much of the day locked in his chambers. He'd left food for her, so it wasn't like she'd been locked in the dungeons to rot, but still. She couldn't learn anything of use if she was trapped inside these walls, lovely walls that they were. And it was boring. She'd have to convince him to allow her to accompany him. Maybe if she used the 'future consort' angle, saying she needed to learn about his duties, he'd allow her to join him.

When the outer door cracked open, Verdria looked up from polishing her axes. Honryn entered, his long stride carrying him across the chamber to her side.

"You're taking me with you next time," she snapped out as he was opening his mouth to say something.

"And good day to you too." He arched a brow at her, and then his lips tilted up at one side in that mischievous way she couldn't resist. And just like that, her angry frown eased, her brows relaxing and the hard line of her mouth softening.

"Sorry. I don't do well with nothing to do." She grimaced, knowing she had sounded whiny.

"And I owe you an apology. Had I known my uncle was going to keep me for so long, I would have left you in the company of my mother, sister, and aunts."

Verdria gave his words a curt nod, eager to leave and do something—anything really—as long as she got to escape these walls for a time. "Where to next? Practice?"

"Ah… yes. It will be practice of a sort. But what we need to practice next is better done in private," Honryn paused and cleared his throat. "There is an upcoming feast, one that we can't avoid."

It was Verdria's turn to hesitate. As much as she wanted to escape, a feast in the great hall, surrounded by full-fledged soul mages, was not what she'd had planned. She'd been hoping for a walk in the gardens or along one of the beaches. Any sort of outdoor activities that would allow her to study the infrastructure and find weaknesses she might be able to use as an escape route, or even just good places to spy from. At this point, she'd even settle for more phobia training if it got her outside.

But then she clued into Honryn's nervousness, which raised her curiosity and her own unease.

"I will not like this 'practice' overly much, will I?"

"I think that depends on my skills. Either you will really like it…. or not, if I'm as rusty as I fear."

She arched an eyebrow at him, doing her best to keep her face neutral.

"You will be required to sit by my side," he started.

Now she was just confused.

"That doesn't sound like some kind of terrible trial." Then, with growing suspicion, she asked, "Will I be wedged in next to some other powerful soul mage?"

"No. But it will be a formal feast, where we'll be on full display."

It didn't sound like she'd get many opportunities to map out the palace and the surrounding city today.

Unaware of her thoughts, Honryn continued with his halting, one-sided conversation.

"Our formal feasts often devolve into less… formal activities as the night advances and drink flows. We'll need to appear to… er…"

"To appear what?" she asked, her suspicions growing.

"We'll need to appear familiar with each other. At least to some degree. Like I said, after the formal feast there will be much drinking and dancing. And other more intimate things…"

Verdria jerked her head in his direction, his words finally sinking in. "You mean… you and I are expected to… to… In public?"

"Fuck in public?" Honryn supplied, his face giving nothing away, which suggested he wasn't any more comfortable with the conversation than she was, but she was too focused on what he'd just revealed.

"Yes," she agreed, proud her voice was almost as neutral as she was working to keep her face. "That."

"No. I don't have a reputation for exhibition, obviously." He gestured down at his groin. Not that she could see so much as an outline of anything since he was wearing his robes, but she got the idea. "So, it won't seem strange if we don't partake of the usual late-night activities in public. But others will watch us closely. They will expect us to be familiar with each other's bodies by this time. We will need to show some affection or intimacy toward each other, or at least not seem like we're completely unfamiliar with each other. Because I've led everyone to believe that you are enjoying my body regularly as part of our agreement."

Verdria frowned at him, not hiding her anger about that. "I can't believe that's the best you could come up with. 'Taming' me with your sexy body. They'll all think

I'm a spineless… an absolutely spineless—" Words failed her.

Honryn shrugged. "It worked. And they likely think I'm weaving some subtle spell over you when we're intimate."

She grunted in response.

"I need to start by asking you a few awkward questions," he said almost apologetically. "So, I'll know what we have to work on."

Her suspicions continued to grow, but she was curious as well. Honryn was referring about a practice session in being intimate, in some ways at least. And she wouldn't lie to herself and pretend she wasn't interested in Honryn in that way. He was beautiful to look upon. And it sounded like he wanted them to practice…

What?

Touching each other?

She found that far more titillating than she probably should.

"Go on. Ask your questions."

"I assume since you were still a scout or border guard, you have not yet begun your training to become one of the mothers of your people?"

"No."

"So, you've never had a male lover."

"No."

"A female lover?" Honryn asked and then rushed on. "I swear I'll not be judgemental. I know it is a common enough arrangement with so few men. Even here, with a balanced population, we have an abundance of same-sex partners."

"None," Verdria said, then added, "I'm not against it. I've just never been attracted to my own gender."

"Fair enough." Honryn cleared his throat. "Not even kissing?"

Verdria shrugged. "Three different times. Didn't like it."

"All right, at least I know." Then under his breath, she heard him mumble 'no pressure' so softly she was certain she wasn't meant to hear.

He cleared his throat again, a nervous gesture. "Well, at the minimum, we have to get used to touching each other. Can't have you jerking away in startlement every time I brush up against you."

She snorted. "I fell asleep on you. I'd say that I'm pretty comfortable with touching you at this point."

"We are talking about an entirely different sort of touching." But he seemed prepared to go ahead with his plans anyway because he gestured her forward. "Let's sit."

She allowed him to lead her to another of the long, padded bench-like seats that seemed to be all the fashion here. Though, at least this one had a back and was very comfortable. She'd already spent a good amount of time on it, lazing around earlier, leafing through some books she'd found in Honryn's private library. She couldn't read the language yet, but there were illustrations. From what she'd gathered it had been a book about farming, of all things.

But as Honryn guided her to the seat and urged her down next to him, her thoughts about farming were swiftly forgotten.

She could feel his body heat from how close he sat, the short bench forcing a kind of intimacy before they were even touching. To her utter and absolute surprise, her traitorous fingers didn't care that he was half soul mage. They itched to reach out and touch him, but she was also feeling suddenly shy and so very big and awkward, like if she allowed herself to reach out and touch him, she might get carried away and knock him clear off the end of the bench in her eagerness or do something else equally stupid.

But not one to allow her fears and uncertainties to rule her, she squared her shoulders.

"This isn't a battle, my Fierce One," he murmured softly, and he reached out and touched the back of one hand as he leaned closer.

Moons. He smelled so good. Screwing up her nerve, she reached out and touched him in return, her hand coming to rest against his shoulder. The material of his robe stopped her from feeling the softness of his skin, but somehow that made her want to explore him all the more. She wanted to push the robe off his shoulders, slowly bare him to her gaze.

So, she did exactly that, gently pushing the robe off both his shoulders and allowing it to pool around his waist. He inhaled sharply but didn't do or say anything to stop her. But she'd clearly surprised him. Liking his reaction, she continued to be the aggressor and pressed her hands to his flesh.

He was so warm, his skin silky under her fingers, like he'd never been exposed to a bitter winter wind, or a harsh cold air so dry it was even devoid of ice crystals.

Confidence growing, she trailed a featherlight touch over his shoulder and down his bicep until she could curl her fingers around his. Then, with a gentle tug, she guided that hand onto her cloth-covered thigh.

That was all the encouragement Honryn needed. He slid his fingers up her thigh, circling around to caress her hip as he continued to his destination, his hand soon coming to curve around her back. Once there, his fingers skated back and forth along the waist of her skirt before stroking up her spine until their progress was hindered by the glorified scarf that criss-crossed her chest and pretended to be a top. His other hand joined the first and now both thumbs traced up her sides. Her breath hitched and her skin broke out in goosebumps as the delicate hairs on her arms stood at attention.

The light caress of his fingers along her spine made her body thrum and her breath hitch.

Leaning closer, he crowded her and slid his other

hand higher, up under her top at the back to continue his teasing along her spine. Eventually, he had to reverse and stroke his way back down. She'd never imagined it could feel so good just to have someone stroke her, but he didn't stop there and dipped his head down to rub his face against the side of her neck.

His breath was hot against her skin and little shivers of pleasure raced down her body. When his lips brushed against her skin and the tip of his tongue licked a path down the side of her neck, she groaned. Her nipples hardened as if he had been playing with them and they hadn't even been touched yet.

Groaning low in the back of her throat a second time, she tipped her head back to give him better access. She instinctively pulled him closer, one hand buried in his thick hair, as if to hold him in place. Though, by the way he was holding her tight, his hands roaming her back and sides, he didn't seem interested in pulling away.

His kisses along her neck became more heated, and he groaned, his exploring hands stroking lower until he cupped her ass and dragged her closer. He wanted her in his lap, and at the moment, that sounded like a splendid idea, Verdria decided. Besides, this was a training session, and they both needed the practice so they didn't betray their lack of intimate knowledge of each other at the festival.

Decision made, she crawled into his lap, settling

with her knees to either side of his hips. Even clothed, she liked the feel of his heat and warmth trapped between her thighs, though it left her feeling off balance and vulnerable at the same time.

And that was a weakness and Verdria hated weakness, so she shifted her knees farther apart and lowered herself until there was no space between them and all she could feel was Honryn, the warmth of his body and hard muscles.

He groaned in her ear and nipped her earlobe. "This escalated quickly."

"Too much?" she asked even as she admitted she loved how husky and deep his voice had turned.

"No," he groaned, even as his lips continued to worship her skin, kissing in a downward path toward her cleavage. "This is perfect."

This was what a man in need sounded like, Verdria mused.

Another part of her consciousness warned that this couldn't be allowed to go farther, that her reactions were from the effects of going without her hormone suppressing tea.

But that didn't lessen her enjoyment of hearing the cool, collected Honryn come undone for her. Some wicked part of her wanted to keep pushing. It wasn't wise, it wasn't safe, and it certainly wasn't rational.

Spurred by a renewed sense of bravery, she trailed her fingers down his chest, stroking the twitching muscles of his abdomen in gentle caresses as she worked her way lower.

Her stomach fluttering with nerves, she halted, and that seemed to unleash something in Honryn. His hands abandoned her sides to capture her face and then his lips were crushing down on hers.

Lips parting, she gasped, and he took advantage, his tongue darting out and then he was invading her mouth. He tilted his head more, seeking a better angle to ravage her mouth, then his hands were buried in her hair.

Verdria's eyelids fluttered close, the darkness allowing her to focus on the sensations his body was drawing from hers. Foreign sensations, but divine.

She pressed her chest to his, rubbing her heavy breasts against him, wanting to know what it felt like to be skin to skin with him, but there were too many layers of clothing between them.

His deep moan suggested he thought the same thing. Their lips mimicked what was denied to their lower bodies. Honryn kissed her like he was trying to devour her, his tongue urgently thrusting against hers. His hands left her hair, and she protested that loss against his lips, but a moment later his hands landed on her hips, gripping hard as he urged hers into motion.

With a gasp, she broke the kiss, burying her face against his shoulder, and she clung to him and melted.

"Moons!" she groaned out the curse even as she

wrapped her arms around his neck and rocked against the thick bulge she felt trapped against her core.

"Hmmm," Honryn uttered and then his large, long-fingered hands left her hips to slide up her torso and cup her breasts. "I like the sound of your cursing, my Fierce One. I want to hear more of it."

Then he began fondling her, cupping and squeezing and teasing her nipples until her breasts were more sensitive than she'd thought possible. Her core clenched, empty and heavy with an indescribable need. She took it as a challenge and wanted—no needed—to get him burning as brightly for her touch as he'd made her burn for his.

Her hips rocked more firmly against him, partly to release the aching tension building within her and partly to inflame him. It worked, drawing a desperate groan from him.

"Verdria… I think this is enough…"

She ground against him, and his words morphed into a moan before he continued, "enough practice for this…"

He panted against her neck before he managed to finish his sentence.

"For this session."

He wrapped his arms around her and pressed her firmly against his chest, trapping her, but that didn't stop the rocking of her hips, so he grasped them instead, locking them together.

But she enjoyed the feel of him under her too much to stop just yet and returned to kissing him, wooing him with her lips even as her right hand slid under his robe and cupped the bulge inside his loincloth. He twitched and gasped at her exploring touch. Even soft, he was almost too generous for her fingers to fit around, and the loincloth hampered her, so she settled for listening to the deep, throaty sounds he made as she palmed him, her fingers tracing over his impressive length. Such a shame that he couldn't perform, but Verdria decided she still enjoyed the feel of Honryn very much.

"Goddess! Verdria s-stop," Honryn stammered, his back arching and the tendons of his neck standing out.

She released him, uncertain if she'd hurt him. "Honryn, I'm sorry."

But then he turned and bucked sharply.

Caught off guard, Verdria rolled off him, coming to sprawl against the other end of the padded seat.

By the time she'd leaped to her feet, Honryn was already standing with his back to her, stiff and unmoving except for his rapid panting breaths.

"I'm sorry," he murmured and then retreated to the bathing chamber, walking with a stiff-legged gait. The door slammed behind him.

As she stood staring after him, her lust beginning to cool, her brain started to work again, and she didn't like what it was telling her. She blushed furiously and stared down at the floor.

Had she really just tried to seduce Honryn—a soul mage?

A touch-starved, impotent man. She'd all but slapped him in the face with the reminder of what he could no longer enjoy. Males were prideful creatures. No man liked to be reminded of his shortcomings and a man unable to get a cockstand would see that as his greatest shortcoming.

Verdria hung her head in shame. She hadn't meant to be cruel to him, but that didn't change what she'd just done to him when he'd been nothing but kind to her. Even if the training session had been his idea, he couldn't have expected her to practically try to ravage him.

"Good going, Verdria," she muttered, doing her best to ignore the throb between her legs.

Even if he wasn't her greatest ally, she still wouldn't leave things as they were. She needed to apologize and somehow ease whatever embarrassment and emotional pain he must be feeling now.

With new determination, she started toward their bathing chamber.

HONRYN ARCHED HIS BACK AS HE GRIPPED HIS TWO cocks, holding the bases in a futile attempt to prolong the glorious sensations as he saw again in his mind's eye what Verdria had looked like in the throes of passion, her head and shoulders tilted back, her breasts thrust forward into his hands, her hips rocking against his.

The damned suppressant tea he'd drank earlier had been no match for the lust that had roared through his blood at seeing his Fierce One lost in her passion.

He groaned and began shuttling his hands along his cocks, twisting and squeezing just how he liked, but imagining it was Verdria's long, strong fingers wrapped around his members. His hips snapped forward sharply, driving his aching cocks into his fists, his copious amounts of pre-cum acting as all the lubricant he needed.

So close. His back arched again, and a soft groan slipped between his lips.

So close now.

"Honryn." Verdria's hesitant voice called through the door.

He clamped his fists around the base of each cock, praying she'd give him just a few moments more if he didn't respond.

"Honryn. I'm sorry. I didn't mean to get so carried away." She fell silent, and he felt a little thump against the door.

His magic told him she was pressed against the other side. He couldn't be sure, but he thought she stood with her forehead resting against the door, her shoulders slumped. She was ashamed and upset at how she'd reacted. At least that's what he could read from her soul.

How *she'd* acted?

How could she blame herself. It had been his idea.

And he'd been the one close to losing control and unleashing that part of him no one should ever see, that dark beast sleeping in his soul,

"Honryn, I didn't mean to remind you about… that. I never would have intentionally humiliated you… or anything."

Oh. Right, she thought his problem was because he couldn't get a cockstand. He gave both of his cocks a hard stroke. There was something stirring and deviant about listening to her talk to him through a door while he was on the edge of spilling a double load of his seed all over the floor. His toes flexed, hips snapping forward again as his eyes nearly rolled back in his head. His ball sacks twitched and drew up.

"Honryn, please talk to me," she called and then fell silent, listening. "Honryn, I came to apologize, but now I'm getting worried. If you don't answer me, I'm going to assume something bad happened, that you're unconscious on the floor, and I'm going to break this door down."

Honryn gave a mental curse while gripping the base of both cocks harder.

Leave it up to his warrior-woman to make an awkward situation even more embarrassing. He dropped his chin to his chest and muttered.

"I'm fine." Then, in a louder voice, "You have nothing to be sorry for. My issues are my own."

"But my thoughtless actions made it worse." Guilt was clear in her voice.

"Oh, my Fierce One. I very much enjoyed what we were doing. I just..." What could he say without revealing that he'd been lying to her?

"I was on the edge of losing control," he said, going for a partial truth. "My power. I'm dangerous to others when I'm like this."

"I didn't... I didn't cause you..." He could feel her searching for the right words. "Emotional distress by my—"

"No, Verdria. Yes, we got carried away. But I assure you, I liked it. Very much. I'm just sorry I couldn't give you... more. But I did like it. So much so, you made me nearly lose control."

There was a long pause and then her voice came again, softer. "I nearly made you lose control of your magic, eh?"

"Yes," he said with a shaky chuckle as he stroked himself.

"My Pretty One, I enjoyed making you lose control."

Her voice came low and husky, reaching through the door as if to wrap around his cocks. The climax he'd been fighting rolled over him, his cocks jerking with the force of his balls emptying themselves of every drop of seed. Only clamping his teeth together kept his shout from escaping.

"I liked watching you come undone for me." At her words, he gave himself another stroke and a soft moan hissed past his lips. And he decided, she'd probably have liked watching him make the mess all over the floor he'd now have to clean up.

"Verdria," he called through the door.

"Yes?"

"I liked coming undone for you."

"Hmm," she purred. "I'm glad."

He chuckled again. "I'll be out soon. I almost have my magic back under control and we can talk more about what will be expected during the feast and after. But compared to what we just did, anything we might need to do at the festival will be much tamer."

"That's good, Mage," Verdria called through the door, her voice low and husky and wicked sounding again, "Because I don't like the idea of you coming undone where others can see."

Honryn's cocks gave another half-hearted twitch as more seed splattered the floor.

CHAPTER 28

Verdria

$\mathcal{H}$onryn had not lied about the festival. It was early still and already half the nobles were drunk by what she could see. Verdria avoided anything alcoholic and only nibbled at her food, not really hungry but also not wanting to reveal the depth of her unease to the surrounding soul mages. One benefit with being so focused on the other soul mages, she didn't have time to go over and over what she and Honryn had done earlier. She could barely look at him without her cheeks going up in flames. And she was still deeply ashamed of how easily she'd gotten lost in her hunger for Honryn, a soul mage. But that was a less dangerous problem to deal with later.

Now she had a part to play and if she didn't play it well, it might be her doom. Hence, she pretended interest in her food while studying the soul mages and their servants. One thing she'd been quick to pick up was that not every human within the palace was what she'd label as a soul mage.

Which came as a surprise. She'd assumed everyone in the soul mage kingdom was one of those morally and spiritually corrupt individuals. But there were far more nuances in this place than she'd been expecting.

That bothered her.

For one thing, the young children she'd glimpsed over the last day and a half seemed just as innocent and precious as the few born to her people each year. Somehow, she'd never thought about soul mage children.

But there were many to be seen here. Even in the great hall.

She watched as children wove their way among the older servants, carrying drinks and dishes of food from the kitchens. Verdria craned her neck and attempted to watch them for as long as she could until they vanished from the hall again, using some kind of servants' entrance. Soon, another youngling would emerge from that side door, carrying another dish.

Her instincts shouted that she should be watching for danger, not watching the children, mesmerized by their sheer numbers, by their healthy, glowing skin and bright eyes.

"I should have remembered that you likely haven't seen so many children in your entire life as you've seen tonight in this hall," Honryn mused, his gaze having followed hers.

He glanced over his shoulder and gestured to where several Elites stood behind them, half hidden in the foliage of tall palms and tree ferns. But it wasn't an Elite he was summoning forward.

"Renan, isn't it?" Honryn asked as a young boy with beautiful dark eyes and curly black hair approached them and prostrated himself on the floor. Verdria nearly choked to death on her food, seeing the boy—who couldn't be more than seven or eight summers old—cower before Honryn.

For his part, Honryn frowned at the boy's bowed head. "This is an informal setting. I hardly think such formality is necessary in this situation, young one. Please stand."

The boy swiftly scrambled to his feet but wouldn't look up at Honryn.

The priest-king elect merely smiled and then reached out to ruffle the boy's hair, startling the youth.

"I'll let you in on a secret," Honryn said in his deep, calming voice. "I have never harmed an innocent. And certainly never a member of my House. And moreover, if anyone picks a fight with one of my House, they've picked a fight with me. I *am* rather protective of my people." He patted the boy on the shoulder. "I assure you Renan, as a member of my House, you have nothing to fear from me."

Renan glanced up, uncertainty morphing into adoration as he shyly met Honryn's gaze. Verdria saw then that the boy hadn't been cowering. He was in awe of the priest-king elect.

"And as I understand it, you were the newest member of my household until Verdria arrived. Now that she has joined us, she holds that title. Perhaps you can help her settle in? Show her around? Give her a tour of the palace grounds? Keep her company when I am busy?"

The boy was speechless for long moments. But after vigorously bobbing his head and swallowing hard, he blurted out, "Of course, Your Holiness." Then added so swiftly he nearly ran the words together. "You honor me greatly."

Honryn laughed. "You might change your mind once Verdria sinks her claws into you. She'll likely have you trained up to be a powerful warrior in a few months."

The boy's mouth fell open and then he glanced at Verdria for the first time, his eyes widening when they gazed at the width of her shoulders and her muscular arms.

"Though," Honryn mused, his tone turning thoughtful, "perhaps you are too young to start a warrior's training just yet." Now his gaze snapped to Verdria, amusement dancing in his eyes. "Perhaps I have a better use for you. Verdria doesn't know the first thing about being a mother, and I don't know the first thing about being a father. Maybe we should adopt you and you could teach us how to be good parents?"

Adopt the boy?

The silence at the table and surrounding hall was so intense, Verdria's ears twitched. Shock ruled for several more moments and Honryn continued like he didn't care that the entire hall was straining to hear every word.

"Yes," he said, thumping the boy on the shoulder again. "You could help us learn some parenting skills before Verdria and I have little ones."

"Babies?" She might have sat there frozen in shock for half the evening if Honryn hadn't snapped her out of her shock by laughing at her expression.

"We don't spring forth from the ground. We start out as babies," he said between chuckles. "We're human, same as you."

'No,' she thought, *not the same as the rest of humanity.*'

But as she gazed on in shock at Renan, she could see that he was a perfectly healthy boy. It only stood to reason that soul mages started out as humans. At least until they started practicing tainted magic that twisted their souls into a new and corrupt form of life.

But adopt the boy? Babies? What was Honryn playing at?

Was the boy even an orphan? Or did he have living parents, and Honryn was just stealing the boy away?

Honryn chuckled in delight. "Your face is entirely too expressive, my Fierce One." Then he leaned toward her until he was deep in her personal space. She sucked in a nervous breath, and he leaned closer still, burying his nose in her hair and nuzzling at her neck and then the line of her jaw.

Her breath sped and then froze in her lungs when his warm breath brushed along her overly sensitive skin. His lips nipped just below her ear. "We're about to get some unexpected visitors. My apologies. Just playing the part."

Honryn pulled away, but she was so flustered, it took her mind far longer than it should to sort out the meaning of his words. But a commotion at the back of the room drew her gaze.

A man of medium height and a slim build strode up the main pathway through the center of the room. Like many other soul mages, this man had several geometric patterns painted on his skin with ink. As he drew closer, she noted a message satchel slung over his shoulder. When he was almost at the high table, the breeze carried a hint of horse.

He was likely some kind of message runner. Whatever news he carried must be important for him to interrupt the priest- king elect during his evening meal. Once the messenger reached their table, he bowed low to Honryn and then straightened to present a sealed letter.

Verdria noted the glow of magic. More than wax sealed it.

Honryn pressed his thumb to the wax seal. After a swiftly muttered spell, he cracked open the letter and read its contents.

"Delightful," Honryn said, sounding anything but. "My sire, Emperor Zarkyn, has sent word that he is returning early. He is less than a half hour behind the messenger."

CHAPTER 29

Verdria

*H*onryn didn't look unduly concerned by the development. Neither did his sister or mother, so Verdria remained alert but not at full battle readiness. Honryn waved over a tall man dressed as a servant. Verdria assumed he was a senior servant, perhaps overseer of the royal kitchens? For after Honryn was finished speaking, the man rushed off and ordered a few other servants to attend.

Honryn chuckled. "I sent him to collect some of my sire's favorite desserts. I'm sure the news will cause a bit of a stir in the kitchens, but I might as well put my sire in a good mood when I introduce him to my new consort. He'll not be pleased that I've already publicly claimed you."

Verdria arched a brow, keeping an outwardly brave face when internally she was more than a touch concerned whether Honryn could live up to his bold plans of making her his consort if his father, the emperor, had other plans. And if she was handed off to some other soul mage, that would hinder her own plans of escape with valuable information about this place. Honryn, even though he was the most powerful soul mage, seemed to trust her and because of that, he would be much more lenient with her. Another mage wouldn't be as lax.

"And what if your father doesn't agree with your choice of consort?"

"Sire," Honryn corrected and then sighed loudly. "Not father. A father is someone who cares for you." Honryn leaned forward and propped his head on his hands. "And I expect my sire to be very displeased, since I will be effectively annihilating his plans for a powerful marriage for me. But unlike my older brothers, I am rarely a thorn in my sire's side. And he knows I do not back down. Even if I can't give you the protection of the title of priestess-queen to the next priest-king, I will not allow you to be taken from me."

"Well, that's a reassurance," Verdria murmured with heartfelt enthusiasm.

"I'm sorry," he said and placed his hand over hers, where she'd rested it on her thigh. "I had hoped to give you a few more days' worth of peace to settle in before you were exposed to these particular blood relatives."

Verdria swallowed back a retort, deciding mentioning that it would take her a lot longer to 'settle in' than a few days wouldn't serve any purpose. Instead, she merely grunted in acknowledgement of his comment.

As it turned out, they didn't have long to wait. Within a few minutes, servants were hurrying back with more trays from the kitchen. Swift on their heels, another messenger raced into the hall and made for the high table.

He hastened his way through a courtly bow and sprang back up to approach the table at Honryn's gesture.

"Your Holiness, the Emperor—" He was cut off by the deep tones of a gong ringing.

Verdria wasn't sure if she or the messenger startled worse. She'd not even noticed the gong. And that was unacceptable for a warrior- priestess.

Even before the gong had echoed to silence, a well-groomed man with a neatly trimmed beard and impeccable robes strode into the room, his voice booming out with as much authority and composure as the rest of him. "Our Glorious Emperor, his excellency Zarkyn of the Garnet Islands, has returned safely from his journey."

Honryn leaned close, once again crowding into her personal space. "That mouthpiece is Lord Vondrak. He has the much less known distinction of being my father's spy master. Also of note, his niece, Lady Bykenstra is my oldest brother's spy master."

Before Verdria could ask Honryn the name of his own spy master, a man of indeterminable age and average height walked in, flanked by several other lavishly dressed individuals.

"Ah. And here comes my sire," Honryn muttered.

Her gaze swiftly took in Honryn's father. Zarkyn's figure was that of a man only a little past his prime, his middle a little thicker than his son's, but otherwise he was lean and muscular like Honryn. Though unlike his son, the emperor was not as broad across the shoulders. Both men had the same thick black hair, though the emperor's was trimmed far shorter in the style favored by mages to show off as much of their tattoos as possible. And unlike his son's untouched skin, Zarkyn's pale flesh was covered in black tattoos.

But there were enough similarities Verdria could see the family resemblance, and the reminder stirred unease in Verdria's middle. That Honryn's father was a soul mage had been a sort of abstract thing. Yes, she knew he'd been spawned by the enemy, but Honryn and his twin lacked the usual trappings of soul mages, and their mountain heritage shone through in their height, the proud way they carried themselves, and their temperaments. It was easy to think of them as being of the mountains and trapped here in this place like her.

But seeing Honryn's father drove home what she'd known all along. Honryn's heritage was as much of the mages as it was of the mountains. And, she reminded herself, Honryn *was* a soul mage.

He wasn't one of her people.

Though not an overly tall man, the emperor was strongly built, his sturdy frame heavily muscled, and she would bet he knew how to use the sword at his belt and the row of throwing knives tucked into a harness that crossed his chest.

As he moved closer, Verdria decided that Honryn must have inherited his prettier features from his mother's bloodline.

Unlike his youngest son, the emperor had a long square face, a large forehead that overshadowed his eyes, and boasted a thick beard. It was well trimmed, as seemed to be the fashion. Once again, she glanced around the room, noting most of the males old enough to grow one had beards of some style or other.

Glancing at Honryn's clean-shaven face, she marveled at how much he openly went against what was normal for most soul mages. But now that the emperor had returned, how would Honryn's behavior change? Would Honryn change how he treated her?

Verdria wasn't given long to mull over what her immediate future might look like because Honryn was once again pointing his chin toward the back of the room, where a group of servants and nobles were gathering around the royal entourage. "And now you'll see the spy masters of my father and brothers attempting to subtly weaver their way through the various royal advisors, garrison captains, even the city steward and his aids, all in order to deliver all they know about my various escapades. You'll be a feature in their reports."

Verdria nodded and nibbled on a bit of chilled fruit, copying some of Honryn's mannerisms. After all, nothing good ever came of allowing your enemies to see your fear. Then, casting Honryn a savage grin, she tilted her head toward the newcomers.

"So about now they'll be hearing how I tore out the throat of one of the High Nobles?"

"Oh, that will have already spread. But I imagine they'll deliver a more detailed version in person."

"And how you slayed over half the mages in the room and harvested their souls?"

"Most certainly," he replied in the same lighthearted tone.

"Aren't you even a bit concerned about how your father will react?"

At her words, something glinted in his eyes briefly before he smoothed his features back into an unreadable mask. "It's hardly the first time I've killed half the people in a room. Besides, my father and I have long since come to an understanding."

Verdria glance back to study the emperor and noticed what could only be called a thunderous expression directed at Honryn.

"You sure about that understanding?"

"Er...," Honryn murmured and leaned forward to prop his elbows on the table, "I may have to remind him about our understanding."

But if he was concerned about that development, he didn't show it, continuing on with his introduction to his family and a bit about court politics.

"Ah. There's my oldest brother," Honryn said, indicating a young man near his own age. "Crown Prince Rydorth."

Verdria studied the male, looking to see if she could spot the family resemblance. Rydorth shared his youngest brother's dark hair, but that was about all they shared. Rydorth was short and heavily muscled like his father, but he had a paler complexion than even the emperor. If he had a pretty face under all that facial hair, Verdria couldn't tell, but it did look like he shared his father's square jaw. In short, oldest and youngest brother had little in common.

"Like what you see?" Honryn asked, a hint of a laugh in his tone.

"Not really. Never been attracted to shaggy mountain bears."

Honryn laughed boisterously this time. "Good. Because my oldest brother and I don't care for each other. And he'd absolutely be delighted if he was more to your taste than I am. He'd see it as a blow to my standing."

"Why doesn't it surprise me that you and he don't get along?" she said and then paused. "Come to think of it, you don't seem to like many people."

Honryn shrugged. "What can I say? I tend not to like people who try to kill me."

Verdria arched an eyebrow in question. "Is your oldest brother going to try to kill you tonight?"

"It's always on the table. Thought I'd explained that bit to you." He made a humming sound.

He didn't say anything more, his gaze locked on his approaching father. She gave him a verbal prod. "You were talking about how you and your brothers don't get along."

"Yes, having one's brothers hire assassins to assassinate you as a child will do that."

Honryn and his family rose from their seats and shuffled down the long table. Verdria moved with them but watched as servants brought more seating for the new arrivals. One chair was a throne-like monstrosity of dark wood and inlaid gold with crimson red upholstery.

That ghastly throne must belong to the emperor.

Verdria was happy to see Honryn had been herding her and his family farther away from the center of the table and the emperor's seat.

"That sounds like some kind of interesting family dynamic," Verdria said as she walked farther down the table between Honryn and his twin sister.

His twin leaned forward, joining the conversation with a mischievous grin gracing her lips. "And Honryn hasn't even told you about Marduk, our middle brother yet." Nadraya pointed a finger at another young man following close on the emperor's heels.

Verdria briefly took in the tall, slim man with walnut brown hair and a face with more delicate features and an almost pointed chin.

In short, he looked nothing like Zarkyn or Rydorth. And though he was prettier than either of those men, he didn't share much of a resemblance to Honryn, either.

She didn't have time to learn about Honryn's relationship with the middle brother, but it was likely just as bloody. Seemed to be a theme here.

Everyone remained standing at the emperor's approach, even Honryn. Verdria straightened to her full height, squared her shoulders, and rested her hands on the hilts of her axes—not in threat, it was just the most natural place for them, and she figured if she moved the axes now, it would only draw more attention.

Emperor Zarkyn reached the table and halted in front of them, his gaze taking her in from head to toe, the table seeming to provide no hinderance to his perusal. While he seemed speechless at her size, his sharp gaze hadn't missed her two axes. He made no comment about them, merely glancing at Honryn.

"And I thought your mother was outlandish in her towering height. This one is even bigger."

Honryn shrugged. "It's nice for a change, not getting a kink in my neck from looking down at people all the time."

Now that the emperor was on the dais at the same level as Honryn, she noticed how much taller Honryn was than the rest of his family.

"I await your tale of taming this great beast of a woman so quickly. I couldn't trust your mother not to lop off a body part for… well… I still don't trust her not to attempt an amputation upon me."

Honryn snorted. "My approach is very divergent from your methods and proving much more efficient."

The emperor grunted and then smirked. "Be sure to tie her down in bed and most definitely never allow her on top. Even if she doesn't intend you harm, she might crush you to death by accident. Hardily a dignified death for the future priest-king."

"Better big than some delicate little thing I might split in half on the first thrust," Honryn replied, sounding bored.

The emperor leered at Verdria's cleavage for a long moment and then turned his attention back to Honryn, his expression darkening.

"So, the reports and rumors are all true. You only managed to capture one priestess?"

Honryn barked out a laugh. "I hadn't been expecting to be capturing any priestesses. I was called to salvage that disaster of a raid. By the time I was involved, the ship was already lost, the dragon eggs rescued and most of our men were already dead." Honryn took a sip of his fruit juice and gestured at Verdria. "This priestess was an unexpected blessing in what otherwise would have been a complete waste."

"A blessing?" Honryn's oldest brother snapped out the question as he stomped behind them on his way to his seat at the table. "I was just told she killed more than a dozen of our men on this side of the portal before you contained her power, and even that spell she managed to escape, then killed Lord Nuran. And if that wasn't bad enough, you killed almost everyone else in the room for touching the priestess."

"Touching?" Honryn asked in a soft voice that was downright chilling.

Crown Prince Rydorth must have heard that chilling warning, because his superior grin vanished.

Honryn continued in his chilled voice. "They were doing more than touching her, which would have been enough to earn a strong punishment. But when I arrived, they were doing their best to beat her to death, attempting to kill a woman I'd taken into my House."

Verdria glanced away from Honryn's brother to take in his father's expression.

The emperor looked utterly entertained and merely took a gobbet of some drink from a passing servant.

Crown Prince Rydorth wasn't giving up so easily. He was either stupid or trying to save face in front of the emperor, Verdria decided.

"Surely one female, even if she is the most fertile womb on the island, isn't worth that many of our own dead."

"No. Of course not. But she is the Serpent God's choice for my High Priestess. Our offspring will be more powerful than any born before me."

The Crown Prince looked like he was going to swallow his tongue. After a moment, he recovered and asked, "She's that powerful?"

"Yes," Honryn all but purred. "If I asked it of her, no doubt she could kill you, father, and Marduk," Honryn added as the middle brother joined them, "before the Elites could stop her."

What the emperor thought of the boast, Verdria didn't know, for he had continued to his seat and was now partaking of dinner. Other members of the royal house had also taken their seats. Only she, Honryn, and his two brothers were still standing.

Verdria might have sat down, so as not to draw any more attention to herself, but she didn't like the way both older brothers looked upon her with surprised expressions that soon shifted to thoughtful and then cunning. Besides, Marduk was already busy trying to peer down her cleavage, and she wasn't going to give him a greater opportunity. Nor would he meet her eyes. If he'd looked up and saw what she was planning to do to him if he leaned any nearer, he wouldn't be standing so close. When the middle brother finally got his fill, he at least looked into her eyes briefly before studying her other features.

"That hair," he murmured appreciatively to Honryn, "I'd enjoy getting a good grip..." He let his sentence drift off as his gaze turned as calculating as his older sibling's.

"And I've always liked a good challenge in bed," Rydorth added.

Honryn made a huffing sound and Verdria glanced at him in time to see him roll his eyes heavenward.

"Really?" He muttered something else darkly, and then in a louder voice, "You're both going to go there?

She is my future Consort. I suppose if you both want to try for her, I could always use more soul crystals."

On the heels of Honryn's words, Verdria felt a harsh power tingle along her skin in a creeping sort of caress. But by the reactions of Honryn's two older brothers, they were the targets of Honryn's spell, and it wasn't anything like a caress by the time it reached them. Both brothers stiffened, clearly equal parts fearful and angry.

Rydorth snarled out what sounded like a curse, but it was said too fast for Verdria to catch the words. Honryn raised one hand and made a flicking motion. It was only then that Verdria realized Rydorth had spat some spell at Honryn, which the priest-king elect had simply brushed aside like it was of no more importance than an annoying insect.

Rydorth's expression darkened more. "You're bluffing. You can't kill us both without father retaliating. One of our bloodline must live to succeed father."

Honryn laughed in utter delight. "You seem to forget I have a twin."

Marduk turned enough to stare over Honryn's shoulder at Nadraya. "Rydorth is correct. She isn't anywhere near powerful enough to hold that position, nor does she want it, clearly. Her actions have never been ambitious."

Honryn chuckled again. "Oh, you'd be correct about the lack of ambition, but also greatly mistaken about the level of our sister's power."

While Honryn took a sip of his drink, Verdria glanced back at the emperor to see what he thought about this little tiff at the table. But Emperor Zarkyn looked just as amused as before.

"And since when does one's ambition or lack there-of," Honryn continued, "influence our destiny? The Serpent God does not care what we might want. He moves us where we are needed. If he decides Nadraya must one day rule, then she will, since you both will already be dead if you cross me in this."

"Thank you, my beloved Twin," Nadraya bit out as she waved a spoon in his direction as she joined the conversation. "For turning the attention of our older brothers to me once more."

Honryn shrugged.

"You've been training with me. You know you're more than capable of taking them on."

"It's the aggravation of having to deal with overeager assassins popping out of every shadow for the next few weeks," Nadraya whined.

"Well. You won't have to worry about them being Guild assassins, at least." Honryn sipped from his goblet again before grinning at his twin. "You will be pleased to know I've had the assassin guild's allegiance for some months now."

It was Rydorth's turn to bark out a laugh. "You've gone too far with your bluffing this time. No one owns the assassins."

Honryn aimed his now chilly smile and otherwise emotionless face at his oldest brother. "I never bluff. And I'm always plain-spoken when I'm discussing death and power." Honryn picked up a bit of cheese and nibbled at it while his older brother stewed.

Seeing others eat and deciding she was hungry despite the new company, Verdria popped a chunk of warm bread in her mouth and chewed thoughtfully before saying in an offhanded manner, "Did you want me to kill the oldest one for you?"

His older brothers both made strange sounds. Marduk's turned into a delighted laugh while it sounded like Rydorth might really have swallowed his tongue this time.

"Silence your whore, little brother or I'll—"

Verdria's powerful punch rendered the mage mostly silent, only a wheezing issued from his mouth for a moment. It was likely good he had eaten nothing yet, but Honryn and Verdria both stepped back, just in case. When it appeared Honryn's oldest brother wasn't going to vomit in front of them, Verdria resumed her seat. Honryn did the same a moment later.

Emperor Zarkyn snorted with humor, the first response he'd made since Honryn and his brothers had started bickering. "Honryn, you really must share your secrets for gaining a warrior-priestess's loyalty. If I had known such secrets all those years ago, I'd likely have had fewer scars from your mother."

The emperor looked at Verdria in a way she didn't like as he rubbed a scar on his upper arm, the scar's smooth, pale pink flesh disrupting the pattern of a tattoo there.

"Well, this differs from the usual bickering about who gets my throne before I'm even dead. I never thought I'd see my sons fighting over a woman, especially my youngest. Perhaps I should kill all my ungrateful whelps and start over with this new warrior-priestess." The emperor stood and walked over to Verdria.

She stayed in her seat, since no one else had stood when the emperor had. Apparently, that was only necessary when he entered a room. Unfortunately seated, she had to crane her neck to meet his gaze.

"You're a big, powerful female," Zarkyn grinned down at her. "You'd likely drop more impressive offspring than my first two mates."

Honryn pushed back his chair and stood. Verdria wondered if they were about to get in a fight over her, of all things.

If so, she'd side with Honryn in the coming blood-bath. After all, hadn't she crossed that portal back on the ship because it might give her more time to kill a few more Soul Mages? And what better way to go out than taking the Soul Mage Emperor with her?

But then fate dashed her hopes in the next moment when Honryn stepped closer to his father and Emperor

Zarkyn placed his hands on his son's shoulder, thumping him in a way that was clearly proud.

"Ah, my strongest son," Zarkyn said with a laugh, "I will not attempt to take your great hulking mountain of a woman for my own. I've had my fill of battling mountain women. I like a softer bed partner. One I can trust when she has my cock in her mouth."

While Verdria was fighting to keep her expression neutral, Honryn merely relaxed and nodded in acknowledgment to his father.

A moment later, Emperor Zarkyn turned his full attention upon Verdria. "My spies tell me you're a fighter. I can see in your eyes the rumors are true. That's good, since having all three of my sons fighting over the same woman would likely leave me with only one son. As much as they sometimes act like young fools, I am fond of them all. Lucky for me, we have a tradition where all young, fertile women can take part in a competition where the strongest fighter gets to take her pick of any male of legal age."

When Honryn made a low growling sort of sound, she knew this was what his father had planned all along, likely long before Verdria arrived. He wouldn't battle Honryn directly, but he also wouldn't allow Honryn to dictate how this was going to go in this situation. The competition was Emperor Zarkyn's revenge against his youngest son's gumption.

Verdria arched an eyebrow at the emperor, then coolly glanced around the hall, taking in all the soul mages watching the high table in silence. They had a rapt audience. Verdria knew she had to play a part here, but she knew herself to be a terrible liar. Better she was just her brash self still.

"If I understand you correctly, I get to kill all my rivals and pick the prettiest male to be my husband? And I don't have to share him?" Verdria's lips stretched across her face in a genuine grin at the thought of destroying more of the enemy in the name of a competition.

"That is correct," Zarkyn agreed.

"Eviscerating more soul mages to win pretty Honryn?" she said, with a happy little lilt in her voice. "When do I start?"

Emperor Zarkyn's eyes widened, and he laughed in delight. "She's even more bloodthirsty than you, Honryn. I see why you want her, even if she's the biggest, coarsest woman I've ever laid eyes on."

"Bloodlust calls to bloodlust. And I'm pretty enough for us both." Honryn's words were said in an amused tone, but the mirth didn't reach his eyes. He was worried about this competition. Or maybe 'displeased' was a better description of the emotion brewing in his eyes.

Emperor Zarkyn turned his attention back to

Verdria. "My three sons will have to vote on when to hold the competition, but once they agree to a date, I'll announce the competition well in advance to give all the interested women time to travel to the capital."

Verdria didn't know what kind of timeframe she'd be looking at but would ask Honryn later.

"No point in postponing the vote when all my sons are in one place," Zarkyn said with a hint of glee in his voice as he leveled an intense stare at Honryn. Oh, yes. This was his revenge against Honryn's cockiness. "What say you to a vote now, my sons?"

Honryn cleared his throat. "What would be the point? Verdria clearly favors me, and I already know she will best any woman in the competition."

"Because it will be greatly entertaining to watch a hundred of our most skilled and powerful women from every noble House battle in a winner-takes-all competition." His father's expression turned colder. "And it will *please* me to watch the greatest priest-king elect in a thousand years squirm and worry while he watches and wonders if his chosen one will prevail against the most vicious, powerful, and cunning women of the empire. What say you, my sons? How do you vote?"

Rydorth gloated, seeing his chance to make a strike against his more powerful youngest brother. "I look forward to it. I vote to allow the competition to take place as soon as possible."

Honryn grimaced and then bit out his next words. "I vote no to this foolery."

"Your vote is noted," his father said and then turned to the middle brother.

"Sorry, Little Brother," Marduk said. "But my vote is with Rydorth this time. Yes, I know. How unusual for me to side with him. However, Father is correct. Crossing you will be worth it to see you sweat. I wonder what female you'll be forced to take to wife when your mountain woman trips over her enormous feet. I'd bet my weight in crystals that it will be one of the three sisters from House Stormwater. They are as powerful as they are brutal."

Verdria's battle magic stirred in sudden warning. She jerked her head up from where she'd been focused on her food while the conversation washed over her, but now she was scanning the crowd, hunting for the danger—her food and the conversation forgotten.

She reached out and slapped her left hand against Honryn's arm.

"I sense danger," she murmured in a soft voice, not wanting to give away to the assassins that she sensed their approach.

Sort of.

Her magic usually flagged the direction that the danger was approaching from, but this time, she only had a vague sense of emotions, dull and uninformative. She couldn't pinpoint the direction this time.

Was someone working a spell upon her to befuddle her battle magic? But Honryn would have felt something.

"Where?" he asked, leaning forward as if to whisper secrets in her ear. "I sense nothing. My magic always senses danger."

"It's…"

Her gaze raced around the area, searching for the danger. The other guests were eating or deep in conversation, or still watching the high table with rapt attention for the next bit of gossip. But nothing she saw matched up with the danger she felt closing in on them.

"I don't know. But something isn't right." Frustration had her wanting to leap up and hunt out whatever was causing her magic to stir when no clear enemy was within sight.

The only bodies moving toward the high table were a group of servants carrying more trays.

Assassins posing as servants?

"The servants? Do you recognize that group?"

Honryn couldn't possibly know every servant, but it was their best hope.

"I don't know any of them," he replied, calling his magic, a rush of it flowing around her.

"It's an attack!" He shouted in warning just as the servants tossed their trays away and sent tiny blades flying toward the high table.

Honryn raised a wall of power, shielding the entire

high table, but the blades still struck their targets. Honryn grunted in pain, and she jerked her gaze away from the assassins for a moment to see he had a slash cutting across one bicep. It was just a minor flesh wound. The blade must have gotten through before Honryn could get his shield up.

Verdria lunged from her chair even as Honryn and his twin were doing the same. The twins were the first to counterattack, flinging sharp black magic tridents toward the not-servants. Verdria launched her own attack, sending her smaller axe arching through the air.

She inhaled in surprise as the battle magic in the axe snuffed out just before it struck her target. The sharp blade still cut through her attacker's defenses—the assassins were wearing some kind of strange leather or bone armor under their clothing—and embedded itself in the chest of the woman she'd targeted.

But unlike her axe, Honryn and Nadraya's purely magical attacks did nothing, merely blinking out of existence as soon as they encountered the strange armor.

"Elites! Skin Weaver bones!" Honryn bellowed, but his warning was cut short by a gasp of pain. As he staggered back, Verdria glimpsed a throwing knife sticking out of his chest, far too close to his heart for her to be certain it wasn't lethal. But he was still standing, and dead men did not stay on their feet.

Verdria roared in rage and leaped over the table,

using her heavy boots to kick plates and platters and bowls at the assassins, to distract them. And then she was in their midst, towering over them, her great axe singing through the air before a brief wet, meaty sound was followed by a crunch as she decapitated each body. But even as she killed two more, the remaining three continued to throw their deadly little blades at their targets seated at the high table.

She understood they were willing to die for their cause, whatever it was, and they only fought her to slow her from killing them. But the Elites had shoved their way through the crowd of nobles fleeing and were now aiding Verdria, and the last two assassins were swiftly gutted.

Whirling back to face the high table, she took in the damage, her heart pounding. Honryn was still fighting to get out from underneath the bodies of three Elites. They'd forced him down and were shielding him with their own bodies, but Honryn was fighting to be free, screaming his twin's name.

"Nadraya!" he roared, his voice breaking with strain.

Locked in battle with the enemy, she'd been deaf to all other noise in the hall and didn't know how long Honryn had been screaming to be freed, to reach his twin.

But for whatever reason, he wasn't using his magic. Then she knew.

He couldn't use his magic.

Whatever a Skin Weaver was, its bones either stopped magic, absorbed it, or rendered it impotent.

Honryn couldn't call upon his vast stores of magic. He couldn't even reach his twin.

Verdria was already searching the swarm of Elites surrounding the high table looking for other casualties. When she spotted Honryn's mother, she noted Jardeen seemed unharmed, but she was crouched over the still body of Nadraya.

When an Elite made to block Verdria's approach, she bared her teeth. "I need to share my power with Royal Consort Jardeen if she has any hope of healing Princess Nadraya and Priest-King Elect Honryn. So unless you want to explain to Honryn why you held me up while his twin was dying…"

The Elite spun on his heels and motioned her to follow.

She did and swiftly made it to Jardeen's side and placed her hand on the older woman's shoulder, willing her substantial battle magic into something tamer, something a healer could use.

"Thank you!" Jardeen sobbed in relief and then continued in a rush. "The Skin Weaver poison is spreading throughout her body, absorbing my magic before I can use it to heal her."

"Take what you need from me," Verdria said as she began looking for the other aunts. She spotted them being held back with the other nobles. Glancing at her new Elite shadow, she barked at him, "Get the Aunts! All mountain women can share power. Move it!"

The Elite hesitated for only a moment but pulled two more Elites in to watch Verdria and then he was racing across the hall, shouting for the other guards to allow the aunts to approach the high table.

When they arrived, Verdria grabbed the nearest woman's hand and felt when the older woman sent the magic flowing through her into Jardeen.

On her knees, Jardeen cried out, "It's not enough. I need Honryn. Now!"

Verdria nodded and jumped up, running full out toward Honryn. With despair in her heart, Verdria admitted she didn't think Jardeen knew both of her children had been injured by the Skin Weaver blades.

Mortally?

Verdria hadn't gotten a chance to get to know Nadraya yet and now she wasn't sure if she ever would have the chance. But then she arrived at Honryn's side and skidded to a halt. Her heart contracted painfully at what she saw.

Honryn's skin was covered in sweat. Unnatural dark shadows had discolored a large patch of the skin around the knife wound and blood flowed freely from both his chest and his lips. When more blood bubbled with each laboured breath, she knew his lung had been punctured. And he was so pale, almost grey, she feared he was hemorrhaging internally from where the blade might have clipped an artery. He was using his magic to bind the chest wound but it wasn't enough.

"Tower," he managed, with an accompanying wave of blood coursing over his lower lips.

What he needed was in his tower.

Verdria didn't need to be told twice. She lunged at Honryn and hoisted him over her shoulder and then bolted into a run.

"Bring Nadraya to Honryn's tower!" She shouted to the three mountain women trying to save the other twin. "Now!"

But Verdria didn't slow. She couldn't heal Honryn or Nadraya, but if she got Honryn where he needed to be to heal himself, then maybe he'd be able to heal his twin in time.

Behind her, the Elites were shouting for her to stop, but she'd given her word to Honryn. She would serve him as long as he remained true to her. He hadn't gone back on his word.

He had honor.

And he was her…

He was her friend?

What a strange thought. To call a Soul Mage her friend.

If she survived long enough to escape, she would have the strangest of tales to tell her family back home. But in that fuzzy vision of the future, Honryn was sitting next to her while she told her tale to her family.

"You're not dying on me, Mage," she growled between panting breaths as she ran full out. "You hear that? You don't get to die on me!"

Thank you for reading Soul Mage.

The adventure continues in Warrior-Priestess, coming soon.

In the meantime, you might enjoy Master of the Hunt. It takes place in the same Huntress vs Huntsman world and is another
enemies-to-lovers tale, this time featuring a centaur huntsman and
member of the Warrior-Priestess sisterhood.

You can get it here https://books2read.com/u/bzd1Z9

If you wouldn't mind leaving an honest review, that would be greatly appreciated.

I also have a newsletter where you can receive book updates, free books, and other bookish goodies. Just signup below:

https://lisablackwood.com/join-the-newsletter-here/

BOOKS BY LISA BLACKWOOD

Gargoyle & Sorceress

Dawn of the Sorceress

Sorceress Awakening

Sorceress Rising

Sorceress Hunting

Sorceress at War

Sorceress Enraged

Legacy of the Sorceress

Sorcery & Firedrakes

Scion of the Sorceress

Sorceress Eternal

In Deception's Shadow Series (Epic Fantasy Romance)

Betrayal's Price

Herd Mistress

Maiden's Wolf

Death's Queen

The Prince's Gryphon (forthcoming)

Ishtar's Legacy Series (Epic Fantasy Romance)

Ishtar's Blade

The Blade's Beginning (short story)

Blade's Honor

Blade's Destiny

The Blade's Shadow

First Queen of the Gryphons

The King of the Anunnaki (forthcoming)

The Anunnaki's Blade (forthcoming)

Huntress vs Huntsman (Epic Fantasy Romance)

Master of the Hunt

Night Huntress

Dragon Archer

Soul Mage (forthcoming)

ABOUT THE AUTHOR

Lisa Blackwood is the author of the bestselling Gargoyle and Sorceress urban fantasy series. Her work has also landed on the Wall Street Journal and the USA Today Bestseller lists as part of the Dominion Rising Anthology. When she's not reading and writing, she also enjoys gardening and spending time with her horse and her dogs.

At present, she grudgingly lives in a small town in Southern Ontario, though she would much rather live deep in a dark forest, surrounded by majestic old-growth trees. Since she cannot live her fantasy, she decided to write fantasy instead.